Death in a Little Town

A Matilda Perks Mystery

By R. C. Woodthorpe

A unique murder ... a mad tea party ... an extraordinary courtship ... an amazing parrot.

Originally published in 1935

Death in a Little Town

© 2015 Resurrected Press
www.ResurrectedPress.com

Published by Resurrected Press

This classic book was handcrafted by Resurrected Press. Resurrected Press is dedicated to bringing high quality classic books back to the readers who enjoy them. These are not scanned versions of the originals, but, rather, quality checked and edited books meant to be enjoyed!

Please visit ResurrectedPress.com to view our entire catalogue!

ISBN 13: 978-1-943403-06-6

Printed in the United States of America

Resurrected Press Books by <u>R. C. Woodthorpe</u>

Resurrected Press Books in A. E. Fielding's *The Chief Inspector Pointer Mystery* Series

RESURRECTED PRESS CLASSIC MYSTERY CATALOGUE

Journeys into Mystery
Travel and Mystery in a More Elegant Time

The Edwardian Detectives
Literary Sleuths of the Edwardian Era

Gems of Mystery
Lost Jewels from a More Elegant Age

Anne Austin
One Drop of Blood
The Black Pigeon
Murder at Bridge

E. C. Bentley
Trent's Last Case: The Woman in Black

Ernest Bramah
Max Carrados Resurrected:
The Detective Stories of Max Carrados

Agatha Christie
The Secret Adversary
The Mysterious Affair at Styles

Octavus Roy Cohen
Midnight

Freeman Wills Croft
The Ponson Case
The Pit Prop Syndicate

J. S. Fletcher

The Herapath Property
The Rayner-Slade Amalgamation
The Chestermarke Instinct
The Paradise Mystery
Dead Men's Money
The Middle of Things
Ravensdene Court
Scarhaven Keep
The Orange-Yellow Diamond
The Middle Temple Murder
The Tallyrand Maxim
The Borough Treasurer
In the Mayor's Parlour
The Saftey Pin

R. Austin Freeman

The Mystery of 31 New Inn from the Dr. Thorndyke Series
John Thorndyke's Cases from the Dr. Thorndyke Series
The Red Thumb Mark from The Dr. Thorndyke Series
The Eye of Osiris from The Dr. Thorndyke Series
A Silent Witness from the Dr. John Thorndyke Series
The Cat's Eye from the Dr. John Thorndyke Series
Helen Vardon's Confession: A Dr. John Thorndyke Story
As a Thief in the Night: A Dr. John Thorndyke Story
Mr. Pottermack's Oversight: A Dr. John Thorndyke Story
Dr. Thorndyke Intervenes: A Dr. John Thorndyke Story
The Singing Bone: The Adventures of Dr. Thorndyke
The Stoneware Monkey: A Dr. John Thorndyke Story
The Great Portrait Mystery, and Other Stories: A Collection of Dr. John Thorndyke and Other Stories
The Penrose Mystery: A Dr. John Thorndyke Story

The Uttermost Farthing: A Savant's Vendetta

Arthur Griffiths
The Passenger From Calais
The Rome Express

Fergus Hume
The Mystery of a Hansom Cab
The Green Mummy
The Silent House
The Secret Passage

Edgar Jepson
The Loudwater Mystery

A. E. W. Mason
At the Villa Rose

A. A. Milne
The Red House Mystery

Baroness Emma Orczy
The Old Man in the Corner

Edgar Allan Poe
The Detective Stories of Edgar Allan Poe

Arthur J. Rees
The Hampstead Mystery
The Shrieking Pit
The Hand In The Dark
The Moon Rock
The Mystery of the Downs

Mary Roberts Rinehart
Sight Unseen and The Confession

Dorothy L. Sayers

Whose Body?

Sir William Magnay
The Hunt Ball Mystery

Mabel and Paul Thorne
The Sheridan Road Mystery

Louis Tracy
The Strange Case of Mortimer Fenley
The Albert Gate Mystery
The Bartlett Mystery
The Postmaster's Daughter
The House of Peril
The Sandling Case: What Would You Have Done?

Charles Edmonds Walk
The Paternoster Ruby

John R. Watson
The Mystery of the Downs
The Hampstead Mystery

Edgar Wallace
The Daffodil Mystery
The Crimson Circle

Carolyn Wells
Vicky Van
The Man Who Fell Through the Earth
In the Onyx Lobby
Raspberry Jam
The Clue
The Room with the Tassels
The Vanishing of Betty Varian
The Mystery Girl
The White Alley
The Curved Blades

Anybody but Anne
The Bride of a Moment
Faulkner's Folly
The Diamond Pin
The Gold Bag
The Mystery of the Sycamore
The Come Back

Raoul Whitfield
Death in a Bowl

And much more!
Visit ResurrectedPress.com
for our complete catalogue

FOREWORD

The 1920s and 1930s have been called the "Golden Age" of British mysteries. It saw the flowering of a new style of detective fiction that went beyond the puzzle based stories of the late Victorian and Edwardian eras. It was clever, witty, often not very serious in tone, and the emphasis was much less on the crime than on the people. And it was incredibly popular on both sides of the Atlantic. It has been said that during this period one fourth of all the books published in Britain were mysteries.

With such of wealth of books to choose from, it was inevitable that some would be lost to obscurity in the subsequent decades. Agatha Christie, who wrote some of her best works in this period, has remained the "Queen of Mysteries, and her works have remained in print almost continuously. The works of Dorothy Sayers and Anthony Berkeley have enjoyed cycles of popularity as each new generation has rediscovered them. Unfortunately, other authors such as A. E. Fielding, Cyril Hare, and others have gotten lost in the shuffle with their novels only available in second hand book shops.

R. C. Woodthorpe is one of those authors, who, while well known at the time, is now largely forgotten except by students of the genre. This is unfortunate, as he was quite a good writer, and his works give an interesting insight into small town life in England at the time.

His mystery novels were written exclusively in the 1930s, with the first one *The Public School Murder* coming out in 1932, and the last *Put Out That Light* being published in 1940. He knew a number of the other mystery writers of the period, especially Margery Allingham and her husband Philip Carter, who was one of his former pupils.

On the surface, *Death in a Little Town* deals with the

murder of one Douglas Bonar in the south English town of Chesworth. Bonar, a wealthy landowner, was also an outsider, having made his fortune in the north of England before moving to Chesworth and buying the manor. His body is found after a night in which a party of villagers had torn down a barricade that he had built to block a footpath that crossed his lands.

In reality though, *Death in a Little Town* is not so much concerned with the process of detection or achieving justice for Bonar, which no one in the village really seems to care about anyway, as with the actions and reactions of the villagers as they wonder which of their neighbors might have committed the deed and how they can avoid incriminating themselves. As with any good village mystery, there are an assortment of characters, officious constables, bumbling Scotland Yard detectives, busy bodies, and a few loonies, all of which Woodthorpe describes with a dry wit.

At the center of everything is a retired schoolmistress, Matilda Perks. Other than the fact that she is elderly and a spinster, Miss Perks bears no resemblance to that more famous village sleuth, Miss Marple, Miss Perks is only too glad to vent her opinions and she shows little patience for fools, which includes just about everybody but herself. She also possesses a parrot that quite literally swears like a sailor. Furthermore, having had several of the chief suspects as pupils in her school, she is only too aware of the weaknesses and foibles. Miss Perks later would also feature in a later Woodthorpe mystery, *The Shadow on the Downs*.

All this adds up to a delightfully entertaining mystery.

Though little known today, R. C. Woodthorpe is an author that deserves to be more widely read, and it is with pleasure that Resurrected Press offers this new edition of *Death in a Little Town*.

About the Cover

The cover art includes a reproduced image of the original dust jacket for the hardcover first edition published in 1935.

About the Author

Ralph Charles Woodthorpe (1886-1971) was a British author who wrote eight mysteries in the 1930s, including *The Public School Murder (1932), A Dagger in Fleet Street (1934), Death Wears a Purple Shirt (1934), Death in a Little Town (1935), The Shadow on the Downs (1935), The Necessary Corpse (1939), Rope for a Convict (1939),* and *Put Out That Light (1940).* Many of these are set in small towns in the south of England. Several feature Matilda Perks, a retired schoolmistress, and *The Public School Murder* was made into a television episode in the UK. It is interesting to note that Woodthorpe was himself a teacher of English and that one of his pupils was Philip Carter, the husband of the mystery writer Margery Allingham.

Greg Fowlkes
Editor-In-Chief
Resurrected Press
www.ResurrectedPress.

NOTE

Topographically, the "Chesworth" of this story resembles an existing town in Sussex; but the reader acquainted with the original would, I need hardly say, search it in vain for my characters. Nor, in real life, do the townsmen of "Chesworth" behave like those in my book when selfish landlords stop up footpaths. I wish they did. An incident in the story was suggested by an episode in Mr. Louis Marlow's Swan's Milk.

TABLE OF CONTENTS

I. Party On The Footpaths

MISS PERKS glanced first at the clock and then at the new wireless set. The clock said eleven, but it was a doubtful witness. The wireless set said nothing. It stood in the corner and looked very knowing. A week ago, so far as Miss Perks was concerned, it had existed only in the generous imagination of an old pupil. The old pupil had taken pity on Miss Perks living almost alone in the big house which had once echoed with the shrill voices of little boys. He expressed surprise and indignation when he found that Miss Perks had no wireless: it was a wonderful source of entertainment and instruction, he said. Miss Perks grunted. She remembered her old pupil as an ill-conditioned, sailor-suited little boy who had not taken at all kindly to the process of instruction. Now he had a double chin and a rolling stomach and proposed to instruct her. She said she had got along very well hitherto without a wireless and saw no reason why she should not continue to do so. Nevertheless, the wireless set had arrived.

It had arrived in a great wooden crate. The delivery man declined to bring it upstairs. He said he could not leave his motor, but the real reason was that he had delivered things at Miss Perks's house before and knew its awkward geography. So the case had stood partly blocking up the stone passage just inside the front door until Frank Thornhill sent his man Jennings along with a book which he thought Miss Perks might like to read. Jennings had come when Miss Perks was out, but Elizabeth had told her all about it. Jennings had picked up the packing-case as though it were a baby and carried it round the stone passage and through the kitchen and up the steep and awkward stairs on to the dark landing. There he had set it down and dispatched Elizabeth in search of a hammer and a chisel. Extricating the wireless set from the interior of the crate, he had borne it through the bathroom into Miss Perks's sitting-room, and when it was established in the corner he had inserted the valves and made a connection to the electric point and switched on. Lovely it had sounded, said Elizabeth.

Miss Perks glanced again at the clock. The clock said five minutes past eleven, but it was five minutes fast. Or was it ten? Miss Perks scowled. She was a plump little old woman in black. Had it not been for her face, she might have been described as a comfortable old body, but her face was anything but comfortable. Its central feature was a remarkably prominent hooked nose. A dark down grew thickly on her upper lip. Her sharp eyes seemed to comment caustically on all that they saw. Her voice was deep and gruff, and the things it said were too often uncomplimentary to the persons it addressed. Charitable people said of Miss Perks that her bark was worse than her bite, but that is the sort of thing that charitable people say. Miss Perks really gave them little grounds for the compliment.

On a table in the corner between the wall and the window stood a large bird-cage covered with a dark red shawl. Next to it was the chair in which Miss Perks was accustomed to sit. Beside this, on the floor, rested a large bell provided with a strap for a handle. Miss Perks looked once more at the clock, stooped, picked up the bell, and rang it impatiently.

In the kitchen below, Miss Perks's servants, William and Elizabeth, sat on opposite sides of the enormous, old-fashioned fireplace. It was past their usual bedtime, but they lingered on in the hope of hearing the new wireless in action. Elizabeth heard the bell, rose yawning from her chair, and clumped up the staircase, across the landing, through the bathroom, and into her mistress's presence.

"Mr. Robert not back yet?" demanded Miss Perks. It

was an unnecessary question. She knew very well that her brother had not come in. She had supped by herself at nine o'clock and listened intently since.

"Not yet, ma'am," said Elizabeth, avoiding her mistress's eye.

Miss Perks hesitated.

"Did Jennings show you how to turn this thing on?" she said at length, nodding her head towards the new wireless set.

"Yes, ma'am." Elizabeth, requiring no further invitation, stooped and did something to the handsome box of mysteries.

"I should have liked Mr. Robert . . ." began Miss Perks. "However," she added, "if people won't come in when they should, they can't expect to be considered."

The wireless set emitted a low hum which died away as the programme gathered strength. Miss Perks, who had not listened to music since she gave up going to church (and that was a number of years ago), heard what seemed to her a jangled and discordant noise. Presently a female voice detached itself from the din in the background and began to croon a song of which the refrain was, "Oh, You Nasty Man."

Miss Perks glanced at Elizabeth in bewilderment.

"Are you sure Jennings understands these things?" she asked. "It doesn't seem to me the sort of noise it ought to make."

"Oh, yes, ma'am, it's all right," said Elizabeth. Her face wore a pleased expression.

"Then perhaps this is a foreign station," suggested Miss Perks. "I know nothing about wireless, but they tell me there are foreign stations."

"No, ma'am, this is London Regional. Jennings left it tuned in."

"I understood that the wireless was a wonderful source of entertainment and instruction," remarked Miss Perks. "Well! . . . Do you remember, Elizabeth, when we spent a holiday at that farmhouse in Kent, and were kept awake all night by a sick heifer in a neighbouring meadow? This woman's voice . . ."

Elizabeth had no ears except for the music. Miss Perks glanced at her sharply.

"What on earth are you swaying those great haunches of yours about for in that indecent manner?"

"Sorry, ma'am." Elizabeth blushed and stood still. "It's the dance music."

"Oh!"

"Many people are very fond of it, ma'am," said Elizabeth defensively. She went on, revealing unexpected stores of information: "They say the players earn at least a thousand a year each. All the bands have their own special arrangements of the tunes they play, and they pay as much as ten guineas a tune to the man who arranges them."

"Indeed!" said Miss Perks ironically, as the last strains of "Oh, You Nasty Man" died away. "And how much do they pay to the man who arranges the words?"

Elizabeth was unable to say.

"Following that," said a man with a nasal twang, "the boys will play 'Let's Have a Basinful of the Briny.'"

"Indeed they won't," said Miss Perks indignantly. "Not in my house. Turn the wretched thing off, Elizabeth."

Elizabeth reluctantly obeyed.

Miss Perks looked once more at the clock. The clock said a quarter past eleven.

"How fast is that clock?"

"Twenty minutes, ma'am."

Miss Perks grunted.

"You can go to bed, Elizabeth. I shall go out for a short walk. A little fresh air will do me good." Catching a certain look in Elizabeth's eye, she added hastily, "I expect Mr. Robert will be in before I come back. Is the water hot?"

"Yes, ma'am."

"Very well. You and William are not to wait up. Good night, Elizabeth."

"Oh, ma'am," said Elizabeth suddenly, "I meant to tell you. They're up on the footpaths."

Miss Perks appeared to understand this cryptic remark.

"I'm very glad to hear it," she said. "God knows I have a low opinion of the people of Chesworth, but even I could not believe that they would sit down calmly under . . ." Miss Perks broke off. She snorted. "That man Bonar!" she said, in tones of the most savage contempt. "Well, don't stand there like a gawky. Be off to bed, and William too."

"Yes, ma'am. Good night, ma'am."

Elizabeth clumped away through the bathroom. Miss Perks followed her as far as the landing, and then went into her bedroom, and put on her bonnet and her long black mackintosh. Presently William and Elizabeth heard her unlock and unbolt the front door and slam it after her.

"That Mr. Robert's up to his games again," said Elizabeth. "Pity, and such a nice gentleman too: you wouldn't think it of him, that you wouldn't."

"He's a fair cough-drop, Mr. Robert, and that's a fact," returned William, removing his waistcoat. "But there'll be rain before midnight, or I'm a Dutchman, and that'll send him home all right. It only needs a drop o' rain to put a stop to Mr. Robert's pranks and bring him to his senses."

2

The town of Chesworth, which housed Miss Perks and the fellow-inhabitants of whom she had spoken in such disparaging terms, is in Sussex. As late as 1814 the townsmen baited bulls, tying the animals to an iron ring which is still to be seen in the Square. The baiting of Parliamentary candidates, another time-honoured sport, continued to a much later date. Nowadays the community is particularly sober and well-governed, and it is only on rare occasions and under great provocation that the people take the law into their own hands and demonstrate. Such a demonstration was going on as Miss Perks first sampled the joys of wireless. It had every excuse, and things were done decently and in order; but indirectly it led to a dreadful event which has been a topic of conversation in Chesworth for the past year, and will remain one for years to come.

It is now necessary to go back an hour and join Michael Holt, a novelist, who is standing at his garden gate on the outskirts of the town.

3

There was no moon that night. The scent of wall-flowers and lilac and laburnum filled the garden of the Vineyard. Michael Holt stood with his elbows resting on the gate. The air was so still that he could hear the murmur of the little Denne, flowing behind the low stone wall on the opposite side of the lane.

The church clock struck ten. It sounded unusually close at hand. Michael stirred.

"It will be a wrench to leave all this," he said, unaware that he said it aloud.

Walter Chrystal, who had dropped in for an hour after dinner from his "semi-bungalow" farther up the lane, was still standing by the half-open gate. He appeared to have something on his mind. He could bring himself neither to confide in Michael nor to go. Michael had almost forgotten that the little man was still there.

Chrystal pricked up his ears.

"Who is leaving it?" he asked sharply.

Michael's thoughts came back to his neighbour. He wondered what was troubling Chrystal, and why he never bothered to change his clothes in the evening, and whether he really did not know how ill that knickerbocker suit became him, making him look even thinner than he was . . . and what it was like to be married to a woman like Daphne Chrystal.

"Who is leaving it?" Chrystal repeated his question

eagerly. His voice had a metallic edge. Oxford had given him, not her own traditional accent, but this imperfect disguise of a provincial origin.

"I may be, pretty soon."

"What, you, Holt? Why, you've only been here two months!" Chrystal's tone now had the joyous note of one who suspects a dark secret: even, with special luck, a scandal. "Leaving the Vineyard! What on earth for?"

"I'm not at all sure that Chesworth suits us."

"Extraordinary!" Chrystal ruminated for a full ten seconds on the extraordinariness of the notion. "Really, I should never have thought . . . Why, Holt, there's nothing wrong, surely? The boys look as fit as possible."

"Nothing's definite." Michael tried to convey his unwillingness to discuss the subject. He repented of having said what he had. "We may stay."

"Extraordinary! . . . Really, if anybody had asked me to name an ideally happy couple I should at once have thought of you and Mrs. Holt."

Michael did not answer.

"There's nothing wrong with the Vineyard, surely?" persisted Chrystal. "I think you lucky to have such a place. Many people covet it."

"No, there's nothing wrong with the Vineyard," echoed Michael without enthusiasm. "There are people who would like to take it from me."

"Really, I . . . But perhaps you find it difficult to write here? You authors are so temperamental."

As a professional author, Michael resented the imputation.

"On the contrary, it is possible to write anywhere."

"Well, I can't understand it. It seems extraordinary to me."

A shaft of light fell across the lawn. Mary had gone upstairs. The ray reached as far as the border and revealed a spade which had been left among the wall-flowers. Michael reminded himself that he must put it back in the tool-shed when Chrystal had gone.

Mary adjusted a curtain and all was dark again.

"I can't understand it, Holt, really I can't. Here are you, to all appearance as happy as possible, with a most enviable house in delightful surroundings, and you talk of leaving it all. Extraordinary!"

Michael stretched out his hand and rested it on the spade. His fingers traced the initials M. H. stamped in the handle. He was tempted to silence Chrystal for ever by dealing him one sharp crack across the skull with the flat of the blade. The verdict should be Justifiable Homicide. In dealing with bores like Chrystal it ought to be permissible to waive the ordinary restraints of civilized society.

"And," Chrystal added, "you have such heaps of friends."

"Heaps of friends! Yes, heaps of friends!"

Michael's tone startled Chrystal and stopped his tongue.

In that blessed silence they began to hear unusual sounds. There were distant voices that grew louder, and the heavy tread of men coming up from the town. At least a score of men, judged Michael, listening. What brought them up this way so late? His mind leapt to the reason.

"Good! There's public spirit in Chesworth still. They are doing what I hoped they would."

"Doing what?"

"And I'm hanged if I don't join them."

Michael flung the gate open wide, but instead of going out into the lane he hesitated, as though he had been seized with a misgiving.

"I don't know . . . Yes, I will, though. I will go up and watch the fun. Just a minute, Chrystal. I must run upstairs and tell Mary."

He hurried into the house. The marching men drew near. Chrystal stepped back into the little drive and peered curiously as they passed. One of them carried a lantern. By its light Chrystal recognized the bearded man who walked at the head of the party. It was Bisgood, the jeweller in the High Street, one of Chesworth's leading tradesmen and author of a learned little book on the antiquities of the place. The light of the lantern did not carry far enough to make sure of the others. They tramped past the Vineyard in silence.

Chrystal stood waiting for Michael to come back. He thought about Michael. He had fastened upon the hint that Michael had dropped, and worried it as a terrier worries a bone. He would have enjoyed a malignant satisfaction in extracting from it some conclusion damaging to Michael.

Michael came out of the house wearing a hat and a light coat. He had also put on a pair of nailed shoes.

"Oh, there you are. . . ." said Chrystal. "Those fellows were carrying tools, Holt."

"Of course they were. By the same token, I might as well bring this along. It may come in handy." Michael drew the spade out of the wall-flower border. "You'd better join the party."

"Really, I still don't see . . ." began Chrystal. He broke off and made the dry, cackling sound that passed with him for a laugh. "Oh, I suppose they are going up to the Park."

"Direct action," said Michael.

"Extraordinary business! Really, I should have thought it impossible for a man to behave like that."

Suddenly he stopped dead. "I don't think I'll come with you. I don't want to run into Bonar."

"I don't wish to do that myself," muttered Michael. He added: "But I've thought of that. Even if he comes along, he won't know any one in the dark. Anyhow, he'll have his hands full with his own affairs."

"All right," said Chrystal reluctantly. "I'll come."

They went on in silence, each occupied with his own thoughts. They passed the semi-bungalow, where the light shone through Mrs. Chrystal's flimsy red curtains. Ahead of them, at the end of the lane . . . or, rather, where the lane went rural and passed through gates and

across fields, leading to a surprising number of farms and
cottages . . . Thornhill's house was brilliantly lit as usual;
but they turned sharp right and followed the party from
the town up the by-way which led to the footpaths across
the Park.

4

Bisgood halted his little band at the first barricade
and turned to address them. He was in his element. He
loved justice and he loved his own oratory: here he could
use the one in the service of the other. He saw himself as
a Chesworth Hampden,

> *that with dauntless breast*
> *The little tyrant of his fields withstood.*

His eyes shone earnestly behind his gold-rimmed
spectacles of thick glass. As he spoke he made sweeping
gestures with his right hand, and occasionally he stroked
his rich brown beard with his left. He wore his coat
unbuttoned, for the night was warm, and the massive
gold chain across his capacious stomach glinted from time
to time as it caught the rays of the lantern.

"Now, men, we are here to redress a just grievance, as
free and independent citizens vindicating our rights. You
do not need to be reminded that these paths have been
freely used by the townsmen of Chesworth from before
my time and yours, aye, and from long before our fathers'
time too."

"Hear, hear," piped a juvenile voice; and there was a
titter.

Bisgood frowned.

"These paths," he went on, raising his voice, "belong to
the people, and if they are wilfully obstructed by a
landlord who takes upon himself, after fair warning, to
stop up public rights-of-way, then . . ."

The harangue was interrupted by a gruff voice from

the back of the crowd.

"We know all about that, Henry, old cock. This ain't no election meeting. Let's cut out the cackle and get on with the job."

Bisgood stiffened himself and glared in the direction of the heckler, whose voice he recognized.

"Walter Hackle," he said curtly, "we all know you for a valiant rascal. Will you take my place, and answer to the magistrates for what is done here to-night? You're more at home in Chesworth police-court than I am. It may be that your word will carry more weight."

The retort that sprang to Hackle's lips was stifled in the laughter of the others. Bisgood's eyes twinkled, and he was tempted to follow up his advantage. Yet he was not too proud to take a hint, from whatever quarter it came. He cut short his address and ordered the lantern to be held up so that the barricade could be inspected.

The men were clustered in the upper corner of an extensive field, at a place where two tall hedges met at right angles. Hitherto an iron swing-gate had offered a passage to users of the footpath, but the gate had been removed and the gap was now closed by a barrier formed of three stout oak posts, laced and interlaced with many strands of barbed wire.

"H'm," said Bisgood, tugging at his brown beard. "Bonar's men have made a workmanlike job of it. The more credit to them, since they knew, none better, that they were building for others to cast down. Now remember, lads, the watchword is no unnecessary damage. First cut the wire, and then dig the posts out, though that'll take longer than chopping them down or sawing them through."

Some of the men murmured against these excessive precautions. Bisgood reminded them that he was their avowed leader. He was willing to bear the brunt of any retaliation that might follow, but he must be obeyed.

"Now then," he added quickly, "those who have wire-cutters can get to work . . . and, don't forget, if by any chance we should be interrupted, we take no manner of notice, but just carry on."

Michael and Chrystal stood in the background and watched the shadowy figures stooping over the wire. Their active help was not needed. The working-space was insufficient to accommodate more than a few of those who were willing to lend a hand. Michael listened to the snapping of the pliers as they cut stiffly through the strands.

"Beastly stuff'," he murmured. "You might have thought the war would have sickened people of it . . . that they would never wish to see the stuff' again, much less use it: yet all over Sussex, all over the country, there's more of it than ever. Barbed-wire entanglements! To serve as a constant reminder of the other war . . . the war that goes on for ever . . . between those who have and those who haven't."

"I suppose it's the cheapest stuff' to use," remarked Chrystal.

Michael chuckled and did not answer.

It was no more than a few minutes' work to reduce the wire to severed lengths strewn upon the ground, but a diversion came before it was completed. An angry voice challenged the Chesworth men from behind the hedge on their right. It cut through the darkness without warning, since Bonar's footsteps could not be heard approaching across the soft turf.

"Who the hell are you, and what the devil do you think you're doing on my land?"

The men working on the wire straightened themselves instinctively. A hush fell upon the others. Then someone began to boo. The man next him clapped a hand over his mouth. The workers remembered Bisgood's orders and calmly went on cutting the wire.

A powerful electric torch shone. It moved round slowly and steadily, picking out faces one by one. Michael shifted his ground, trying to escape the rays. He heard Chrystal dithering about at his side.

Bonar, invisible behind the light, spoke again.

"I see!" he said slowly. "Well, I warn you. You are on private property and doing wilful damage. I order you to stop this destruction at once, and I'll give you exactly two minutes to be off my land and get back where you belong."

The voice retained a trace of a north country accent. It was that of a man sure of himself: harsh but controlled.

"Do you hear, blast you? Get off my land."

The barbed wire was all down. The men were sweeping its tangled remains into the ditch under the hedge. Bonar saw how he was ignored. He grew heated.

"You'll go to gaol for this night's work, you scum. I know your names. I'll have the whole pack of you up before the bench."

Some of the party jeered.

"Now, now, men," muttered Bisgood, uneasily fingering his gold watch-chain.

There was a movement in the crowd. The light swept round again, fell upon Michael and Chrystal, and held them steadily.

"*Mister* Holt and *Mister* Chrystal!" Bonar's voice was mocking. "This is an unexpected pleasure. I didn't think to see either of you here: certainly not you, Holt." The tones took on an edge. "It's lucky for you, Holt, I'm a man of my word, or I might be tempted to say something more: something you wouldn't care to hear mentioned in public, eh? But I promised you twenty-four hours, and the moratorium stands."

Michael's face was hot. He knew that all the others had their eyes fixed on him. They were wondering what Bonar's words could mean. He cursed the impulse that had brought him up to the field.

"As for you, Chrystal," went on Bonar, in a sardonic tone, "wouldn't you be better employed at home, looking after the house?"

Chrystal uttered an inarticulate sound and made an angry movement.

"Now, men," said Bisgood in a loud voice, which he strove to keep calm, "we'll dig out those posts."

"You will, will you, Bisgood?" shouted Bonar. "A fine example you are to your fellow shopkeepers. I'll get you a month's hard, I'm damned if I won't. I'll ruin your business. You needn't seek to hide yourself behind the others. I know you, you see."

"I've no wish to hide myself, Mr. Bonar," retorted the jeweller, stung into answering. "I am perfectly ready to answer for what I am doing. It is you who have reason to think shame of yourself. If you had listened to advice and not acted in this hot-headed way, you would not have found yourself in this position."

"Blast your cursed insolence! We'll see if you sing the same tune to the police and crow as bravely in front of the magistrates."

"Well, Mr. Bonar, you know where to find me, and so do the police, if they want me . . . and now, boys, let's get on with the job."

Bonar swore loudly. A moment later they heard the crackling of twigs beneath his feet as he strode away. They watched his light moving down the other side of the hedge. A volley of abuse followed him, which Bisgood had difficulty in repressing.

"You know, lads," he remonstrated mildly, "that sort of thing does no manner of good. Meanwhile, Bonar, no doubt, has gone to telephone for the police. Whether they will send up is another matter, but we may just as well push on with this business in case they do. Get it finished before they have time to come. Now for these oak posts. Which of you have brought spades?"

Michael among others responded. He was spoken to by a man whose face he could not see, and whose voice he did not recognize. It was a soft voice, with a touch of impudence. "I flatter myself I can handle this implement as well as you, sir, and it so happens I'm not wearing my fine dinner clothes that might take harm from the occupation." Michael yielded up the spade without reluctance.

Bisgood marshalled his forces. There remained two other barricades to be dealt with. In the next field the path forked, and at each exit it had been faithfully blocked by Bonar's men. Two detachments of the party were sent forward, one in each direction. Michael and Chrystal were tacitly omitted from this distribution of forces.

Bisgood approached to exchange a few words with Michael.

"Well, Mr. Holt, this is doubtless a new experience for you, and perhaps you will put something like it into one of your books one of these days. I dare say it's all grist that comes to you novelists' mills, eh?"

"Everything's useful," admitted Michael.

"And as a professional student of character, if I may say so, you must find Mr. Bonar an interesting subject. What a strange fellow he is!"

Michael heard Chrystal, beside him, murmur, "Extraordinary!"

"It beats me how a grown man can behave in such a childish fashion." The jeweller took off his hat and scratched his head in genuine perplexity of mind. "He knows perfectly well he has no right of any sort to close these paths. His own men, the very men who put up these barricades, told him so straight out, at the risk of getting sacked. He hasn't a leg to stand on."

"He's a bit peeved with things in general, and the town in particular, isn't he?"

"You're right. He came here thinking that as he was rolling in money and had bought the famous Forest Park estate, he would be able to boss the town and have ten fingers in every pie that was going. And you know, Mr. Holt"—Bisgood dropped his voice a little—"he had some excuse for thinking so, because we Sussex men are not fools. We shouldn't go out of our way to offend a wealthy man who might do a great deal for the town. But there you are: he has nobody but himself to blame. If he's no sooner here than he builds that ugly brick wall which ruins the view of the town from the top of Chain Hill . . ."

"That put people's backs up."

"To be sure it did. On top of that, he pushes himself forward as a candidate for the Council at the by-election, and finds himself at the bottom of the poll with a mere handful of votes. That was one in the eye for him." Bisgood chuckled and stroked his beard. "He's not got over that yet, and he won't, not for a long time. But if he wanted to get his own back he should have waited his chance. Instead of biding his time, he goes in off the deep end, as they say. Blocking up the footpaths where Chesworth folk have taken their Sunday walks for generations—he's making himself the laughing-stock of the town."

"His temper's none too good?" suggested Michael, offering Bisgood a cigarette.

"No, thanks, I don't smoke. . ... Yes, an ungovernable temper: that's Bonar's trouble. I saw him the other day having a shindy with the police in the Pavement. He had put his car where it ought not to have been, and instead of moving it as directed he was standing up for what he called his rights and cursing the sergeant right and left. If I'd been the sergeant I'd have charged him, but I dare say the police will get back on him in their own way at their own time."

He turned to watch the men digging up the third and last post.

"Really, that was an extraordinary thing that Bonar said to you just now." Chrystal's eager, curious voice took advantage of the pause. "About something you would not care to hear repeated in public. And a moratorium of twenty-four hours. Did you understand what he was driving at?"

"Oh, damn the man," said Michael.

"But what an extraordinary thing to say!" persisted Chrystal. "What could he mean?"

Michael did not answer. Chrystal shrugged his

narrow shoulders and walked away. Bisgood, who had missed this interlude, spoke again as something else came into his mind.

"You've had a bit of an encounter with Bonar yourself, I hear?"

"These things get round in Chesworth."

"They do," agreed the jeweller grimly.

"Then you know all about it. Bonar wanted to buy the Vineyard."

"And you sent him about his business?"

"I told him I wouldn't sell."

"History repeating itself," reflected Bisgood. "But you know why your house is called the Vineyard. I needn't trot out that old story again." He added shrewdly: "I imagine he's not the man to take No for an answer when he's once set his heart on a thing. He'll come again with a handsome offer."

Michael stubbed the ground with his toe.

"He has come again, but the offer was not so handsome."

"He'll keep on worrying you, for sure."

"I dare say."

"Do you know those parts?"

"What parts?"

"Where he comes from, where he made his money—up north. . . . Newcastle, isn't it?"

"Y-yes," said Michael reluctantly, "as it happens, I do, to some extent."

"A more robust kind of life up there, a sterner class of men?"

"There's no doubt about that."

"Ah!" As though satisfied, Bisgood moved away.

Michael took out his pocket torch and tried to find Chrystal. He did not wish to be left alone with his own thoughts. Any company was preferable to that, even Chrystal's. He could not see the little man, who had possibly moved on to one of the other fields of action. Michael stepped through the gap in the hedge, where the oak posts lay uprooted, and followed the path. When he came to the fork he turned right-handed (as Sussex people say) and eventually arrived at a second barricade. Here seven of the party, freed from Bisgood's moderating influence, were singing light-heartedly as they made havoc of Bonar's erection with blows from an axe. Chrystal was not there. Michael saw a couple of posts converted into firewood before he picked his way across the field in the direction of the last barricade. From a distance he descried a puny silhouette which he took to be Chrystal's, but when he came closer he could see by the light of the men's lantern that he was mistaken. He stopped and talked to some of the men, conscientious fellows, shop assistants mostly, who were laboriously uprooting the posts with pick and spade. He heard a dozen anecdotes of Bonar's high-handed ways and of his spiteful acts since he had been rejected with ignominy by the electors of the town. Still without Chrystal, he turned towards home. He met Bisgood striving to rally his forces, and evidently anxious to march them back to the town in good order and with as little offence as possible to sleeping citizens. The raucous choruses floating down from the upper slopes of the hill suggested that Bisgood's powers of discipline would be severely tried. Michael bade him good night, and descended the track. As soon as he was alone, his mind was obsessed with thoughts of Bonar. The taunt uttered on the hill rang again in his ears: "It's lucky for you, Holt, I'm a man of my word, or I might be tempted to say something more: something you wouldn't care to hear mentioned in public, eh? But I promised you twenty-four hours, and the moratorium stands." Chrystal had been curious about that. Chrystal had been equally curious about that unguarded remark of Michael's at the Vineyard gate: "It will be a wrench to leave all this." Michael wondered whether the little man had succeeded in putting two and two together: and what dire secret he supposed Bonar to know . . . and whether his shot was anywhere near the truth. "Hell!" said Michael. He kicked a stone down the path.

So he came to the lane. He turned left at the corner, where the curtains in the Chrystals' semi-bungalow still glowed red. Michael smiled as he passed the house and thought of that strangely assorted pair.

He glanced at the luminous hands of his wrist-watch and was surprised to see that they showed twelve minutes past eleven. He had spent over an hour on the hill; and Chrystal no doubt had rejoined Mrs. Chrystal long before. He quickened his step. A few seconds later he stumbled over the dead body of Douglas Bonar.

II. Loss of a Corpse

Michael had almost fallen: recovering himself, he turned on his torch to see what it was that lay in his path. He stood for a moment stunned by the shock. Bonar lay flat on his back, with a little pool of blood surrounding his head. His powerful body, as strong as a navvy's, was stretched full length in the roadway as Michael had seen navvies lying, overcome by beer. But for the significant pool of red, Michael would have concluded that Bonar was drunk.

As soon as the first shock passed, Michael's chief emotion, which overpowered all feelings of horror and compassion, was intense relief. Bonar was dead, and Michael Holt rejoiced. This man, with all his virulence and overbearing brutality and great power for mischief, could trouble him no longer. Michael smiled sardonically as he looked upon the corpse. He could have spurned it with his foot. So there was an end of that. Michael gave thanks for his escape: he exulted, as a sailor exults who sees the wind change miraculously when his vessel has been drifting beyond all hope on to a lee shore.

Outwardly he was surprised to find himself so calm and collected. He bent over the dead man, and the hand that he placed on Bonar's heart did not tremble. It was not until he straightened himself to cast another look round that he found cause for apprehension. The light of his torch fell upon something lying near the body. It was a spade. Michael stooped to examine it. He saw his own initials stamped in the handle. There were ugly stains on the blade. He hastily extinguished his light, and stood listening. Sounds of revelry were floating down from the Park. He could hear men calling to one another, and some of them were singing:

Oh, it's my delight on a shiny night
In the season of the year . . .

The song was drowned as someone started:

Susannah, he's a funniful man;

and voices vied in imitating the grunts of pigs. Very
soon the expedition would be coming down from the hill.

Alarmed at the thought, Michael yet stood motionless.
His mind travelled back to the man who had borrowed
the spade in the darkness: a man he did not know and
could not see, but whose voice perhaps . . . a wheedling
voice, with a touch of blarney and more than a touch of
impudence . . . he might recognize if he heard it again. He
asked himself what he should do.

If he told the police . . . His mind saw all that must
inevitably follow. Bonar had publicly threatened Michael.
Shortly afterwards, Bonar had been killed by Michael's
spade. No need to ask what the police would think. At the
least, they would set themselves to find out what lay
behind those words uttered by Bonar on the hill.
Sedulously, patiently, with minute care they would dig up
all Michael's past: here in Chesworth, back to
Manchester, then to Newcastle . . . Newcastle . . .

"God!" said Michael to himself. "It must not happen."

After all, there was nothing but the spade to connect
him with the death of Bonar. So he persuaded himself.

Common sense had a brief innings. It told him to
behave as any innocent person would: call for help, fetch
Chrystal, telephone for the police. The instinct of self-
preservation mocked at these smug counsels. He stooped,
stretched out a hand, felt about in the darkness, and
picked up the spade.

Yet he found it impossible not to turn on the torch
again for a last hasty look at that prostrate body. Bonar,
reflected Michael, had been a very strong man: self-

indulgence had left traces on that massive frame, but it had still been powerful beyond the average when it had met its end. Odd for a great hulking fellow to have died like that (how Chrystal would have reiterated his favourite adjective!), by a crack on the skull from a spade on a dark night.

Down from the hill floated the chorus of the latest popular dance tune. The voices sounded nearer. That settled it. Carrying the spade, Michael went towards his home. He walked cautiously. He thought for a moment he heard someone walking in front of him, some distance ahead. He listened, and decided he had been mistaken. He felt a drop of rain, like ice on his forehead. The rain fell heavily. He tucked the spade under his arm and quickened his step. He had congratulated himself on reaching the Vineyard without incident and was about to turn in at the little drive when a powerful light was suddenly flashed full in his face. He staggered back as if shot. He made a convulsive effort to hide the spade behind his back, and cursed himself for a fool to think that it might be possible to dissimulate a spade. The falling rain shone like slender rods of steel in the rays of the torch. . . .

"Oh, it's you, Michael Holt!"

It was old Miss Perks. How well he knew her voice! Deep and gruff as a man's. There was some surprise in it, too, as though she had expected to see someone else. He pictured her standing there in her voluminous black mackintosh, a formidable little woman, with her great hooked nose and the dark growth of hair on her upper lip, and those ironical eyes which must now be gazing at him speculatively. He wondered what she was doing there at such a time of night. She in her turn, no doubt, was guessing at reasons why he should be going about in the dark and wet with a spade under his arm.

"You quite startled me, Miss Perks."

"Guilty conscience, eh?" She put out her torch and barked a question: "Have you seen Robert?"

So that was it, thought Michael: poor old Robert was up to his tricks again.

"No." He hurried on nervously: "I've just come down the lane. You won't find Robert there. If he had been, I should certainly have met him." It was, at all costs, necessary to halt her and send her back before she stumbled upon Bonar's body.

"No?" She paused doubtfully. "You're sure? I thought perhaps Robert had gone up to the footpaths with the others." The rain was thrashing down on her umbrella. "That man Bonar!" she exclaimed. "Like a mad dog! It's time somebody put him away."

Lucky, thought Michael, that Miss Perks could not see his face when she said that.

"So you've been joining in the good work too, I notice." Miss Perks appeared to have been considering the spade and to have found a satisfactory explanation for it. Yet Michael wondered for a moment: why the "too?"

"Oh, yes, the spade. Very useful. Yes, rather!" Michael was almost stuttering. "Very good fun it was."

"The excitement seems to have been a bit too much for you," remarked Miss Perks dryly. "You looked just now as if you had seen a corpse."

Michael laughed foolishly.

"Where are the others?"

"Still up on the footpath. They'll be down soon."

"You came back alone?"

"Yes."

"Did you meet anybody?"

"No one at all."

"No one at all?" repeated the old lady.

"No one."

"H'm! . . . Then you haven't seen Robert." Miss Perks concluded her cross-examination, but her tone showed that she was not yet fully satisfied.

"No. He certainly wasn't up there, or I should have seen him."

"Could you be sure in the dark?"

"There was a lantern, and several people had torches, including myself."

Miss Perks grunted.

"Do you know . . . Well, perhaps I ought not to ask you that. If you are perfectly sure it's no use looking for Robert in this direction . . ."

"Absolutely certain," said Michael.

"Oh!" Miss Perks's tone was non-committal; but she added: "Well, however that may be, this rain will send him home. I'll hurry back and get a hot bath ready. . . .Good night, Michael."

"But"—the rain was pelting down: he had to shout—"won't you come in until it stops?"

"I'm not afraid of a drop of rain, thank you," came her man's voice shouting back.

He heard her splashing down the lane, back towards the bridge and the church and her house in the Pavement, where she would turn on the hot bath for Robert . . . poor Mr. Robert, who, as the Chesworth gossips said, was such a nice old gentleman, it was a pity that every now and then he should have one of those queer fits which made him behave in such an odd way that, really, my dear, one didn't know where to look. . . .

It was annoying that Michael should have run into Miss Perks at that moment; but better Miss Perks than someone else, for she could be depended upon to keep her own counsel. Still, he could have dispensed with the meeting, he told himself as he walked up his little drive, while his heart throbbed like the engines of a ship.

2

Michael did not at once enter his house. He spent several minutes in the tool-shed, where he was busy at first with a bit of rag. The rag did not do what he required of it, and he found some sandpaper, which served his purpose. He burned the sandpaper after use, and, leaving all straight in the toolshed, he switched off the light and locked up. On second thoughts, he re-entered the shed, took out the spade, and thrust it back into the border among the wallflowers. Then he went indoors.

The light had been left on in the hall, and as he went upstairs he noticed that the tall clock in the corner stood at twenty-five minutes past eleven. Thirteen minutes had passed since he stumbled over Douglas Bonar's dead body. It had seemed like hours.

The creaking of the stairs or the sound he made when he opened the bathroom door disturbed Mary, and she called out: it startled him and he knocked over a chair.

"Is that you, Michael?"

"Speaking. Sorry I'm such a clumsy ass."

"I hope you didn't get very wet."

"Nothing to speak of."

"Has the deed been done?"

The question came as he switched on the bathroom light. He saw his face in the mirror on the wall and thanked his stars that Mary could not see it too. "Has the deed been done?" The question was sinister in form and of a piece, he told himself, with the melodrama of the moment; but he knew what Mary meant and answered more or less naturally.

"Yes, the barricades are down. All three of them. Old Bisgood was in command: evidently a born leader."

"Did Mr. Bonar show any signs of life?"

"Good God, what do you . . . Oh, I see. Sorry, dear, that was the shaving-brush I knocked off the shelf. I seem to be upsetting everything to-night. Yes, Bonar turned up and had a brief slanging-match with Bisgood. Tell you all about it in the morning."

"Will you be long?"

"I don't know. I'm feeling unusually restless. All this unaccustomed excitement, I suppose. Doubt whether I should sleep if I turned in now. May stay down for a while and write. Perhaps even go out again."

"Not in this heavy rain, Michael!"

"It's passing over. It's too heavy to last."

"Well," came Mary's comfortable, sleepy voice, "try not to upset anything else, or you'll wake the boys up. I shall be asleep when you come: so good night, Michael."

"Good night."

He closed the door with precaution, took off his soaking raincoat and his dinner-jacket, turned up his sleeves, and scrubbed his hands with minute care. He examined his cuffs, held his coat under the light and subjected it to a detailed inspection, scanned closely the rest of his person. He could find no incriminating traces. He put on his jacket and coat, switched off the light and went downstairs. At the front door he paused to light his pipe. His hands were perfectly steady. After looking up at the sky, in which no stars were to be seen, he put his hands into his pockets and strolled leisurely down the little drive and up the lane. There were no longer any sounds coming from the hill. It seemed likely that the working party had found their home, passing the Vineyard while he was upstairs. Their enthusiasm would have been quenched by the rain. On his left the little Denne made itself heard more clearly than usual. It had drunk its fill during the last half-hour.

When Michael had counted two hundred paces he stood still and listened. He could hear nothing but the murmur of the river. He took out his torch and used it cautiously. Keeping the little circle of light on the road in front of him, he walked almost as far as the Chrystals' gate; but he did not see that of which he was in search. He retraced his steps in growing bewilderment, which deepened until he cast discretion to the winds, raking the whole width of the lane with his light. It was some time before he could convince himself that the body of Douglas Bonar was no longer there. He walked up and down several times. The bulb of his lamp grew dim and threatened to go out. By this time he was ready to believe that he had dreamed the whole thing; but at a certain place a little gold brooch gleamed in the dying rays of his torch and, stooping to pick it up, he saw, almost effaced by the rain, yet still unmistakable, the tell-tale smear of red where the pool of Bonar's blood had been.

The rain came on again. After a moment's consideration he threw down the brooch where it had been lying, and went back to the house.

III. Scandal About An Author

Douglas Bonar's body was found at the sluices of Marple's flour-mills, half a mile farther down the Denne, in the early morning. The news was not long in reaching the Vineyard. It was delivered by the milkman with the milk, and the maid passed it on to Mary.

"And it wasn't no accident, mum," said the maid with emphasis. "Nor he wasn't drowned."

"How do you know, Susan?"

"Because he hadn't half had a nasty knock on the head. Dead he was before they threw him into the river. Murdered, mum."

Susan's eyes rounded and her voice became a hoarse whisper as she said, "Murdered, mum."

"Isn't it awful?" she added in shocked tones; and then, immediately, with the liveliest possible interest, "I wonder who done it, mum. Do you think They'll Get Him?"

Michael had slept badly and came down with a headache. It was probably good for him that he had to force himself to make a proper show of surprise at the news of the crime. He said the right things, but his brain was busy all the time, speculating on the discovery of Bonar's body so far down the river. It was curious that the corpse had escaped the snags and the overhanging trees by the stone bridge: the Denne must have risen very quickly during the rain. He assumed, naturally, that the murderer had returned to the spot and committed the dead man to the water. . . lifted that massive body in his strong arms and dropped it over the stone wall into the river. But why the interval? Was this disposal of the body an afterthought? Or had the murderer been disturbed at his work? If so . . . disturbed by whom? By Michael? That was an alarming thought. Michael turned hot and cold as he pictured the murderer in concealment behind the hedge. Everything Michael had done must have been watched. The thought grew no more pleasant as its implications were studied.

Mary talked about the affair in whispers, with significant nods and gestures whenever the boys came within earshot. Michael smiled at this excess of caution. He knew that in half-an-hour's time Hugh and Kenneth would be hearing from their fellow-pupils at the prep, school all about the murder, in gruesome and sanguinary detail.

"And to think, mum," said Susan, coming in with the coffee, "that this very yesterday afternoon Mr. Bonar was sitting in this very room and talking to Mr. Holt."

Michael scowled. He did not want to be reminded of that interview with Bonar. He had hoped that the dead man's second call at the Vineyard could safely be relegated to the limbo of things that one no longer has to worry about.

Mary did not notice the scowl: she herself was too busy making faces at Susan. "Not in front of the children, Susan," the faces said, unmistakably.

Mary was inclined to worry too much about the boys. When, ultimately, they had been dispatched to school, Michael noticed that she had a preoccupied air. His conscience made him uneasy. He asked with some apprehension, what the matter was.

Mary sighed.

"I wish we could afford a better school for Hugh and Ken."

Michael smiled with relief.

"Oh, is that all? I didn't think there was much wrong with that place in the Pavement. Is there?"

"They pick up such nasty language there."

"Nasty language?"

"I went into the garden this morning to tell Hugh to stop jumping off the roof of the tool-shed. I found him picking himself up from among the cabbages, and he said, 'It doesn't half shake your guts up, mum.'"

Michael roared.

"Well, if that's all you have to worry about, old thing . . ."

"But it isn't nice; and you know that what Hugh says and does, Ken promptly imitates."

"My dear, the word you object to is now used in the best circles, and if we sent the boys to Eton they would learn far worse."

Mary looked incredulous, and was not comforted.

"I really don't think you ought to make a joke of it."

"Very well," said Michael sternly. "I'll beat Hugh as soon as he comes home."

"You'll do nothing of the sort!"

Michael looked at her with twinkling eyes. It was so easy to get a rise out of her on some subjects. She blushed.

"I suppose I do fuss too much. . . . Well, poor Mr. Bonar no longer wants the Vineyard."

"You don't think I ever meant to let him have it?"

"But you told me you had said you would think over his offer and let him have his answer to-day."

"I never seriously meant to accept."

"You hesitated over it, though."

"If we want to send the boys to a more expensive school," said Michael, with cunning, "we can't afford to stand on our dignity when rich men offer us money."

"It would have had to be a lot of money to make me even dream of letting you sell the place."

"The temptation is now removed."

"I shouldn't like to leave the Vineyard now."

Michael smiled at her and went off to his room with the intention of working. He was a professional writer of industrious habits, and had no patience with the amateur triflers who boast that they wait for inspiration. His was as much a trade as any other, and he calculated on a certain output every day.

Tasks in hours of insight willed
Can be through days of gloom fulfilled.

The hours of insight were bound to come and could be used for planning ahead. For the rest Michael got on with the job in hand, like any diligent journeyman. Of all things he despised most the fickle mind that calls itself the artistic temperament.

On this morning, none the less, Michael found it impossible to settle down to his task like a good workman. All his self-schooling availed him nothing. After a moody hour spent mainly in studying the wallpaper he put on his hat and went down into Chesworth.

2

For some days Michael had avoided the town because he had encountered a feeling of hostility in certain circles there. He was sensitive: equipped, indeed, with an extra sense which told him at once what other people were privately thinking about him. He did not in the least understand the reason why he was being met in some places with suspicion or positive distrust. It seemed to him impossible that a group of people in Chesworth should have learned of the one thing he wished to keep secret. If they had, then his behaviour of the night before had been unnecessary, idiotic even . . . but it would not matter. Nothing would matter. But they could not know: he told himself again that it was impossible. Then what was there in the wind? What had people against him? . . .

He paused at the stone bridge. There was a path that continued by the Denne, and eventually led across the footbridge and past the church into the Pavement; but it was probably muddy after the heavy rain. He decided to go straight up Forest Lane.

Half-way up Forest Lane stood the new Drill Hall,

which in the intervals of serving the Territorials gave
Chesworth house-room for its dances and whist-drives
and other jollifications. It was the town's one attempt at
modern architecture, a distinguished youngster, with
some of the blood of London's County Hall in its veins;
and it had been tucked away in this semi-rural
thoroughfare, where the average townsman of Chesworth
regarded it with very much the emotions of a small bird,
in a quiet way of life, who had unexpectedly hatched a
fine young cuckoo.

At this moment the Drill Hall was being used for an
exhibition of pictures by Sussex artists. Michael
remembered that he had thought of taking Mary to see
them. He was told that Brangwyn, who lived at Ditchling,
had sent three of his works.

When Michael was abreast of the Drill Hall, he saw
Goodwin, the estate agent, coming down the footpath
towards him. They had been at school together. Goodwin
as a boy had distinguished himself at cricket, though not
in other directions. Cricket and brains did not as a rule go
together: it was otherwise with Rugby football. Yet
Michael and all the clever schoolboys he knew had envied
the successful cricketers, and would have been content to
be half-wits if they could make an occasional century.

Since Michael had returned to settle down in
Chesworth two months before, Goodwin had met him
once. On that occasion Goodwin had been all honey.

He was now hurrying in Michael's direction with his
characteristic quick, springy step, like a dancing
master's. He had seen Michael and a faint smile was
flickering over his brick-red face. Just before they were
due to meet, Michael felt a strong impulse to sneeze and
plunged his nose into his pocket-handkerchief. Out of the
corner of his eye he saw Goodwin, the smile still
flickering over his face, swerve neatly off the path and
cross the road and enter the Drill Hall, as though, quite
improbably, he had been seized with a sudden passion for
Sussex art.

Cut!

Michael blew his nose and put the handkerchief back into his pocket. Goodwin, he told himself, except when he wielded his flashing blade on the cricket field, was negligible. In the rancour of the moment, Michael qualified Goodwin as a worm. But even worms could show which way the wind blew. They would not venture to cut old acquaintances off their own bat, so to speak. They had to be egged on or buoyed up by public opinion before they took action as final as that. The thing was symptomatic, concluded Michael, too serious to be amused by his mixture of metaphors: there was scandal in the air.

Michael had known it for some little time. Luckily, Mary as yet suspected nothing. She had noticed that few people called at the Vineyard now: but she readily attributed this to the fact that the first rush had abated. Partly, too, she blamed her own remissness: she had returned so few of the calls. The family and domestic cares kept her so occupied!

Michael turned into Eastergate. Here something else happened.

Howard came driving his open car very slowly along the street. Howard was another former schoolfellow of Michael's: he had made much money in the broking of stocks, bought a large country house four miles out of Chesworth, and insinuated himself into the fringes of Society, with the assistance of a first-class cook, excellent tennis courts and a few acres of rough shooting. His wife, the daughter of a rich timber merchant, was very proud.

Howard's eyes met Michael's. Without changing his expression or accelerating his speed he rolled by. Goodwin's had been the cut clumsy. This was the cut pseudo-aristocratic.

To be cut twice in swift succession. . .! Michael strode along the pavement with fury at his heart. He cursed Howard. The upstart swine! Michael said in his haste that he would draw a faithful portrait of Howard, "warts and all," make him a character, put him into a novel.

That was the novelist's safety-valve: he could blow off steam that other people would have to keep bottled up. It was one of the compensations of being a novelist. . . .

Then came Sprague.

It was after Michael had passed the point policeman and entered the Cut that he met Sprague. The Cut had once been the Shambles, where, as was customary in medieval times, all the butchers' shops of Chesworth had been huddled together in one fetid alley—probably on the principle that if malodorous trades must exist within the urban precincts it was as well to see that they were segregated. The butchers' shops had given place to establishments of other kinds, but the excessive narrowness of the thoroughfare still persisted. The Cut was not a street in which people could be avoided, and Sprague and Michael met face to face.

Sprague had once been in business as a chemist: he had retired to a small house in the Worthing Road and was now entirely wrapped up in the achievements of his daughters, known throughout Chesworth as the Splendid Sisters. Chesworth possessed no more notorious chatterbox than Sprague, and all his acquaintances were kept fully informed of the progress of his prodigious offspring: how Una, for instance, had wielded a badminton racket for the Ladies of Sussex and defeated the redoubtable female champion of Middlesex; and how Polly was getting on wonderfully with her dispensing in London, where there was a handsome young doctor in the offing.

As a rule, Sprague, meeting Michael in the street, would buttonhole him and keep him standing on the pavement for twenty minutes. On this May morning, when he almost collided with Michael in the Cut, he said awkwardly, "Er, hullo, Holt," went red in the face, turned his head away sharply with a pained expression, muttered, "Get a tie," and blundered into the magnificent new premises of Shilling & Mapp's, outside whose patent non-reflecting plate-glass windows the encounter had taken place.

The cut shamefaced.

Michael, who did not dislike Sprague, hoped kindly enough that Shilling & Mapp's involuntary customer would escape without buying something he did not want or could ill afford. Then, forming a resolution, he turned into the Pavement.

3

Once the visitor has properly penetrated the street called the Pavement, he is ready to forgive the Chesworth Urban District Council, who have turned the entrance into a car park, and even to forget the Wealden Tile Company, who have established their offices in an excessively hideous building and emphasized its unfortunate architectural features by painting them an aggressive shade of green. Having turned his back upon these offences, the visitor sees before him what is perhaps the most delightful street of any country town in England. There is something Continental about it; and yet it epitomizes the Englishman's traditional passion for surrounding himself with grass and flowers and trees and for possessing a roof of his own. The houses are all of different patterns, and each has evidently been built by someone to please himself. There are houses that are plain and dignified, like those the colonists re-created in New England; in others the builders have allowed full play to their wildest whims. A glance at a house, and one forms a clear idea of the man who first owned it. The roofs are all remarkable, and make patterns that would never have occurred to Euclid in his dreams. Two or three of these houses stand within walled grounds, and a few others have tiny patches of unfenced garden in front of them; but for the most part their front doors open plump on to the foot-way, and the passer-by may, if he likes, gaze in at the windows. Even here the line that the houses make with the path is irregular, for some have bay windows and some have bows, and others are straight-fronted; and there are doorways with several steps leading up to them, and doorways with no steps at all. Between the sidewalk and the roadway stands a long line of pollarded trees, which at the time of these events were beginning to send out shoots of green; and these trees are so severely lopped and pruned that they rival in oddness of shape the most fantastic of the houses. The trees, and the triangular fragment of grass at the town end, with its seats where people can laze in the sun, give the finishing touch to this cul-de-sac, which ends at the gates of Chesworth Church: here, says the visitor, is a place where a country-loving people have made the best possible job of living in a town.

In the oddest and most whimsical of all these old houses lived Miss Perks, as it was fitting that she should: together with Robert, her brother, a perfectly charming old gentleman except when he was unfortunate enough to have one of those unaccountable fits that made him do things of which nice people spoke in whispers; as well as William and Elizabeth, whose status was inferior and domestic. It was not Miss Perks, however, whom Michael had come to see. He walked rapidly down the Pavement and turned in at the gate of the rectory.

The Rector of Chesworth, the Reverend William Chandos, was a bachelor. His housekeeper, a sour little woman who kept herself to herself, showed Michael at once into the study, where her master sat at his writing-table. Chandos held a pen in his hand, but he was not writing. He was gazing idly out of the French windows on his left. When Michael came in, he dropped his pen with alacrity, as though he were glad to have someone to talk to.

"Hullo, Michael, hullo. Take a pew, old man. Put a pipe on. You'll find some baccy in the jar. The Store's own special eightpenny blend, popularly known as Desert Sweepings. Most people prefer to smoke their own, and I don't blame them."

"I'm not disturbing you, rector?"

"Glad to see you, my boy. Can't work, anyhow. Mislaid my glasses somewhere. A confounded nuisance, because I need 'em for reading and writing."

Chandos was a fine figure of a man, tall and massively built, with reddish hair and a beard like Sir Francis Drake's. He had begun his clerical career as one of Chesworth's seven curates. Promotion had sent him to Staffordshire, where for several years he toiled in the darkness of a Black Country living: recently, with a deep sigh of relief, he had come back to Chesworth as rector. He prided himself upon being a man as well as a parson. He resented the dog-collar (such he always called it) which branded him as one set apart from his fellows: but he always wore it. To leave it off, as some of his colleagues did whenever they could, was, in his opinion, not playing the game. There was no nonsense about him. In the pulpit he refused to adopt an apologetic tone about the Christian religion: it was so obviously the one solvent for the world's discontents that he failed to see how any decent person could think otherwise. The one difficulty, he said, consisted in living up to it: and that was the very reason why it was such fun to be a Christian. At Cambridge he had rowed in his college boat, and simple analogies from the practice of oarsmanship figured constantly in his sermons: these came straight from his broad shoulders in forcible language and included a great many words like stupendous, amazing, unbelievable, unimaginable, stupefying, colossal, terrific and never-to-be-forgotten. People said that he was marked out for a bishopric. As a townsman he heartily supported the cricket and football clubs and all forms of manly sport. In the Black Country he had come out as a champion of Sunday games: in Chesworth, where circumstances were different and public opinion was not so advanced, he saw no harm in the use of tennis courts on Sunday by those of his parishioners who possessed them, if they wished to play, but he reserved his opinion on the wider issue. The question was about to come up before the Urban District Council, and he was content to abide by their judgment. In his private relationships he was anxious to keep on the best possible terms with everyone: and, as is inevitable in a person whose chief aim is to keep on the best possible terms with everyone, sincerity was not the strongest trait in his character. He was now forty-eight years of age, thirteen years older than Michael, whom he had known as a boy.

"Glad to see you, Michael," he repeated, cramming tobacco into an enormous pipe and moving into an armchair. "Not all my callers are so congenial. I have just had a visit from the police."

Michael's thoughts were shaken into another channel. He stirred in his chair.

"From the police?"

"About this rotten business of Bonar," said the rector, frowning. He lit his pipe. "Feel better when I've got a pipe on. Nice thing for a respectable parson to be mixed up in a murder case, isn't it? I'm in that interesting position which always seems to be considered so important in the detective stories. In all probability I am The Last Person To See The Murdered Man Alive." He chuckled.

Michael began to fill his pipe from his own pouch.

"When was this?" he asked, without looking up.

"At eleven o'clock last night. I can be positive about the time . . . there's another detective story touch for you . . . because I heard the church clock strike during an awkward pause in our conversation."

"You mean in a conversation between you and Bonar?"

"If conversation you can call it." The rector smiled and stroked his beautiful beard. "It came very near degenerating into a slanging match. Against all my principles." He put another match to his pipe and went on, with his eyes twinkling: "Bonar saw fit to relieve his feelings on the subject of Chesworth and its people, their manners and customs and dubious ancestry. He said

some most outrageous things, and even permitted himself
a disparaging reference to the sincerity of our Christian
professions . . . a thing which, hang it all, he couldn't
expect the tamest of parsons to allow to pass. I was
drawn into quite a warm little argument." The rector
laughed as though an amusing thought had just struck
him. "Puts me in a rather awkward position, when you
come to think of it. 'The last person to see the murdered
man alive was the Rector of Chesworth, who was heard in
altercation with him near the spot where the body must
have been thrown into the river.'" He checked himself and
shrugged his shoulders, glanced through the French
windows and sighed. There was a dreamy look in his eyes
as he went on:"It is a staggering shock to our little
community. When such an appalling calamity swoops
down on the calm surface of our little backwater, it forces
us to think of . . ."

Michael recognized Chandos's pulpit manner. The
rector was meditating the incorporation of a topical
reference in Sunday's sermon.

His voice trailed away. He looked round at Michael a
little guiltily.

"Sorry to come the parson over you, old boy. But it is
an unpleasant business. It does make one sit up.
Chesworth won't get over it for a bit."

He fiddled with his fingers. Michael lit his pipe.

"Where did this . . . where did you meet Bonar?"

"Not so very far from your place: just a few hundred
yards farther up the lane. I had been dining with
Thornhill—two bachelors together. Let me see, he's your
nearest neighbour, isn't he?"

"Who, Thornhill? Oh, no. He lives at the far end of our
lane. The Chrystals are between us: at that corner where
the track turns off towards the Park."

"I was forgetting friend Chrystal," said the rector
musingly. "Odd little fellow. Oddly mated. It must have
been almost outside his, er, habitation . . . what do you
call the thing—a semi-bungalow?—that Bonar and I fell

in with each other. I had spent a capital evening with Thornhill. A good chap, Thornhill, English as they make 'em: the right stuff, genuine through and through. A bit too robust perhaps for the taste of maiden ladies"—the rector smiled reflectively—"and inclined to be just a little too fond of the whisky: but a real man. He seems to have struck lucky with his new servants. The wife served us up a thundering good dinner, and Thornhill told me that Jennings, the husband, works like a Trojan in the garden. Yes, I passed a jolly evening and enjoyed a good yarn: Thornhill and I, you know, have a good deal in common. We both rowed for our college, for instance. A splendid fellow in everyway." The rector halted, and looked at Michael with a deprecating smile. "Not that I claim to be on level terms with Thornhill as an oarsman, or, for that matter, in any other field of sport. He had a marvellous athletic record. That wonderful collection of cups on his sideboard is enough to prove that."

"An impressive show," murmured Michael.

The rector's grim little housekeeper knocked at the door and came in with a small parcel.

"From Mr. Thornhill, sir. Jennings brought it."

She went out silently. The rector undid the wrapping.

"Aha, my glasses! So that's where I left them. Very good of Thornhill to send them back so promptly."

Chandos glanced at the clock on the mantelpiece. It seemed to occur to him that Thornhill might have sent them back even sooner, since he knew how indispensable they were. The rector coughed, as though to delete the implied criticism of his fellow athlete.

"Let me see. . . . Oh, yes. I had my bicycle with me, but I was in no hurry and I strolled back, pushing the machine. I met Bonar in the lane. As you say, it must have been very near the Chrystals' semi-bungalow." He uttered the word "semi-bungalow" with relish, as though he found it a delicious expression. "Bonar had been witnessing the destructive efforts of our public-spirited fellow-townsmen, and he was filled with a sense of grievance." The rector glanced sadly at the great bowl of his pipe. "A regrettable affair that, from several points of view, especially in the light of what followed: but, *de mortuis* or not, one cannot help feeling that Bonar brought it on himself. It seems that he had hurried away from the footpaths to telephone to the police. He took it for granted that they would promptly send up and arrest every man Jack of the demonstrators. Instead of that, he found 'em positively rude, or at least not very helpful: they told him it was a matter for civil action and declined to interfere. Got on their wrong side, I expect. He would. It was my ill luck to run into him at such an awkward moment. He exploded on my unoffending person. I bore it with Christian resignation for a few minutes, but, hang it all, even a downtrodden parson sometimes turns, and at last I rounded on him and let him have a few home truths. I said he was a disturbing element in the community, and ought to have more sense. I believe I let him have it good and strong"—the rector chuckled—"and before he had a chance to reply I jumped on to my bike and buzzed off, leaving him standing."

Michael looked down his nose.

"Do you know where he telephoned from?"

"I hadn't thought of that. Not from his own baronial halls, evidently. He very likely found it quicker to come down the hill into the town."

It was a fresh subject of speculation for Michael; but the rector did not show any interest in the question, and went talking on.

"I never knew what to make of Bonar. He was a strange bird, new to my experience. Naturally I tried to rope him in . . . it's a good thing to get these big magnates interested in the Church if possible . . . but then he put himself at logger-heads with the town, and . . . well, a parson has to mind how he goes when things are like that. I walked like Agag, delicately. We were quite friendly when we met, however, quite friendly."

Chandos glanced shrewdly at Michael. "I hear that

you had a little encounter with him yourself?"

Michael wrinkled up his eyes.

"Bonar wanted to buy the Vineyard," he said.

"I believe, my dear Michael," said the rector, puffing out a cloud of smoke, "that I put the idea in his head. You came to the Vineyard in March, just before Bonar bought the Park? . . . It must have been very soon afterwards that I encountered him in the lane outside your house. I told him the stock story: why your place was called the Vineyard, because in former days the owner of the Park had cast covetous eyes upon it. The old story of Naboth. I can quite understand it, because the Vineyard is a sort of slice cut out of the Park and prevents it from stretching down to the river. . . .. I saw that Bonar was interested: a predatory gleam came into his eye. I confess I did not understand at the time what the gleam portended, but when I heard he had been pressing you to sell, it dawned upon me. He had promptly formed the resolution to win back the Vineyard for the Park: he had made up his mind to succeed where his ancient predecessor had so ignominiously failed. That, I suppose," said the rector, shaking his head, "is the sort of man he was. I imagine he would have left you no peace until he got what he wanted."

Michael leaned back in his chair.

"He pressed me pretty hard," he admitted. "In fact he made me another offer only yesterday, and gave me twenty-four hours to think it over."

"Which offer now falls through, presumably," said the rector dryly. "It saves you the trouble of having to make up your mind, eh?"

"I should have been sorry to leave the Vineyard, if only for Mary's sake," said Michael, dropping his eyes. "Last summer, you remember, we came through Sussex on a motor tour. Mary wanted to see my old haunts. She liked Chesworth, and when she saw the Vineyard she fell in love with it."

"And worried you until you bought it for her?"

suggested Chandos humorously. "I am a bachelor, my dear Michael, but I am not altogether ignorant of the ways of women. . . . You have been very happy there?"

"I don't think Mary would have let me sell. Not even," Michael added carefully, "if Bonar had offered considerably more than he actually did."

"Well, the question has been settled for you." The rector stretched out his long legs and yawned: yawned and apologized. "I have had a trying morning, old fellow. The police were quite nice, of course: still, it's all very unpleasant and tiresome."

"How did they get to know?"

"About my row with Bonar in the lane? I rang 'em up. Instinct of self-preservation." Chandos stroked his beard and winked. "I said to myself that my little scrap with Bonar might have been overheard, and it behoved me to weigh in with my story first. So they interviewed me. For that matter, I suppose they will be interviewing all the good fellows who so very excusably took the law into their own hands last night."

"Oh! I hadn't thought of that." Michael's face showed that he was disconcerted.

The rector smiled at him.

"Aha, Michael! So you were one of the bold fellows. Prepare yourself for a domiciliary visit, my lad."

"Confounded nuisance," muttered Michael, with genuine feeling.

"And what were you armed with?" asked the rector slyly. "Pick and shovel?"

"I had a spade."

"H'm," said the rector thoughtfully.

There was silence for a few seconds. The object of Michael's visit returned to his mind. He put the question he had come to ask.

"Look here, rector," he blurted out, "as man to man, what's this scandal that's going the rounds about me?"

Chandos looked down into his beard, and then raised his eyes and fixed them on Michael.

"Scandal, my dear fellow? What scandal? Is there any scandal?"

It dawned at once upon Michael that the rector was the last person he should have asked. He had come to the wrong quarter: he would get no information here. The rector was too wily a bird. At the same time, Michael, who had intuition, realized that Chandos knew exactly what he meant: but was not going to be drawn. He set too high a value on a peaceful life.

"If you haven't heard anything . . ." said Michael, rising.

The rector kept his seat, smiled indulgently, and waited.

"Oh, well," concluded Michael, "I dare say they don't tell you these things. Sorry to have bothered you about it. I must be off. I've already stayed too long."

"Don't go, my dear fellow, don't go," said the rector, briskly jumping to his feet. "If you can spare a few minutes I want you to cast your expert eye over my garden. I should like your opinion on what is best to be done. I am afraid my predecessor neglected it shamefully. Mind the step under the French window. Now, this border. . . ."

It was a quarter of an hour before Michael escaped from the rector, who talked the whole time . . . and without swerving from the subject of gardens. Michael started for home in a complicated state of mind, but he found a glimmer of comfort before he reached the Vineyard. This curious and inexplicable scandal which circulated in the town was not pleasant, but it could be used to his own advantage.

IV. MISS PERKS WRITES A NOTE

Mary announced at lunch that she intended to call on Miss Perks, and Michael, after a little hesitation, encouraged her. Mary needed encouragement. She had to be braced for the ordeal. She liked Robert Perks, who had seemed to her a gentle-mannered scholar . . . none of the gossip about Robert had reached Mary . . . but Matilda Perks was a formidable proposition. Mary well remembered Miss Perks's formal call at the Vineyard. The old lady had sat like an extremely ferocious edition of Queen Victoria, and made the most alarming conversation. Her deep bass tones were intimidating in themselves; and she had said exactly what came into her head and asked the most direct questions without the least beating about the bush. That parting remark of hers . . . could Mary ever forget it? Miss Perks had risen, regarded herself in the glass over the mantlepiece, apparently approving the ensemble, hooked nose and hair on upper lip included, and then turned to Mary and delivered herself of this pregnant saying: "People are fond of deluding themselves into the belief that a rough-tongued old woman like me has a heart of gold. Don't you believe them, my dear. Mine isn't a heart of gold, not by any means. I have long since lost any faith I had in human goodness. What I have got, something even rarer than a heart of gold, is a passion for the truth. That is, when it suits me, my dear. The truth is a sharp-edged weapon, and often it's best kept locked up." Whereupon she had departed. A terrifying little woman, thought Mary. However, since calls had to be returned, Miss Perks must be called upon; and since she was the fiercest dragon on the list, she might well be disposed of first.

Michael was a very old acquaintance of Miss Perks. As a little boy he had attended Miss Perks's school, in common with many other little Chesworth boys, as well as little Chesworth girls. The school had been abruptly closed two years after Michael had passed on to a more advanced institution, and the story of its ending was characteristic of Miss Perks. She had boxed a little boy's ears. The little boy's mother came to complain. Miss Perks listened to the complaint and then rose to her full height, which was not great, although her dignity of bearing enhanced her stature. "Mrs. Smith," she said, "I have come to the conclusion that I am growing too old to suffer fools gladly. I can educate the Chesworth children, but I cannot educate the Chesworth parents, nor can I suffer them any longer, gladly or otherwise. I have all the money I want, and I shall close the school at the end of this term."

Such was Miss Perks's prestige in the town that a deputation of parents called upon her to desire that she should change her mind, but on learning the object of their visit she showed them to the door herself and hurried, almost pushed them into the street. When the last day of term came, Miss Perks expressed the pious hope that her pupils would grow up better men and women than their parents, wished them farewell, and locked up the classroom for ever. Rumour insisted that the room had never been entered since: that the desks stood thick with dust, and that the atmosphere was still charged with the unmistakable odour of school, arising from a blend of powdered chalk and the perspiration of little bodies. Thenceforth Miss Perks cultivated her garden, took a caustic interest in the affairs of the town, kept a parrot, collected china, and looked after her brother Robert, who had himself been a school-master until, not unreasonably, he had been asked to resign.

On this afternoon Mary climbed the four steps to Miss Perks's front door and pulled the wrought-iron bell-handle. She heard a kind of ghostly pealing far away in the interior, and presently the echoing tread of footsteps advancing down a stone corridor. When this was followed by the sound of bolts being thrown back, Mary began to feel that she was paying a call on a medieval fortress. The sight of Miss Perks's housekeeper reassured her. Elizabeth was a comfortable, elderly person, broad in the beam as good cooks so often are: and she had a comfortable face and a welcoming smile which helped to nerve Mary for the encounter with her mistress.

"Miss Perks is at home, ma'am. Please to come in. Four steps down. Yes, ma'am, it is peculiar," she went on, as if Mary had spoken aloud what she could not help thinking. "You have to go up four steps to the front door and then come down four steps again immediately. The whole house is very peculiar. Even the bathroom has four doors, and you have to remember to lock them all and sometimes visitors forget, which makes it rather awkward. Though it is not often we have guests staying in the house now. Then all the rooms are on different levels, and there are so many ways in and out that it is easy to get lost. A very peculiar house, altogether, ma'am."

Elizabeth bolted the front door, top and bottom, and then, with a "Please to come this way, ma'am," clattered along the stone passage, which stretched for some distance and took two turns at right-angles before it arrived at a badly lighted hall from which opened several doors.

"This is my kitchen, ma'am," said Elizabeth, letting in a ray of sunshine from one of these. "There's a step down."

Mary found herself in a room full of dressers and tables and pots and pans and crockery which seemed to her to be beautifully kept; and she was wondering whether she was expected to say so when she noticed Elizabeth holding open a narrow door in the wall.

"This is the way upstairs, ma'am. Yes, it is a peculiar house."

The steep and narrow stairs wound like a corkscrew until they came out in an apartment which reminded

Mary of a stage setting for a farce, so extravagantly was it furnished with doors.

"I think at one time, ma'am, this was one of the bedrooms. But, of course," remarked Elizabeth, with a shake of the head, "nowadays that would be rather awkward, and so it is not used at all. Please to come this way. Two steps down."

This room was obviously the bathroom, and Elizabeth made no comment. She rapped smartly at a door on the opposite side. Miss Perks's gruff voice was heard answering, "Come in."

"Come in, curse you," supplemented another voice, in rasping tones.

"That's only the parrot, ma'am," whispered Elizabeth reassuringly. "Two steps up and two steps down. . . . Mrs. Holt, ma'am."

Miss Perks was posted in a chair at a large window overlooking the garden.

"Come in, Mrs. Holt," she barked, without troubling to turn her head. "Elizabeth, have you found my brooch?"

"No, ma'am."

"Have you looked everywhere?"

"Everywhere, ma'am."

"Then you are quite sure it is not in the house?"

"As to being quite sure it is not in the house, that I cannot be, ma'am," said Elizabeth, "for a little thing like a brooch may have slipped through a crack or anywhere, but I have searched for it, ma'am, and William has helped me."

"I suppose you are trying to suggest," said Miss Perks coldly, "that I lost it out of doors."

"Well, ma'am, even the most careful of us, with a little thing like a brooch . . ."

"And perhaps you're right," snapped Miss Perks. "That will do. You can go, Elizabeth."

Elizabeth smiled indulgently and retired through the bathroom.

During this interlude Mary had been left standing in

the middle of the room. It was a large and cheerful room, given plenty of light by a great window which jutted out over the garden. The walls were hung with an interesting paper, evidently not of modern pattern, in which the figure of a bird was constantly repeated amidst a background of green trees. The new wireless set stood facing the window. Two framed silhouettes of gentlemen in eighteenth-century costume were stationed one at each side of the fireplace, and there were no other pictures. But crockery was everywhere: it filled two glass-fronted corner cupboards and numerous brackets and overflowed on to the mantelpiece and the sideboard. Mary saw that none of this china had any special value: it just happened to amuse Miss Perks to surround herself with cups and saucers and bowls and vases and soup-tureens. When other people had a fling and went up to town for a restaurant and a theatre or down to the seaside for a few days, Miss Perks sent a cheque to the Potteries for a new tea-service. It was her way of celebrating.

Miss Perks, clad in her usual black, sat facing the window, with all this profusion of porcelain behind her. The parrot occupied a large cage on a table at her left hand. It had observed Mary's entrance with a disgusted air, and now hung its head and appeared to be brooding on the boredom of a parrot's life. On Miss Perks's right stood a little table which supported her work-basket. A large hand-bell, provided with a strap for a handle, rested on the floor beside her chair.

"What are you standing there for?" demanded Miss Perks suddenly. "We have chairs."

She dropped her work into her lap and stretched out a gnarled forefinger to indicate a particular chair, which was wedged between her work-table and the side frame of the window. Mary inserted herself into the allotted position with some difficulty. The window, raised aloft above the garden, gave Mary the impression that they were on the bridge of a ship of which Miss Perks was the captain. She had the odd feeling that she would be promptly clapped in irons if she misbehaved herself.

"You walked here?" demanded the fierce little woman in" black.

"Yes."

"I suppose it's no use asking you if you found a little gold brooch on your way?"

"I'm afraid I didn't," said Mary. She spoke apologetically, since Miss Perks's tone suggested that anyone but a born fool would certainly have found the brooch.

"No," said Miss Perks. "I didn't suppose you would. I have lost my little gold brooch forever, it appears." Miss Perks expressed emotion by wrinkling up her enormous hooked nose and pursing her down-covered lips: which made her look still more forbidding.

"I hope it wasn't of great value," ventured Mary.

"It was of value to me, or I shouldn't trouble other people about it. . ... Have you any objection to parrots?"

The change of subject was so abrupt that Mary turned a startled glance to the big cage; but its occupant was silent and pensive and appeared to be taking no notice of her.

"None at all," said Mary. "I think yours is a very handsome bird."

"H'm! Some foolish people are afraid of parrots. They talk about psittacosis: something the doctors invented a few years ago. Doctors are so much better at inventing fresh diseases than curing the old ones. Quacks and humbugs! . . . So you think Ramsay MacDonald is a handsome bird. That depends. Handsome is as handsome does, and unfortunately he received his early education on board a tramp steamer. His conversation consists almost exclusively of oaths. His mind has been contaminated by association with men. However, if you are squeamish, you can set your mind at rest. Ramsay MacDonald is not allowed to talk when strangers are present. He knows he will be promptly covered up if he does. That is why he looked at you in such an old-fashioned way when Elizabeth brought you in. . . . And that reminds me, Mrs. Holt," added Miss Perks severely, "you are very late in returning my call."

"You really must forgive me. It is so difficult to get away from the house when one has a husband and children to look after, and only one maid."

"Only one maid," repeated Miss Perks sarcastically. "You poor thing! . . . How I love to hear you young wives talk of the domestic burdens that weigh you down! One would suppose women had never endured husbands or borne children before. . . . How many children have you? Two, isn't it? I thought so. And how long have you been married?"

"Ten years."

"Then you've been wasting your time, my dear," observed Miss Perks. "However," she added, with an air of endeavouring to be just, "I don't know your circumstances. It's no use saying that young women nowadays shirk their responsibilities, because the poor things often can't help it. But I do think they needn't make such a song about it. A girl slaves all day in an office, and struggles to stand in overcrowded buses, and lunches off a bun and a cup of coffee in a fetid tea-shop: but she needn't call it Living Her Own Life when she knows very well that she only does it because her parents can't afford to keep her in idleness at home. I have no objection to a woman limiting the size of her family, but it's sheer rubbish to call it Emancipation, when everybody knows that children are not encouraged by husbands because they cost money to keep, and there are too many people in the world already." Miss Perks snorted, and considered Mary through her keen grey eyes. "My former pupil Michael has blossomed out into a literary man, I hear. He hangs about the house all day long, I suppose?"

"He works at home," admitted Mary good-humouredly.

"Then you have one cross to bear," said Miss Perks. "I grant you that. I should never dream of allowing it. I should refuse to have a man moping about my house all day. It's against the decencies. Every man ought to get out to his work. If I were married to an author, which God forbid, I should put my foot down. I should insist on his taking an office in the town and going there at regular hours to do his work, like any other decent husband."

"I shall have to suggest it to Michael."

"I met your husband last night," said Miss Perks, thoughtfully, "when I was looking . . . when I was out for a walk. A most unpleasant evening altogether. Apart from the loss of my brooch, I got thoroughly drenched by the rain and was nearly killed by a bicyclist who came tearing across the stone bridge like a madman. They're worse than motorists: you can hear a motor-car coming. . . . I should have given him a piece of my mind if he had waited to hear, but he rode on without stopping. I can only hope that he broke his neck. . . . What do you think of the garden?"

"It looks lovely," answered Mary, her eyes running down the beds and borders to the summer-house at the end.

"It *is* lovely," declared Miss Perks, as though Mary had flatly contradicted her. She added in a complacent tone: "Robert is a great gardener, and William is competent to follow his instructions. I hope Robert may come in presently, but he . . . but we were out rather late last night." The old lady took up the piece of knitting on which she had been engaged. It looked as if it might be a pull-over for Robert, but Miss Perks did not display her work or discuss its technicalities in the usual feminine way. She simply went on with it, and appeared to forget that she had a visitor.

Presently she said: "I have informed the police of the loss of my brooch . . . if they have any time to spare at the moment for a trifle like that."

"Michael is expecting a visit from the police," said Mary, frowning. Michael had thought it wise to warn her of this.

"Michael?" demanded Miss Perks. She dropped her knitting, and glared at Mary. "For goodness' sake, why Michael?"

"He was one of those on the footpaths last night. The police are expected to interview them all."

"H'm!" said Miss Perks. She pushed her chair back suddenly and rose. "I have remembered I must write a note. Don't disturb yourself. It will not take me a minute."

She went to a little desk and wrote: having written, she returned to her chair and rang the handbell.

"Tell William to take that note immediately on his bicycle," she commanded Elizabeth.

Elizabeth glanced at the address and her eyes showed some surprise.

"Don't argue," said Miss Perks peremptorily. "Find William at once and tell him the matter is urgent."

Elizabeth obeyed.

2

Mary's eyes, fixed on the garden, saw an elderly white-haired gentleman appear and stroll towards the summer-house. It was Robert. He stood for a minute or two in the sun, as though absorbed in thought.

"I am not going to waste any false sentiment on an ill-conditioned person like Douglas Bonar," declared Miss Perks abruptly. "No doubt in the long run it will prove to be a blessing that he was put out of the way before he caused any more mischief." She clicked her needles. "From all accounts, he was a most objectionable man. If somebody had to be murdered, there could not have been a better choice."

Mary, a little shocked by this plain speaking, did not answer. She watched Robert. The old gentleman was slowly taking off his coat. She supposed that he was going to do a little gardening.

"In the circumstances," said Miss Perks, "I can

scarcely expect the police to bother very much about my brooch . . . or my complaint of the reckless way in which bicyclists are allowed to fly through the lanes after dark."

Robert had taken off his coat and was now removing his waistcoat too. Evidently he intended to put in a spell of really hard work. Mary noticed how neatly he folded his discarded garments and laid them on the bench in the summer-house. She smiled as she thought how far Michael was from being as tidy as that.

Miss Perks looked up from her knitting for a moment, stretched out a hand, seized the bell by its strap, and rang it vigorously.

Elizabeth was heard approaching: she knocked and entered.

"Elizabeth," said Miss Perks, "I think Mr. Robert may be requiring some assistance in the garden. As William has gone out with my note, you had better see what you can do."

"Very good, ma'am," said Elizabeth. She let her eyes wander for a fraction of a second in the direction of the garden, and recalled them as she felt Miss Perks's stony glance upon her. "I think I shall be able to manage."

"Of course you can manage," snapped Miss Perks. "Don't pretend you're a fool."

Elizabeth smiled quietly and went away.

Robert was removing his collar and tie. Mary, considering his scholarly head, his gentle expression, wondered that he should differ so greatly from his sister . . . this old vulture whose conversation was so truculent. . .. And Elizabeth helped in the garden too, she reflected. That was interesting. . ..

Miss Perks cocked her head on one side and considered Mary with a dubious expression.

"Robert in some ways is a child," she said suddenly. "You're a married woman. You're not a silly girl. You have a husband and children, and presumably you've acquired some sense. You know it doesn't always do to take too much notice of childish behaviour." She clicked her needles again. "I suppose they are bound to call in Scotland Yard."

"Who? Oh, the police," said Mary. "Yes, in a case like that I suppose they will, though I don't understand these things."

She was interested in the behaviour of Robert. The old gentleman had sat down on the bench in the summer-house and he was taking off his shoes and socks. This puzzled Mary. In her experience it was an unusual preliminary to work in the garden, and she speculated as to the reason.

"Not that I have much faith in Scotland Yard," remarked Miss Perks. "Still, no doubt the local police will be only too glad to shift the responsibility from their own shoulders. I sometimes read detective stories that Frank Thornhill lends me. In a case like this, I suppose the first thing to do is to compile a list of suspects. I believe that is the word: suspects."

Mary scarcely heard her. The developments at the foot of the garden had reached an embarrassing stage. Robert was now unfastening his braces. It appeared that he was about to take off his trousers. He went through his acts very methodically, as if he were going to bed. Mary glanced shyly at Miss Perks, and then, suddenly the implication of the old lady's remarks about childish pranks struck her with full force. She felt herself blushing. The grim old woman, whose shrewd eyes took in everything that went on in the garden, continued her knitting with the greatest calm.

"Suspects," repeated Miss Perks, as though the word comforted her. "Who were the people with reasons to wish this man Bonar out of the way? Of course we know that he was justly disliked and despised by the whole population of Chesworth, but dislike and contempt are not very strong reasons for murder."

Robert took off his trousers and the garment beneath them, and stood up.

"Gorblimey! Well, I'm . . ."

The events in the garden had become too much for the parrot, who, with his head cocked on one side, had been following them with the most earnest attention, and he could not refrain from making his own comment in his rasping voice; but before he could complete his sentence Miss Perks swiftly stooped to the floor and picked up a dark red shawl.

"Oh, hell!" said the parrot. "That blasted thing again." He gave a squawk of disgust before night descended upon him and he relapsed into rueful meditation.

"So much for you, Ramsay MacDonald," said Miss Perks sternly. "If you insist on meddling in other people's business, well, so much the worse for you."

She took up her knitting again and clicked the needles savagely.

Meanwhile Robert had folded his trousers and the other garment with great care and placed them upon his coat and waistcoat, forming an orderly pile of clothes on the bench in the summer-house. He stood in his shirt, with his white, lean legs exposed to the sun. He was removing his cuff-links. . . .

Mary realized two facts. One, that Robert had periodical attacks of absent-mindedness in which he undressed himself wherever he might happen to be, and Miss Perks and her household were used to them. Two, Mary was expected, like the parrot, to take no notice of what went on before her eyes, but to behave as if nothing was happening. Otherwise there might be a dark red shawl for her, too!

Taking this second deduction to heart, Mary made an effort to be collected and matter-of-fact. Miss Perks had said something about suspects. So Mary remarked brightly: "Ah! That's the point. Why should anyone hate poor Mr. Bonar enough to want to kill him?"

The old lady gave her one swift glance of congratulation and approval.

"You've met him, I believe? They tell me he wanted to buy the Vineyard."

Robert had undone the buttons of his shirt. He was on the brink of pulling it over his head . . . Mary let a little sigh of relief escape her. Rescue was at hand. Upon the sunlit stage of the garden there entered Elizabeth. She carried over her arm a bright blue dressing-gown. Unhurried, and with the most ordinary air in the world, she walked up the path towards her master. Robert looked up as she came, and paused in the very nick of time.

"Yes," said Mary bravely, but her voice sounded to her as though it belonged to some other person, "Mr. Bonar wanted our house. Only yesterday he came again and made such a handsome offer that Michael was tempted. Mr. Bonar gave him twenty-four hours to think it over."

At the bottom of the garden, Elizabeth, like a plump and kindly nurse tending a well-behaved child, held out the dressing-gown. Automatically Robert inserted his arms in the sleeves. Elizabeth buttoned it for him. Then with one swift sweep she gathered under her arm the neat pile of rejected garments, and in five seconds more Robert and Elizabeth and all traces of this scandalous episode had disappeared from the garden, and the unruffled wallflowers and tulips and forget-me-nots slept as tranquilly as though nothing had happened. The incident was all over, and Mary realized that not by a word or a look would Miss Perks betray that she knew it had taken place.

"How much was this handsome offer?" asked Miss Perks after a slight pause broken only by the clicking of her needles.

"I . . . I really don't know."

"H'm!" Miss Perks gave her a searching glance, but refrained from comment. "Isn't your husband happy in Chesworth?"

Mary was surprised at the suggestion.

"We are both very fond of the place."

"Michael knows the place better than you do," said Miss Perks quietly. "He knows people can be as uncharitable in Chesworth as in any other town."

Mary did not understand her. She looked at the old lady inquiringly.

Outside the room the voice of Elizabeth could be heard quite distinctly: "No, Mr. Robert. You can't have a bath now. You must go to bed." Robert's voice murmured something placid and indistinguishable. Their footsteps receded.

"You know, or perhaps you don't know," said Miss Perks, "that Michael left the place very abruptly in his youth."

A door closed. Elizabeth clumped downstairs.

"I never got to the bottom of that," added Miss Perks thoughtfully. "Michael was very reserved, even as a little boy."

The front-door bell pealed through the house.

"So it may be," continued Miss Perks, "that he does not return to it with unmixed feelings. No. I dare say he's not quite so pleased to be back in Chesworth as you think."

Elizabeth could be heard steering a caller up the stairs.

"He was a quiet little boy, but he had fits of impulsiveness." Miss Perks had become reminiscent. "He often did a foolish thing on the spur of the moment . . . but he stuck to the consequences. I will say that for him. He was willing to abide by his acts. . . . Come in! And, Elizabeth, you can bring the tea."

It was a capital tea, with several kinds of sandwiches, two attractive home-made cakes, *petits fours* and chocolate biscuits. Miss Perks clearly did herself well, and in Elizabeth she had an excellent cook.

The new arrival was the wife of an Urban District Councillor, and she had news for Miss Perks. The Urban District Council had only that afternoon ordained that the new swimming-pool in the public park should be opened to the public on Sundays, before the hour of breakfast and between the hours of midday dinner and afternoon tea. This decision, marking an epoch in Chesworth history, had been come to by a very small majority. Several members had abstained from voting, including the husband of Miss Perks's caller.

Miss Perks seemed to find all this very amusing. No doubt cleanliness was next to godliness, she observed in her most caustic manner, but if bathing, why not lawn tennis and clock golf, and, indeed, cricket and football? Where were they to draw the line? Did not logic dictate that they should go the whole hog and introduce the Continental Sunday lock, stock and barrel into their quiet Sussex town? As for Mrs. Councillor So-and-So's husband, had he no convictions of his own, or was he really foolish enough to think he would placate both parties by sitting on the fence?

"And this bathing immediately on top of Sunday dinner!" exclaimed Miss Perks. "One knows what Sunday dinners are in Chesworth. Have preparations been made for coping with the numerous attacks of apoplexy that may be expected from bathing on top of a heavy meal? Have the Council bargained for that?"

They were still at it when Mary rose to take her leave.

3

At about the same moment that Ramsay MacDonald so far forgot himself as to utter speech in the presence of a visitor, a man in police uniform jumped from his bicycle at the gate of the Vineyard and walked up the little drive. It was Sergeant Whalebone of the West Sussex Constabulary.

The sergeant softly whistled a little tune as he pushed his bicycle past the wallflowers in the border. He was feeling pleased with the variety of his life. His week had been full of events and he had done himself credit. On Monday morning, bicycling down the Worthing road, he had spotted something which would not have been obvious to the untrained eye in the outward appearance of a large house whose lawful inhabitants had gone out for the day. Following the trail, he had discovered the best bedroom in possession of a young tramp, who had shed his clothes and put on the mistress's silk lingerie, and was admiring the effect in the tall mirror of the wardrobe. "I am a police officer," said the sergeant. "I can see that," said the tramp. "You must come along with me to the station," said the sergeant. "That's O.K. with me, big boy," said the tramp. It tickled the sergeant to recall that dialogue: he supposed he would have to retail it in court. On the afternoon of the same day, the sergeant had gone out with the ambulance to the scene of a motor accident on Toat Hill, and had identified the injured men as bandits whom the police had been anxiously wanting for several weeks. Then, on Tuesday, the sergeant had been detailed to look for a flashy young man who had absconded from Chesworth after running up a considerable bill at the Blue Boar, and was supposed to have gone to Brighton: on Wednesday, the sergeant had traced the fugitive, by a brilliant piece of detective work, to a lodging-house in Tunbridge Wells, and brought him back in triumph. . .. And now a murder! Quite an interesting week, thought Sergeant Whalebone.

Susan opened the door to the sergeant and, all of a most agreeable flutter, showed him in to Michael's study.

Miss Perks had been perfectly correct in her diagnosis of her former pupil. Michael had resolved to keep silence concerning his discovery of Bonar's body. This was a risky course of action, and might well prove to be disastrous; but Michael had strong reasons for his peculiar conduct, and, in any event, having once made up his mind, he had no intention of changing it. As for the story he intended to tell the police . . . well, what is the use of being a successful writer of fiction if one cannot produce a water-tight tale for use in such an emergency?

In this connection, the mysterious scandal that passed from lip to lip in Chesworth was going to be of unexpected service. Michael had thought a great deal about this since his call at the rectory. He felt confident that the rector (a) had heard the story and (b) was not sure whether he believed it or not. Far more important, the story that went about could not be the one that Bonar . . . Or, Michael knew, the rector would have adopted a very different attitude.

One danger Michael refused to face. Bonar's knowledge implied the existence of at least one other person who knew the secret and was willing to part with it.   Michael shut his mind to this thought, and braced himself to deal with his immediate fears. He bade the sergeant take a chair.

Sergeant Whalebone was tall and slim. Since he was not of powerful build it might have been assumed, and correctly, that he owed his promotion to the possession of brains. When he sat down and put his peaked cap on the floor beside his chair, Michael saw that he had sandy hair above a pleasant, freckled face. His manner was cheerful.

"Sorry to disturb you, sir," he said, with a glance at the sheets of manuscript which Michael had pushed to one side. "As you may guess, I have come about this unfortunate business of Mr. Bonar."

He paused, and Michael ventured a question.

"I expect you have Scotland Yard helping you on that job?"

"We have, sir," said Whalebone, readily enough. "Two of the high and mighty ones are quartered on us, and they're sending us small fry running here, there and everywhere for them, like a pack of errand-boys." He grinned and returned to business. "Well, sir, I am sure you will be glad to give us any help you can, and I don't think I need detain you long. You know what happened last night, sir, and you will understand that we wish to interview all those who took part in the proceedings up yonder in the Park. You were present, I believe?"

Michael nodded.

The sergeant opened his notebook and turned over some leaves.

"I have had several accounts of what happened, and I suppose you can add nothing to them, unless . . ."

Sergeant Whalebone hesitated. He added: "Did you remain with the party and return at the same time as the others?"

"No," said Michael. "I left before the rest of them."

"Did you come back alone?"

"Yes."

"What time was this?"

"I think I must have left the others soon after eleven o'clock."

The sergeant made a note.

Susan tapped at the door and came in blushing. She spoke to Michael but her eyes were on the sergeant.

"I don't know whether I done right to interrupt you, sir," she said, "but Miss Perks's man has just brought this, and it's marked 'Urgent,' and I thought . . ."

Michael apologized to the sergeant, and read Miss Perks's letter. It ran as follows:

Dear Michael,—I understand you may be favoured with a visit from the police. There is no need to say anything about meeting me last night. I want to keep out of this business.

Yours sincerely,
Matilda Perks.

Michael read this communication twice, and thought rapidly. On the whole, it simplified matters. He smiled at Susan.

"There's no answer."

Susan left the room reluctantly, with sidelong glances at the handsome sergeant.

"I'm sorry, sergeant," said Michael, thrusting Miss Perks's letter into his pocket. "Please go on."

"That's all right, sir. . . . You were saying you left the others soon after eleven o'clock. Did you come straight back to your house?"

"Yes."

"And did you meet anybody on your way back?"

"Not a living soul," said Michael.

The sergeant seemed satisfied with this.

"There's another thing, sir. Most of the party carried tools and implements of one kind or another." Whalebone looked at the page in front of him. "So-and-so, a pair of wire-cutters. So-and-so, a saw. You yourself, sir, perhaps . . ." He made a delicate pause.

"I took a spade," answered Michael readily.

"A spade," murmured the sergeant thoughtfully. He appeared to be considerably interested.

"I took it with me because it happened to be in my hands when the party passed my gate. As a matter of fact, I never used it." He went more slowly, for he saw that the sergeant was writing this down. "Someone borrowed it from me on the hill in the dark. He said he would probably be a better hand with it than I."

"Who was this?"

"I have no idea."

"Would you know him again if you saw him?"

"No. You must remember the night was very dark."

The sergeant made no comment, but he added after a little consideration: "Do you think you would recognize his voice if you heard it again?"

Michael had no doubt about that: there was a certain individual quality in those tones that he would know again anywhere. To the sergeant, however, he said without hesitation: "I very much doubt it."

"Did you get your spade back?"

"Yes. I found it sticking in the border just inside my gate when I went into the garden this morning."

"You don't know who put it there?"

"No. I can only suppose," said Michael indifferently, "that the fellow who borrowed it returned it on his way back."

"Then he knew who you were and where you lived?"

"There were plenty who could tell him that."

The sergeant nodded.

"We have not been able to identify all the members of that party. It seems there were a few hangers-on, strangers in the town, who had come to see the fun." He made a careful note of the very inadequate description which was all Michael could give him of the man who had borrowed the spade. "I should like to have a look at that spade later, sir."

"It's still in the border."

"Very good." Whalebone looked up from his notebook. "There's one thing more I must ask you about. What Mr. Bonar said to you up on the footpath."

Michael heard Bonar's voice again: "It's lucky for you, Holt, I'm a man of my word, or I might be tempted to say something more; something you wouldn't care to hear mentioned in public, eh? But I promised you twenty-four hours, and the moratorium stands." He said nothing.

The sergeant read aloud a fairly accurate report of Bonar's words.

"Can you explain what he meant, sir?" he asked, poising his pencil in his hand and looking keenly at Michael.

"It's a rather difficult matter," said Michael. He leaned back in his chair and frankly returned the sergeant's gaze. "I'm a good deal in the dark myself. I used to live in Chesworth as a young man, as perhaps you know. Two months ago I returned, and settled down here. In the last few weeks I have come to know that there has been gossip in the town about me. Some scandal. What it is I have no idea. But it is plain from the attitude of some of my former friends that there's a slanderous tale going the rounds. I can only suppose that Bonar had heard it. That must have been what he was referring to."

"You've no idea what this gossip is?" asked the sergeant. His manner was sympathetic.

"None whatever. I'm completely in the dark." He added dryly: "I have no doubt you will be able to find out."

"Chesworth is a great place for scandal," said the

sergeant. "Though no worse than other small towns in my experience." He made no further comment, but closed his book and stood up. "If I might see that spade, sir?"

Michael took him out to the wallflower border. Whalebone looked at the spade and hesitated.

"Of course, it was out in all that rain," he said. "Still, perhaps . . ."

He considered the spade with a speculative air, and yielded to temptation. He pulled it up, struck the flat against the wall, took out a large knife and scraped away the mud that clung to the surface, and carried out a thorough examination. With a look of disappointment he thrust the spade back into the soil; then caught Michael's smile and smiled back.

"Not a trace," he said. "Still . . ."

He hesitated again.

"May I borrow it?" he said at length.

"Certainly," answered Michael, showing some slight surprise.

The sergeant produced some string from his trousers pocket and tied the spade to the top bar of his bicycle.

"That will give the nobs from Scotland Yard something to play with," he remarked. "Well, thank you very much, sir."

With a friendly grin Whalebone mounted his machine and rode out of the gate: but instead of going back to the town he turned, as Michael noticed with curiosity, in the other direction.

Michael went back to his study and thought of Miss Perks's letter. What did *she* wish to conceal? She was shy of publicity for Robert, probably; or, perhaps, the truth was even as she had said, and she did not wish to be mixed up in a police-court case. He dismissed the matter, and began to wonder whether there were any chemical tests known to Scotland Yard that would detect traces of blood on a spade which had been carefully cleaned with sandpaper and then left out all night in heavy rain. He did not know.

V. Dangerous Riding

Meanwhile Sergeant Whalebone rode a couple of hundred yards up the lane and dismounted outside the Chrystals' semi-bungalow.

People who live in semi-bungalows do not keep maids, and it was Mrs. Chrystal herself who opened the door after the sergeant had rung three times. The sergeant knew her by sight: she was a thundering pretty woman in his estimation. It displeased him to see that her beauty was now marred. She had a black eye. Also she was extremely untidy. She looked as though she had been disturbed in an afternoon nap. Her hair was all awry, and her hands clutched a loose wrapper which had been hastily flung on.

"Good afternoon, madam," said the sergeant with hearty politeness. "Is Mr. Chrystal at home?"

"He is not, and I can't say when he will be in, but I shouldn't be surprised if he's rather late. I am sorry. I don't think it will be any use waiting, and I'm afraid you'll have to call again some other day." Mrs. Chrystal smiled vaguely, and made to shut the door.

"Just a minute, madam," said the sergeant quickly. "If Mr. Chrystal is not at home, perhaps I may trouble you yourself for a few minutes."

"Me?" Mrs. Chrystal held the door ajar and poked her head coyly out. "You wish to speak to me?"

"Well, madam"—the sergeant coughed deprecatingly—"I have come about this unfortunate business of Mr. Bonar. We think you may be able to give us a little help."

"This unfortunate business of Mr. Bonar?" repeated Mrs. Chrystal in a puzzled tone. "What unfortunate business of Mr. Bonar?"

It occurred to Sergeant Whalebone that the Chrystals, living all alone, in a remote dwelling unequipped with the sensitive antennae of a maid-servant, might conceivably be ignorant of a matter which was the talk of the town.

"If perhaps I might come in . . ." he murmured tactfully.

"Of course you may come in if you wish to," said Mrs. Chrystal dubiously. "Yes, I think you had better come in."

She held open the door for the sergeant, and showed him into the front parlour, keeping behind him as she murmured directions: then, with a mumbled excuse, she disappeared, and the sergeant heard her ascending to the one upstairs apartment of the semi-bungalow.

The front parlour, like Mrs. Chrystal herself, was *en deshabille.* A chintz-covered sofa with rumpled cushions proclaimed itself the recent scene of Mrs. Chrystal's nap. The morning paper lay dismembered on the floor. A cup that had contained tea was on a pouf. The sergeant's eye noted that the room had been neglected for days, and he found himself thinking how strongly Mrs. Whalebone would have disapproved of it all.

It was ten minutes before Mrs. Chrystal returned, with her hair more or less in place, and looking generally a little tidier. In the meantime the sergeant had run his finger through the dust on the mantelpiece and frowned, inspected the rest of the room from sheer force of habit, and remarked that two cigarette-ends lay under the sofa, while another had been trodden into the carpet in a conspicuous place. There was also a cigar-end in the fireplace. The sergeant decided that all this argued careless and slatternly habits and possibly loose morals, but not necessarily criminal tendencies, and sat down to speculate upon the possible origin of Mrs. Chrystal's black eye. If he had met with an eye like that on the Council's housing estate at Roughey, or among the slummy cottages in the squalid by-ways opening off Victoria Road, he would have taken the cause for granted; but middle-class husbands did not as a rule assault their wives, and he knew nothing about Chrystal to suggest that he was likely to prove an exception. A puny fellow like that!

Mrs. Chrystal's first act on her return was to offer the sergeant a cigarette. When he politely declined, she lit one herself, and lolling back upon the sofa, regarded the sergeant dreamily through half-closed eyes.

"So you think I shall be able to help you about something?" she asked in a tone of mild surprise. "I can't imagine why you should think so. I've never had anything to do with the police before, but of course, if you think . . ."

"It's about this bad business of Mr. Bonar," began the sergeant, sitting bolt upright in his chair.

"Yes, you said that before," answered Mrs. Chrystal placidly. "I understand it's something about Mr. Bonar, though what it is I don't know. What is it?"

"Perhaps you have not yet heard the news, ma'am," said Whalebone, leaning forward slightly, and on the alert. "Mr. Bonar was found dead last night. He is believed to have been murdered." He was quite prepared, as he made this blunt announcement, to be called upon to administer first aid to the lady. He would not have been surprised if she had fainted or become hysterical. That he should have risked precipitating such a crisis was a witness to the efficacy of his training, which had taught him that shock tactics are often the most humane in the end.

Mrs. Chrystal, however, took it quite calmly.

"No," she said, shaking her head, "I hadn't heard," and the sergeant was much more perplexed than he would have been if she had risen from the sofa and bestridden the carpet like Lady Macbeth.

He kept his expression under control, and brought out his notebook.

"I am sure you will be glad to give us any help in your power. There are one or two questions I must ask you, but I shall be as brief as I can."

Mrs. Chrystal paid no attention to this. She was considering something in the half-light of her mind. She raised an inquiring face.

"Did you say that Mr. Bonar had been murdered?"

"I am afraid that is so, madam."

"Mr. Bonar murdered?" She thought it over again. "Who did it?" she asked.

"That is what we have to find out," said the sergeant curtly. He did not know what to make of this inconsequent woman sprawling on the sofa; and, being in doubt, he took refuge in firmness. "Still, madam, I am here to ask questions, not to answer them. Would you kindly tell me one or two things that may help us in our inquiries? For instance, at what time did Mr. Bonar leave this house last night?"

"Leave this house last night?" echoed Mrs. Chrystal. "Let me see, was he . . . but of course he was. But how did you know he was in this house last night? How clever of you to find that out!"

The sergeant was tempted for a moment to surprise Mrs. Chrystal with a bit of Sherlock Holmes deduction from the cigar-end in the fireplace; but he resisted the temptation.

"I'm afraid there's nothing clever about it," he said. "At half-past ten last night Mr. Bonar rang up the police station. On inquiry at the telephone exchange, we found that the call was put through from this house."

Mrs. Chrystal looked at him with round eyes.

"Oh, I see. I didn't know you could do things like that. I always thought the telephones were secret, like the Post Office Savings Bank, and the Income Tax, and . . . and things like that." She contemplated the telephone under this new light and added vaguely, "It must be a great help to you."

"Would you kindly tell me," said Sergeant Whalebone patiently, "exactly what happened when Mr. Bonar came to your house last night?"

"Why, he asked if he could use the telephone."

"Yes, yes. And then?"

"I said certainly he could."

"So he did?" suggested the sergeant ironically.

"Yes. I couldn't help thinking how clever he was at it, too, for he just said 'Police' and got through to somebody at once, while I can never get any reply at all from the thing at night. I often wonder where they all get to."

"Never mind where they all get to," said the sergeant, not unkindly. "Please tell me what happened next."

"He talked to somebody at the other end. I didn't hear all he said, but he seemed to be very angry about something, and the police wouldn't do what he wanted them to do, and that made him angrier still. So he threw the thing down in a violent temper, and told me he'd been talking to a pompous jack-in-office who didn't know his business."

"That would be the Inspector," murmured Whalebone. "And then?"

"I said to Mr. Bonar, 'You seem to be a little upset, and you'd better sit down and let me make you a cup of tea.'"

"Yes?"

"He didn't sit down, but walked about the room, talking about the police and saying something about his footpaths. So I made him a cup of tea and coaxed him to sit down on the sofa and drink it, though I didn't know what my husband would think."

"Why should your husband think anything?"

"Well, it was getting on towards eleven o'clock, and . . . well, naturally. . . .." Mrs. Chrystal smiled blandly, as one person of the world to another.

"I see, ma'am. Your husband had not come in?"

"Not then."

"How long did Mr. Bonar stay?"

"Perhaps half an hour, perhaps a little more or a little less. I know I kept wishing he would go, and at last I said I was sorry, but I really did think he ought to go. So in the end he went. I thought it was a pity he could not stay until he felt better, but there you are, you see" —Mrs. Chrystal threw out her arms in a helpless gesture

—"it was getting so late."

"Until he felt better? Was he unwell?"

"Not exactly unwell. No, I didn't mean that. I shouldn't say that he was unwell. Not strictly speaking."

"He was still very angry," suggested the sergeant, "and you thought it would have been better if he could have composed himself?"

"Yes, I think that is what I mean," said Mrs. Chrystal gratefully. "You are very kind and helpful, and you express things very nicely." She gazed with appreciation upon the sergeant's fair hair and honest freckled face: she was thinking that he was one of the nicest looking policemen she had ever met.

The sergeant annoyed himself by blushing: he blushed rather easily, as persons of his complexion do.

"And when did Mr. Chrystal come home?" he went on hastily.

"Oh, not until later."

"Can you give me some idea of the time?"

"You are so very particular." Mrs. Chrystal smiled indulgently. "I am afraid I can't tell you the exact time. I only know I was very sleepy when he came in. It must have been past my usual bedtime."

"That's a nasty eye you've got, madam," said the sergeant suddenly.

"Isn't it?" returned Mrs. Chrystal complacently. "I shan't be able to go out for a day or two. People will think Walter has been knocking me about." She smiled.

"How did you get it?" Whalebone made the question sound like a sympathetic inquiry addressed to a child which has hurt itself.

"Oh, I fell off my bicycle. So stupid of me. The silly thing skidded as I turned in through our gate."

"Most unfortunate," murmured the sergeant. He added thoughtfully: "I should like to interview Mr. Chrystal."

She gave him a sudden frightened look.

"But it was my bicycle that did it," she exclaimed.

Whalebone stroked his upper lip and smiled quietly.

"I quite understand that, madam. All the same, I shall have to see Mr. Chrystal, I'm afraid." He looked at her, and added: "But don't be alarmed. I understand that Mr. Chrystal was one of those who went up to the footpaths last night, and, of course, we shall have to ask him what he saw, just as we are asking all of them. You say you do not expect him back until late?"

"Well," said Mrs. Chrystal reluctantly, "as a matter of fact he may not be back for a few days. I don't want everybody to know it, because you see I shall be all alone in the house, and . . ."

"Quite," murmured Whalebone understandingly. "Where has Mr. Chrystal gone?"

"Oh, he's staying with his sister. He went up to London by the first train this morning."

"That would be the 6.12 *via* Three Bridges."

"Really," said Mrs. Chrystal in frank admiration, "you are quite a walking encyclopaedia."

"Then he didn't get much sleep, I'm afraid," pursued the sergeant.

"He didn't "Mrs. Chrystal bit her lip. "No, he didn't get much sleep. It meant getting up very early."

The sergeant was making entries in his notebook. "And his sister's address?" he asked, looking up.

"Park Road," said Mrs. Chrystal, with the pleased smile of a bright scholar who has answered a stiff question correctly at the first attempt.

"Number?"

"Number? Oh, you mean the number of the house? I'm afraid I've forgotten."

"You may have it in your address-book?"

"I don't keep an address-book."

"You may have one of your sister-in-law's letters somewhere?"

"I don't think so. No," went on Mrs. Chrystal more

confidently, "I know I haven't. I always tear up her letters, because they annoy me so. She is one of those people who are always criticizing. I expect you know what I mean." She realized that she had been betrayed into a confidence, and shook her head. "Of course, this is between you and me. . ... Besides, now I come to think of it, she never puts her address on her letters. She seems to think I ought to know it."

The sergeant refrained from comment.

"Well, anyhow, it's Park Road, and what district?"

Mrs. Chrystal looked at him inquiringly.

"What district?" repeated the sergeant. "N.W. 3 or S.E. 27, or what?"

Mrs. Chrystal made a gesture indicating ignorance.

"Park Road is not an uncommon name," said the sergeant. "There may be any number of Park Roads in London. What part of London is it in?"

"Let me see. I wonder if I can help you at all." With her arms clasped behind her head as she lay on the sofa, Mrs. Chrystal appeared to be thinking deeply. "I've got it. At least, this may help. It's a threepenny omnibus ride to the Crystal Palace. I remember that quite clearly, because once when we were staying there we went to the Crystal Palace, to see a firework display," she concluded triumphantly.

"If you have stayed there, madam, surely you must recollect the name of the suburb. Forest Hill, Dulwich, Streatham, Penge . . .?"

"No, it's no good firing a list of names at me. I shall never remember if I go on trying to think all day. I am not the least good at remembering things like addresses."

"But surely, madam," repeated the sergeant in desperation, "if you have stayed there you must have some idea . . ."

"It was a double-fronted house," recollected Mrs. Chrystal.

The sergeant looked at her suspiciously. Her eyes were as innocent as a baby's. He abandoned that line of approach and essayed another.

"You can tell me your sister-in-law's name?"

"Viola," answered Mrs. Chrystal promptly, and somewhat disdainfully, as if she thought it was a ridiculous name for the person who bore it.

"And her surname?"

"Surtees."

"How do you spell it?"

She spelled it correctly, with an effort.

"And her husband's Christian name?"

"Frank." Mrs. Chrystal smiled cheerfully: she was acquitting herself well. "He's much nicer than she is," she added gratuitously.

"Are they on the telephone?"

At this question she shook her head despondently.

"What is the husband's business?"

"Oh, he's something or other in the City."

"What exactly? Accountant, broker, underwriter, merchant . . ."

"Rich man, poor man, beggar-man, thief?"

Sergeant Whalebone looked at her sternly. It seemed, however, that Mrs. Chrystal was not attempting to make fun of him: her fluid mind had merely been stirred by an irresistible association of ideas. He gave up the attempt to get any sense out of her, and shut his notebook and rose.

"Well, I am sorry to have kept you so long, madam. Please ask your husband to communicate with us directly he comes back. That is," he added mentally, "if we don't lay our hands on him for ourselves before then."

Mrs. Chrystal removed herself languidly from the sofa.

"Oh, not at all. Oh, certainly. Pleased."

"I wouldn't mind betting," said Sergeant Whalebone to himself as he mounted his bicycle, "that her husband gave her that black eye . . . and if I were her husband I'd be tempted to do the same." He pedalled rapidly back towards Chesworth police station, and as he rode he hummed a cheerful little tune.

Mrs. Chrystal watched him go. She thought the sergeant quite a nice man in spite of his disagreeable way of pressing for precise information. She always liked big men with freckles. It gave them such a fresh, healthy, country sort of look. She sighed, and went into the kitchen to make herself a cup of tea. She felt she had earned it. How stupid of her not to have offered one to the sergeant!

2

After tea that afternoon, Michael walked up the lane. He passed the Chrystals' semi-bungalow and continued straight on to Frank Thornhill's place. Thornhill was a well-to-do bachelor and had built himself a largish modern house, all straight lines, white paint and green shutters. The garage continued the line of the house and for once did not look like an unhappy afterthought. In the front stretched a large lawn, fringed on three sides by a rock-garden. This garden was the pride and joy of its owner. Thornhill did not stick at larceny to embellish it. Unlike some keen gardeners, he did not steal other people's plants; but he had no conscience where rocks were concerned. He never set eyes on a stone which appeared suitable for inclusion in his rockery without forming plans to possess it. As he always knew a corner of his garden which could do with an additional rock, he was always being tempted. He had many a time removed his neighbour's landmark. People accused him of keeping a car entirely for the purpose of enlarging his field of theft and facilitating the removal of stolen boulders. His justification could be seen in the use he made of his thefts. His rockery was not at all to be compared with the despondent, fern-fringed dusty-looking scrapheaps to be seen in the corners of suburban gardens and sometimes in public parks. It was a magnificent affair, a superb and zealously tended piece of work, in which the rocks were used for their proper purpose of providing each tender plant with its own coign of vantage, its own niche of soil, its own tiny valley to inhabit in the shelter of the miniature mountains.

Thornhill was not on view among his rocks, but a thin thread of blue smoke rising from beyond the the hedge suggested his whereabouts; and presently he came into sight, clad in sweater and shorts, and carrying a fork.

"Come, fill the Cup," he quoted, striking an attitude, "and in the Fire of Spring the Winter Garment of Repentance fling. . . . Or, more prosaically, Burn All You Can and Keep Down the Rates. See notice on the Urban District Council's dust-carts."

He dropped the fork and stooped to pluck out a weed which had recklessly chosen to plant itself among his rocks.

Michael looked round on all this loveliness.

"And gardens are not made," he quoted in his turn, "by saying, 'Oh, now beautiful!' and sitting in the shade."

Thornhill straightened his powerful barrel-chested body and gave Michael a friendly grin.

"Glad to hear anyone quoting Kipling at this time of day, even Kipling at his rum-tum-tummiest. . . . Had a couple of beardless but side-whiskered youths over to see me last week, undergraduates, and one of them had never heard of Kipling, and the other said in a la-di-dah voice, 'Oh, Kipling!' . . . meaning to convey that Kipling was Victorian and moribund and altogether out of date and beyond the pale. Whereupon I told him that Kipling was the last of the English poets, except perhaps for Masefield, and that the present generation was incapable of stringing together a couple of tolerable lines. He giggled in his feminine way, and said I was being left behind, and murmured reverently a list of names I had never heard of. Incidentally," added Thornhill thoughtfully, "he quoted something about 'the damp souls of housemaids sprouting at area gates.' Rather a good line, don't you think? I feel I must have a shot some time at the man who wrote that, though I imagine the rest of his works are unreadable. But as for the young man who quoted it, I turned and rent him. I said he had probably never read Kipling, but if he had read Kipling and could make nothing of him, then his soul was damper than the soul of any housemaid, sprouting or otherwise. To which he answered, perkily enough, that all he knew of Kipling's was 'Land of Hope and Glory,' and when I told him that Kipling didn't write that he expressed surprise, and said it was the sort of thing he had always understood that Kipling wrote. 'Oh!' said I. 'You must be one of those intellectuals I have heard about. Are you a pacifist?' He said he was. 'And have you solemnly pledged yourself not to fight in the next war?' He said he had. 'Not even if you are unjustly attacked?' I asked. He said that made no difference. 'Oh, doesn't it?' said I, and I sat down on the wheelbarrow and turned him over and 'six I give 'im with me large flat 'and.' Outrageous breach of the laws of hospitality, but the only way to deal with youngsters like that. . . . Come in and have a drink."

They entered a large room which opened on to the garden, and Thornhill crossed to an enormous mahogany sideboard and took a decanter, glasses and a siphon from a cupboard. Not for the first time Michael marvelled at the load the sideboard bore: a great weight of silver in the form of cups and shields, testifying to Thornhill's athletic prowess in his youth and early manhood.

"You know, Frank," he ventured to remark, "it's not safe to have all that valuable stuff in such a vulnerable place. It's tempting burglars. You ought at least to lock it up."

"Exactly what the rector said last night," murmured Thornhill with a grin. He mixed the drinks, gave Michael one, and took his own to a deep chair in which he stretched his immense body luxuriously.

"Happy days!. . . As to the silverware, it's as safe as houses. I keep a dog: an intelligent dog, a Chow. The dog sleeps outside the door of this room. Enter burglars in quest of the silver: dog barks, rouses me, rouses Jennings, rouses Mrs. Jennings. I come downstairs with a poker, Jennings follows with a knobkerrie I supplied him with for the purpose, Mrs. Jennings brings up the rear with a rolling-pin. I open the door, dog flies at the burglars, burglars flee, I pursue, Jennings pursues, I knock down two, Jennings knocks down the rest, Mrs. Jennings stuns the prostrate felons with the rolling-pin: when they come to they find themselves locked in the scullery, waiting for the police. It's all cut and dried. Burglars might as well try for the Crown Jewels. They don't stand an earthly chance." Thornhill clasped his hands behind his head, and smiled lazily at Michael. "What have you come to see me about? Always glad to see you. Is it a friendly visit, pure and simple, or have you something in view, some special errand? Go ahead. Only one topic's barred."

"And that is?"

"The death of the late unlamented Douglas Bonar. I'm sick to death of hearing people talk about it, and besides, the matter touches me closely, and I have my own private reasons for not wishing to discuss it." Thornhill half emptied his glass. "Michael, as you are an old friend and schoolfellow, I will tell you a secret. I am engaged to the late Bonar's niece."

"Good Lord!"

"Have been for months. Clandestinely, unbeknownst to the old man. She's the headmistress of a domestic economy centre under some County Council up north."

Michael stared. He could not imagine Thornhill marrying a headmistress. The notion was incredible.

"She's a very capable young woman," said Thornhill enthusiastically, "and you'll like her. Crammed full of culture, and . . . really I was staggered, Michael: I had no idea that headmistresses of domestic economy centres were so good to look at. I was head over heels in love with her before I knew where I was."

"How did you come to meet her, Frank?"

"In the most dangerous place in the world for an

unprotected bachelor: on a cruising liner. The most glorious time of my life, Michael. Nights of romance under a cloudless Mediterranean sky. I expect you know all about that sort of thing."

Michael found himself wondering whether Frank and his schoolmistress had had any meetings outside the enchanting influence of southern seas. He was still boggling at the notion of such a marriage of inharmonious particles.

"The snag," said Thornhill carefully, "is that she inherits all Bonar's possessions, unless he has altered his will in the last twelve months."

Michael whistled.

"She was his favourite niece," Thornhill explained.

"He was very fond of her as a little girl. He had no nearer relation. He took pride in her success as a school-marm. He had the respect for learning you sometimes find in the half-educated even now. He greatly approved of her common sense, too. He felt she would manage his estates admirably. His ambition was that she should find a husband worthy of her, a man who had made his way by his own exertions. That is why we kept our engagement secret."

"I congratulate you," said Michael belatedly.

"Thanks, old man," said Thornhill. "I suppose I shall have to reform now," he added, as he got up to mix himself another drink, "but I could scarcely do it under more favourable auspices. She's a remarkable young woman, Michael."

Yet he sighed as he sat down. He swallowed half the whisky and sighed again.

"So you see it's rather awkward. We can't possibly announce our engagement now. Not, at any rate, until this murder business has all blown over. . ... Besides, I'm not a bit sure that in common decency I ought to . . . Hang it all, Michael, I don't want to be accused of marrying a girl for her money. Yes, I know what you are thinking: I have money too. But what's a mere thousand a year in the eyes of a girl who has inherited Bonar's sacks of gold? A beggarly pittance, a dole, a schoolboy's pocket-money."

"Oh, nonsense." Michael was driven to remonstrate. "You said yourself, Frank, that she has plenty of common sense. She would never think that."

"No, she never would," said Thornhill vigorously. "She is above that. She is too pure-minded. She would never dream of crediting me with an ulterior motive. . . . But Chesworth people would. They like malicious gossip."

"They do," agreed Michael fervently.

"I can hear what they will say," declared Thornhill. "'Frank Thornhill marrying a schoolmarm! What d'you think of that? But of course everybody knows he's only doing it for her money!' That's what they will say."

"They will," assented Michael with gloom.

"You think the same as I do of our local scandal-mongers?"

"I do, Frank. I have reason."

Thornhill looked at him sharply but said nothing.

"I'm rather glad you introduced the subject of scandal." Michael took some whisky and went on. "It's why I came to see you. There's an uncharitable story going the rounds about me. I don't know what it is. I am only aware of its existence by the behaviour of some of my acquaintances . . . former acquaintances. I thought perhaps. . .. I came to ask you if you had heard anything."

Thornhill, leaning back in his chair, looked at Michael through half-closed eyes.

"Do you mind pressing that bell?" he asked suddenly. "By your elbow. Thanks."

There was silence in the room until Mrs. Jennings appeared in the open doorway. Michael had not heard her approach and was surprised to see her standing there when he looked up. She looked at the carpet, as though she feared her master's eye.

"Oh, Mrs. Jennings," said Thornhill, "please remove this empty siphon and bring a full one. No, send Jennings in with it: I want him. Where is he?"

"Doing something to his bicycle, sir," said the woman, without looking up.

"Then please tell him. Oh, and shut that door."

"Very good, sir."

"There may be a good deal to be said for silent service," grumbled Thornhill, when Mrs. Jennings had gone, "but it gets on my nerves to have a housekeeper who stalks about the house like a ghost. My good woman gets her effects by constantly wearing bedroom slippers. She says her feet hurt her that cruel, it's agony to wear proper shoes. She didn't take at all kindly to a suggestion of mine that she should wear a little bell on a collar round her neck. I had to apologize and assure her that no innuendo was meant. . . . After all, she's a good cook. If I don't bear with her failings and humour her susceptibilities, she will leave me to go to the rectory. The rector was here last night, and she surpassed herself over the dinner she gave him; and you know how utterly devoid the clergy are of scruples when they see a chance of fostering the well-being of the Church. I recognized the light that came into his eye: it was the same glint of cupidity that shines when he hears of a well-to-do old maid taking a house in Chesworth. I shall ask him again soon and give him cold mutton and stewed prunes. I'll teach him to covet his neighbour's housekeeper. . . . Come in!"

Jennings opened the door and stood in the opening, occupying most of it. When Michael had seen him once before, he had been driving Thornhill's car. In a standing position he looked even more formidable, though he was actually less dangerous. He might have been a heavyweight boxer, except that he had a pleasant face; or an ex-Metropolitan policeman, though the quickness of his movements cast doubt upon that; or a Rugby footballer, if his social status had not rendered that improbable in a man of the south country. Whatever he had been, it was easy to see that he would be a useful second line of defence, with or without a knobkerrie, if burglars came after Thornhill's alluring collection of silver trophies.

"You can put that siphon here," said Thornhill, "and, Jennings, I want you to go down to Boot's and change my library book. Here it is. The girls in the shop have my list and are acquainted with my deplorable tastes. If you take your bicycle, you should get there before they close."

"Unfortunately, sir," said the stalwart Jennings, "the bike's punctured, and I haven't finished repairing it yet. Shall I take the Standard, sir?"

Thornhill sighed. "I suppose you must have the car," he said reluctantly.

"Right you are, sir," said Jennings; and he effaced himself before his master had had time to change his mind.

"He's off before I think better of it," remarked Thornhill dryly. "I don't trust that fellow with any machine capable of more than fifteen miles an hour. I let him take me out soon after he came. I wanted to see whether his boasted ability to drive existed in fact . . . or whether it was merely an incident in that form of fiction which we call testimonials, and he calls 'refs.' Once we were on the Arundel road our conversation consisted of my saying at intervals with a white face: 'Steady on, Jennings,' and his replying, in the tones of a dentist dealing with a nervous child: 'This is a lovely car of yours, sir, and if you kept your eyes off the speedometer you would never dream we were touching seventy-five.' We took Bury Hill in our stride: reduced it to a monticule, a pimple."

"Was it no use arguing with him?"

"I remonstrated, I pleaded, I threatened; but Jennings at the wheel of a car is as one possessed, a demoniac, an energumen. I promised myself that the first thing I should do if I returned alive would be to sack him; but when he brought me back to my door I was so limp that I had no strength for anything but to crawl in here and mix myself a drink. Since then I have exercised all my wiles to keep him out of the car . . . and now, against my better judgment, I've fallen."

They heard the car go down the drive.

"Please God it returns intact," said Thornhill piously. "Mix yourself another drink."

"No, thanks."

"About what you were asking just now. . . ." Thornhill hesitated. He rose and trifled with things on the mantelpiece. "Let's take a stroll in the garden."

"I'd like to."

3

They went out through a back door, passing the kitchen in which Mrs. Jennings was moving stealthily among her pots and pans.

"It's a delicate matter," murmured Thornhill, as they crossed the paved yard, "but hang it all, I've known you since you were a fellow-pupil at Miss Perks's, and I see no reason why I shouldn't be perfectly. . . . Hullo!"

"What's the matter?"

Thornhill had paused by the half-open door of an outhouse. Michael's eyes followed his and saw a bicycle propped upside down on its saddle, and surrounded by a litter of tools. The bicycle had been in the wars. The handlebars were twisted, the cranks were bent, and the front wheel had been so badly buckled that it ceased to bear the faintest resemblance to a circle.

"'The bike's punctured!'" murmured Thornhill, reproducing the accents of Jennings. "Which I take to be a pretty example of the figure of speech called meiosis, or understatement. Now you see. . .."

"There, but for the grace of God, goes your Standard," suggested Michael.

"Exactly," said Thornhill ruefully.

"One would have expected Jennings to have several broken bones."

"Typical of the sort of driver he is. He is one of those who strew the roads with dead and dying, but themselves bear a charmed life. Well, if he thinks he's going to mend that wreck, he's an optimist. I wonder now. . . ." Thornhill grew thoughtful. They followed the path down the back garden to a seat under a tall beech tree. "Well, I suppose Jennings has a perfect right to play hell with his own bicycle. . . . Let's sit here and forget about him until the breakdown gang ring up for instructions about the Standard." Thornhill shrugged his shoulders. "Got tobacco? Good."

They smoked in silence for a minute or two, until Thornhill met Michael's eye.

"Get down to it," he said, smiling. "Right. As I was saying, I have known you long enough. To be frank, the rumour you mentioned has reached my ears." He watched for a moment the blue smoke curling up from his pipe. "But let's get this straight first. I am not going to mention any names. I shall not give you the source of my information, not from any sentimental old-school-tie notions of playing the game, but entirely for the sake of my own selfish peace and comfort. That's understood?"

Michael nodded.

"Well, in your industrious youth, long before you began to eat the lotus as a writer of successful novels . . . which, by the way, I am not going to pretend I have read: I never read anything except Kipling, Hardy, a man called Henry Seton Merriman, whom you have probably never heard of, and an occasional thriller from Boot's . . . long before you found the gilded road to competent ease, you earned your living by . . . I admit by your pen, but employed in more prosiac fashion. . . ."

"In other words," said Michael, smiling, "I started life in the office of Nichol & Company, manufacturers of two-stroke engines, here in Chesworth."

"Under the celebrated George Nichol, one of Chesworth's self-made men," recalled Thornhill in musing fashion. "Poor devil! He was killed in a motor smash about twelve years ago. He had a very pretty daughter."

Michael winced.

"She married that fellow Stevens, who afterwards went to Westhampton and started on his own account. From all accounts he has gone ahead like wildfire. Nichol & Company still plods along in its respectable Chesworthian fashion, paying five per cent, with an effort, but Stevens's show in Westhampton is one of the brightest stars in the engineering firmament, beside which Nichol & Company hides its diminished head. . . . Stevens and you must have been in Nichol's office here at the same time."

"We were."

"Let me see, how old were you then?"

"I was twenty-one when I . . ."

"Shook the dust of Chesworth off your shoes?"

Thornhill fixed his glance on one of the chimneys of his house. "You know, Michael, you left the town rather abruptly."

"I had reasons."

"No doubt you had." Thornhill still studied the chimney. "Now I meant to be as tactful as possible, but it's not easy to put the next thing tactfully. So let's be brutal. You went away without saying good-bye or telling anyone where you were going. Shortly afterwards the manager comes back to duty, after a long spell of 'flu, and finds that Nichol & Company's accounts are short by twelve hundred pounds, which could not be accounted for."

"Good God!" exclaimed Michael.

Thornhill looked at him sideways.

"The inference was obvious," he said quietly. Then, as Michael made a movement, he added quickly: "I don't believe it, old man. Don't think that. But you must let me tell the story in my own way."

Michael calmed himself with an effort.

"For some reason," Thornhill went on, "the matter

was hushed up. The police were not informed. . . . Nichol was a queer old stick. He often did unusual things: things no other business man would do. Then I fancy he was a good deal under the influence of that beautiful daughter of his. Rose "He caught the look on Michael's face and dropped that subject. "But. . . . Well, you see, Michael, after a long interval you come back to Chesworth and make your home here as if nothing had happened. Whereupon, a certain person ups and says to his pals, 'I have kept quiet about it for years, but if he has the face to come back to Chesworth and brazen it out, why, hang it all. . .!'"

"Rudd," said Michael without hesitation.

"Come, that's not playing the game," remonstrated the other. "I thought we agreed no names were to be mentioned. So far as I am concerned, wild horses could not"

"Sorry, Frank," said Michael. "Thanks for telling me so much. So I am to understand that I bolted from Chesworth at the age of twenty-one after embezzling twelve hundred pounds of my employer's money?"

Thornhill looked at him curiously. "I must say you seem quite pleased about it." Michael indeed was smiling: a smile without bitterness. "I'm glad you take it like that. I was afraid . . ." He did not complete his sentence.

Michael laughed.

"It's a load off my mind. Now I know what is being said, I can take steps about it."

"Well, don't call me as a witness in a slander action," said Thornhill, knitting his brows. "I should be no help to you. In fact I should do you more harm than good. I should flatly deny having told you anything; I should say I live a cloistered existence, and rumours are the last things that reach my ears; I should be afflicted with deafness in court and unable to hear a word, slanderous or otherwise; I should say I never had this conversation with you; I should disclaim all acquaintance with you and declare I had never seen you until you were pointed out to me in court; I should say I had taken the twelve hundred pounds myself."

Michael laughed again.

"I gather that you would rather be kept out of it."

"Right first time."

"Well," said Michael seriously, "I am more grateful to you than I can say, and I certainly shan't trouble you any further in the matter. . .. I don't see why a slander action should be necessary. There's a man called Rudd, who was secretary to Nichol & Company, and took over the business when the old man died. I shall go and see him. . .. I apologize: I'm afraid I'm mentioning names. Please accept my very sincere thanks and . . ."

"And let's drop the subject," said Thornhill with relief. "I hear the car returning. Let's go down and inspect the wings."

They found Jennings expertly backing the Standard into the garage. He gave Thornhill a friendly grin.

"I've put the new book on the hall table, sir. The girl gave me one called *There's Death on the Road*."

"It seems highly suitable," said Thornhill.

He walked with Michael as far as the gate. Michael was still in high spirits.

"Congratulations again, Frank. It's the best news I've heard for some time. I shall look forward to seeing you happily married."

Thornhill glanced back at his bachelor home and sighed.

"There's a fable about a fox who had lost his tail. . .." Michael chuckled.

"One may relinquish one's tail, but there are a good many compensations. If you are as fortunate as I have been so far. . . ."

"Superstitious, Michael?"

"What on earth makes you say that?"

"You touched wood."

"Did I?" said Michael vaguely. "I wasn't aware of it. . . . Well, old man, if the girl is all you say she is . . ."

"She's one in a thousand," declared Thornhill stoutly.

"Then never mind what the gossip of Chesworth is going to say. Marry her. You mustn't miss the chance. It's time you settled down."

Thornhill smiled.

"You're a good fellow, Michael," he said.

4

The nobs from Scotland Yard welcomed Sergeant Whalebone's offering of Michael's spade and its story, but shook their heads gloomily when they heard that the spade had been out all night in the rain. Their hearts leapt up when they heard of Mrs. Chrystal's black eye and Mr. Chrystal's disappearance. They were not the sort of nobs who took anything for granted, but this did begin to look like the old, old story of the jealous husband. As for the little problem the sergeant presented them with . . . that of finding a double-fronted house in Park Road, London, at a threepenny omnibus ride from the Crystal Palace, and occupied by Frank Surtees, who was something unspecified in the City . . . well, it might have come out of Chapter One of *The Young Policeman's First Steps in Detection.* Though, naturally, it did not follow that such a house existed except in Mrs. Chrystal's cloudy imagination . . . or, if it existed, that Chrystal had gone there. Still, there would be no difficulty in tracing Chrystal. The nobs certainly thought that they would like to have a few words with Chrystal. Wheels were set in motion. . . .

The wheels having been set in motion, the sergeant mentioned an idea which had occurred to him during the afternoon. He was diffident about it. There was probably nothing in it, but it might be worth following up.

The nobs quite agreed that there was probably nothing in it, but thought it would not do any harm to Take A Statement. The senior nob remarked rather cynically that it was always a good thing to take as many statements as possible. The public gained the impression that the police were really Doing Something, and it kept the reporters happy and occupied.

The nobs gave a guffaw, and returned to a mountain of papers. Sergeant Whalebone got out his bicycle again and rode slowly and thoughtfully round to the Pavement.

He arrived at Miss Perks's house just as Miss Perks was saying good-bye to the wife of an Urban District Councillor, and he heard her bark, as a parting shot: "And don't forget what I said about the cases of apoplexy that will be littered about the bath on Sunday afternoon. It will be necessary to keep a trained medical officer in attendance. But of course the Council never thought of that. Elected bodies are not remarkable for their intelligence. Remember me to your husband, and tell him what I said. . . . And what," added Miss Perks, turning sharply upon the sergeant, "can I do for you, my man?"

"If you can spare me a few minutes, madam," said the sergeant politely, "I should be obliged to you."

"What's it all about? Have you found my little gold brooch?"

"Not yet, madam, I'm afraid."

"It was too much to hope that you would. . . . Come in," snapped Miss Perks, with a ferocity that made the sergeant jump, "and let me shut the door. I don't want everybody in the Pavement to know that I'm receiving a visit from the police."

Grumbling, she double-bolted the front door behind them, and clumped along the stone passage and through the kitchen, where William and Elizabeth, interrupted in their tea, lifted wondering eyes, and up the dangerous staircase and through the bathroom into the sitting-room that overlooked the garden. She took her former seat, and motioned the sergeant to the chair recently occupied by Mary.

"Well, what is it you want?" demanded the fierce little woman in black. "I suppose I am bound to put up with this . . . this interrogation, or whatever it's going to be;

but please make it as short as possible."

At this moment an elderly man opened the door cautiously and popped his grey head into the room, evidently prepared to withdraw it at once if the omens were unfavourable.

"Has that dreadful woman gone at last?" he inquired. "Oh, I beg your pardon," he added, as he saw the sergeant.

"This is my brother Robert," said Miss Perks, with a mixture of pride and defiance. "He doesn't like Urban District Councillor's wives any more than I do, but I have to put up with them, while he, being a man, can flee when they approach. Robert, this is Sergeant . . ."

"Whalebone," supplied the sergeant.

"This is Sergeant Whalebone, and I don't suppose he wants to see you any more than I want to see him. Have you had your tea?"

Robert thought a moment.

"No. I'd forgotten all about it."

"Then go and tell Elizabeth to give you some in your study."

Robert, smiling deprecatingly at the sergeant, withdrew.

"Well?" said Miss Perks icily.

"We had a complaint from you, madam," said Whalebone in his best official manner, "about the reckless riding of a cyclist who, you said, almost knocked you over on the stone bridge last night."

"You needn't put in 'you said,'" retorted the old lady. "Are you doubting my word?"

"I didn't mean that at all, madam."

"Then you should be more careful how you put things. He did almost knock me over."

"Quite so, madam."

"Well, have you found him?"

"No, madam."

"Nor my little gold brooch. . .. I suppose you are going to ask me a lot of silly questions. Well, I can't describe the man. I can't see in the dark. I only know that he was riding at a speed that should not be allowed if the police . . ."

"What time was this, madam?" asked the sergeant sharply.

"Bless my soul, what does it matter, so long as it was after dark?. . . Soon after eleven, I believe," added Miss Perks grudgingly.

"And in which direction was he riding?"

"I was returning home, and he was coming towards me.

The sergeant looked mildy surprised, and ventured to inquire, in order to make sure: "Then he was riding away from the town and towards the Park?"

"To be sure he was," said the old lady, in a tone which expressed her firm conviction that no one but a born fool would ask such a question.

Whalebone tried the effect of an indulgent smile as he put his next inquiry: "It was a little late for an old lady like you to be out for a walk?"

"Has the man come here to insult me?" demanded Miss Perks of the parrot, which, with its head on one side, was attentively considering the proceedings. Wheeling round on the sergeant, she flashed out: "I am quite capable of looking after myself, thank you, and in any case I fail to see that it is any concern of yours."

"Please don't take offence, madam," said the sergeant good-humouredly. "I am only doing my duty, and you will realize that anybody who was out last night in that part of the town may have some information that would be of use to us."

Miss Perks pursed her downy lips and wrinkled her beaky nose.

"So that's what you want? Why not say so at first?" she said, scowling. "Well, I can't give you any information. I didn't hear anything, except the men singing up on the hill as they chopped down those ridiculous barricades put up by that man Bonar. I met nobody, except the dangerous bicyclist whom you appear unable to lay your hands on. . ... Is there anything else, or may we terminate this conversation, which is exceedingly distasteful to me?"

"Just one or two little things," said Whalebone quietly, "that is, if you don't mind, madam."

"I do mind. I mind very much, but I suppose I must put up with it."

"It is your duty as a member of the public," remarked Whalebone, who was enjoying himself, "to give any assistance you can to the police."

"I don't need to be reminded of my duty, young man."

"Very good, madam. . . . Was your brother, Mr. Robert Perks, with you last night?"

"He was not."

"Where was he?"

Miss Perks trembled slightly. The sergeant had pierced her defences.

"Are you suspecting . . .?"

"No, no, madam." The sergeant's tone was soothing. "But you see, madam, if you were out so late last night, the first thought that occurs to anybody who . . ."

Miss Perks interrupted him.

"Very well, then," she said bitterly. "You must have it your own way. I was looking for my brother."

"Did you find him?"

"No. He came back by himself soon after I was home." The old lady gazed through defiant eyes.

"Then perhaps I could speak with him too, madam."

Miss Perks looked at the sergeant as if she could willingly tear him to pieces, but, meeting his twinkling eyes, she rose, marched across the room, and opened the door.

"Robert," she called.

Without waiting for a reply she returned to her chair in the window. Presently her brother came to the door, with an inquiring look on his handsome face.

"Come in and shut the door, Robert. Sergeant

Whalebone wants to speak to you. Never mind if your tea is getting cold. It seems that satisfying the curiosity of the police is more important than satisfying your hunger."

Robert looked amused.

"What can I have the pleasure of doing for the sergeant?"

"I understands he wants to know where you were last night: and what you heard and whether you saw anybody, and goodness knows what else."

"I didn't know my movements were of such interest." Robert had leaned against the mantelpiece, so that they had to turn their heads to look at him. He was amiably smiling.

"Well, sir," said Whalebone, "you know what happened last night. It's part of our duty to interview anybody who may have information to give."

"'Story, God bless you, I have none to tell you, sir,'" said Robert, still looking very much amused.

"If you would just go over the events of the evening . . ." suggested the sergeant, a little puzzled by the way Robert put it.

"Certainly," said Robert, entirely at his ease and apparently enjoying the situation. "It promised to be a fine night, and I decided to take a walk. I went towards the Forest by way of Doomsday Green." He broke off, murmured something about the night he went to Paradise by way of Kensal Green, saw the look of bewilderment on Whalebone's honest face, apologized, and went on. "At the Sun Oak I turned off to the right along the track that leads to Mannings Heath, but instead of going up the lane into the village . . ."

"Wasn't it difficult to find your way in the dark?" interrupted the sergeant.

"The going is quite straightforward, and I had a torch to use if necessary."

"I see, sir. Well, instead of going up the lane into Mannings Heath . . ."

"I sat on the little bridge and smoked a pipe. I am very fond of the Forest, sergeant," explained Robert. "I like to sit there and smoke a pipe and think of its strange history. Odd, isn't it, to remember that these great peaceful tracts of lonely woodland once formed the Black Country of England?"

"You're right, sir," said the sergeant, poising his pencil, "but . . ."

"*Naturam expellas jure a, tamen usque recurret*" remarked Robert. "And I suppose," he added with a sigh, "there will come a day when Staffordshire itself will have sloughed off man's defilement and returned to its natural beauty. *Adsit omen!*"

"Sergeant Whalebone doesn't understand your Latin," broke in the deeper tones of Miss Perks, "and perhaps you had better get on with your story, since his time, no doubt, is exceedingly valuable."

"All right, Matty," said Robert good-naturedly. "I didn't go on to Mannings Heath, where they charge you one-and-three for a very poor tea, and don't give you a slop-basin . . ."

"The sergeant is not interested in your reminiscences of Mannings Heath," said his sister with asperity, "nor was it tea-time. And, talking about tea, your own tea is getting cold."

"No, indeed," said Robert with a chuckle, "it wasn't tea-time. I was out shockingly late last night. Indeed I was surprised when I knocked out my pipe and looked at my watch to see how late it was. I retraced my steps, and the rain came on, and I took shelter under a tree. When the rain ceased, I made a little further progress, but soon afterwards I had to shelter again. That was near the Sun Oak, and," he added, smiling, "I have a witness to prove it, because a fellow-wanderer came along. I flashed my light and saw it was Walter Chrystal."

The sergeant looked up sharply.

"What time was this?"

"Half an hour after midnight. I know, because

Chrystal had only stood for a minute or two under the tree when he looked at his watch, exclaimed at the lateness of the hour, damned the rain, and hurried off back to the town. I waited until the rain had moderated, and followed him."

"Did he say what he was doing there?"

"He was in a very bad temper," said Robert indulgently. "No doubt the effect of the weather. He was not in a communicative mood. Apart from greeting me and cursing the rain, he said nothing."

"And then, sir, you came straight home? Did you meet anybody else?"

"Not a soul, sergeant."

"Thank you, sir."

The sergeant wrote in his notebook and Miss Perks watched his moving pencil.

"So much for you, Robert," she said. "Your tea will be stone cold. Tell Elizabeth to make you some fresh."

"If Sergeant Whalebone has no further questions to ask . . ." murmured Robert, with his gentle smile.

"Thank you, sir," said the sergeant again. "I think that will do very well for the present."

"Gorblimey, yus," remarked the parrot.

"All this tomfoolery has been too much for Ramsay MacDonald," growled Miss Perks, reaching down for the dark red shawl. "He does not behave like this as a rule."

"That blasted thing again?" exclaimed Ramsay MacDonald. The dark red shawl blotted out an unjust world, and he settled down in darkness to brood upon his grievances.

"He seems very intelligent, ma'am," remarked the sergeant appreciatively, "but it is odd how these parrots pick up such language."

"It is not odd at all," snapped Miss Perks. "Ramsay MacDonald was brought up in a ship."

"And we know what sailors are," observed Robert, surprising Whalebone, who had had the same remark on the tip of his tongue and had thought better of it. "Well, sergeant, if you do not want me any more for the present . . ." Robert smiled and nodded, and left the room.

The sergeant rose. Miss Perks rose too.

"Don't you trouble, madam," said the sergeant politely. "Let me find my way out."

"I'll see you out myself," said Miss Perks truculently.

The sergeant had more than a faint suspicion that she credited him with the intention of pumping her servants on the way out. He gave a little cough to deprecate this unworthy mistrust of him, and obediently followed the determined old lady along the labyrinthine route to the front door.

"I hope the police are not going to make fools of themselves by arresting the wrong man," was Miss Perks's parting remark as she undid the two bolts and unlocked the front door. "Good afternoon, Sergeant Whalebone."

The door closed with a bang, and the sergeant, mounting his bicycle, heard Miss Perks slam the bolts home and turn the key.

VI. Young Blood

Mrs. Chrystal, who occasionally showed symptoms of being musical, had gone to her piano. She sat there untidily for a full minute and then launched a surprise attack on Rachmaninov's celebrated *Prelude in C sharp minor*; but in the pause that followed her thumping of the first three chords she heard someone enter the house, fling a suit-case down in the passage, and slam the front door behind him. She presumed that Walter had come back unexpectedly. Her husband was not accustomed to arrive with such emphasis, but it could be no one else. After a little hesitation she proceeded with the execution of her piece.

"For God's sake, stop that infernal row!" shouted a voice from the passage. It was Walter's voice, lifted far above its normal pitch, and informed with a note which sounded strange in her ears.

She played a few more notes, broke off, and turned her head inquiringly towards the door of the room.

"Really, I never saw such a house," said Chrystal, coming into view. He wore his overcoat over the neat blue suit into which he had changed in the early hours of the morning. It was a heavy winter overcoat, and gave him an appearance slightly more substantial than usual. His features were compressed into a look of resolution. "It's extraordinary what a mess you manage to keep it in," he added, "and I'm damned if I'm going to stand it any longer."

He banged the door of the sitting-room with such violence that one of the many photograph-frames fell from the top of the piano.

Mrs. Chrystal looked at him with a far-away expression in her violent eyes.

"Pick that blasted thing up!"

"What, Walter?. . . Oh, the photograph-frame?" She languidly extended an arm, rescued the fallen frame, and propped it negligently back in its place.

"Really, I never saw such a room! Look at it! Cigarette-ends all over the place! It might be a public bar."

Mrs. Chrystal did not appear to hear. "Frank quite well?" she murmured casually. "And Viola?"

"To hell with Frank and Viola," said Chrystal fiercely. "I'm not talking about Frank and Viola. I said, look at this room, with cigarette-ends all over the place." He folded his arms and glared at her, a little man in a very bad temper.

"You look just like the picture of Napoleon," said his wife thoughtfully. She knew she ought not to have said so; but the comparison presented itself so forcibly to her imagination that she had to let it come out. There was a picture of Napoleon looking like that in Frank and Viola's breakfast-room, she remembered.

Chrystal looked at her and swore. The words he used were very bad ones.

"Has anything upset you, Walter dear?" she asked mildly.

"Really, I . . ." Chrystal checked himself, and added curtly: "Get a dust-pan and tidy the place up."

"It could do with a tidy," admitted his wife, looking round the room as though she saw it for the first time. She sighed and rose lazily from the piano-stool.

"Be quick about it," advised Chrystal. He crossed the room and dropped into the most comfortable armchair, still in his overcoat. "And bring me a cup of tea."

Mrs. Chrystal halted on the threshold of the room and slowly turned.

"Tidy up the room and bring you a cup of tea? Or bring you a cup of tea and tidy up the room? I mean, which would you like me to do first?"

"Don't stand there arguing with me," shouted Chrystal. "There is not going to be any arguing in this house in future. Bring me a cup of tea and then tidy up the room."

He took an evening paper from his overcoat pocket and ostentatiously opened it, to indicate that the discussion was closed. His wife still lingered.

"I . . . I think I . . ."

"My God!" said Chrystal. "Really, you are an extraordinary woman! The extraordinary way in which you stand arguing when you've been told to get on with it! . . . Tell me how you got that black eye."

"But you know, dear."

"Tell me, curse you!"

"All right, Walter, you needn't shout," retorted his wife, with some show of spirit. "You gave it to me yourself. You came in and saw a cigar-end in the fireplace, and you flamed up and said, 'Who's been smoking cigars in my house?' Just as if you were the Three Bears. And then . . ."

"That'll do," said Chrystal, dropping his paper and advancing towards her with the light of danger in his eye. "I just wanted to remind you about it. Now, if you say another word before you bring me my cup of tea, I'll black the other one. Really I will."

He looked as if he meant it. His wife pouted and walked slowly away. When Chrystal returned to his paper he could hear her moving about in the kitchen . . . you could hear every mortal thing in the Chrystals' semi-bungalow. She pottered about with china for what seemed an interminable interval.

"I suppose all the tea-pots and cups and saucers have been put away dirty as usual," he called at last, through the open door.

"They certainly seem to be, somehow," returned the accents of a fatalist from the kitchen.

"Extraordinary! Well, things are going to be very different in future. Hurry up with my cup of tea."

She brought it eventually, with two sweet biscuits in the saucer.

"I didn't ask you for biscuits," said Chrystal, snatching the cup, "I asked you for tea." He flung the biscuits across the room, and they broke to pieces on the dusty glass of a reproduction of Greiffenhagen's *Poppies*. "What are you standing there for, like a fat, stuffed pig? I thought I told you to tidy the place up."

"Yes, dear. I had such a surprise this afternoon. Mr. Bonar has been murdered."

"I know," growled Chrystal. "The paper's full of it. Waste of space on a rotter like that. Extraordinary! Who cares a brass farthing? The man deserved to be murdered. A good riddance to bad rubbish."

His wife still lingered in front of him, with speculation in her eyes.

"I think I ought to . . ." she began.

Chrystal flared up again.

"Hell! The devil take the woman. I told you . . . Oh, you're getting to work, are you?"

He settled down to his tea. A cloud of dust began to rise, due less to the vigour with which Mrs. Chrystal was using her brush than to her inexpertness at the task. Chrystal coughed. After a minute or two he could endure it no longer. He dropped his cup and saucer with a clatter into the brass tray under the potted palm in the window.

"Really, I think you are the most incompetent woman on earth. Extraordinary! Put your brush and tray down. Finish the job when I go upstairs. . . . We're going to have a serious talk, you and I, my lady. Sit down."

Mrs. Chrystal adjusted the cushions on the sofa.

"Not there! Sit on that chair, where I can see you." He indicated the least comfortable chair in the room.

Mrs. Chrystal left the sofa and, picking up *en route* her husband's evening paper from the floor, established herself in the desired position.

"Sit up!" barked Chrystal.

"Have you had a trying day, Walter?" asked his wife sympathetically.

"Sit up, I said. Really, the way you sprawl . . . and still

dressed like that at this time of the evening! These slatternly habits of yours are going to cease. Sit up! Yes, and put down that paper. You needn't think I went up to London to buy an evening paper for you to waste your time with."

"Because I have," added the lady in a weary voice.

"You have what?"

"Had a trying day, Walter."

"It won't be the first trying day you'll have, my good woman," said Chrystal caustically. "I'm going to be master in this house in future. You'll go to bed as soon as I've finished with you, and to-morrow you'll get up at six. At six, do you hear? Instead of your usual nine-thirty. You'll bring me a cup of tea, and then you'll clean the house from top to bottom before I come down to breakfast. You won't say you've run out of bacon and fob me off with a boiled egg. . . ."

"But, Walter, I do believe that's just what we have done," said Mrs. Chrystal, for the first time showing signs of distress. "Run out of bacon, I mean."

"My God! Really, I . . . . Then it's to be the last time . . . and I'll have two eggs. And you can poach them . . . on toast. . . . And you will appear at breakfast properly dressed, not in your usual immodest costume of pyjamas with a loose dressing-gown, in which you delight to bandy jests with the milkboy."

Mrs. Chrystal was stung.

"Walter! That is a thing I have never done. Bandy jests with the milkboy, indeed!"

"No, to do you justice, you're always snoring at my side when he comes."

"And it's a libel to say I snore."

"Slander, Daphne," said Chrystal, unable to resist an invitation to display his learning. "Libel is written, slander is spoken. But you'll be able to bandy jests with the milkboy to-morrow, for you'll be up and hard at it before he comes."

"I should never dream of such a thing as bandying

words with a milkboy."

"No," said Chrystal nastily, "I believe you fly at higher game."

"And if you think," blurted out Mrs. Chrystal, "that I am going to face the milkboy while I have this black eye . . ."

"Oh, tell him who gave it to you. I don't care."

"You may not care, but I do. I was asked about my eye by somebody in this very room this afternoon, and I told him . . ."

Chrystal bounced out of his chair and on to the hearthrug. From that position of vantage, facing her with his hands clenched behind his back and an apoplectic look on his face, he presented a perfect picture in miniature of the Englishman vindicating his right to be master in his own household.

"You told him. . ... So you've had a man in here this afternoon, have you? You think you can carry on in perfect safety, do you? You believe I'm safely packed away to London for a few days, eh? It did not occur to you, I suppose, that I should find my sister and her family gone away to the country, and the house shut up? It's just a piece of luck that I didn't surprise you with a lover in your arms, I suppose? Who was this man?"

"A sergeant," murmured Mrs. Chrystal weakly.

"My God! A sergeant? You sink as low as that? I suppose it will be privates next, and then drummer-boys? You vile woman!"

He raised his fist as though to strike her, but, covering his face with his hands, he walked blindly from the room.

Mrs. Chrystal shook her head, smiled vaguely, and took up her dust-pan and brush. She directed special attention to the cigarette-ends. She heard Chrystal hang up his overcoat in the passage, carry his suit-case upstairs, and dump it on the floor overhead. Sounds suggested that he was unpacking. The process became furious. Drawers were flung open, the wardrobe creaked, things were thrown about. Presently Chrystal clumped downstairs in his shirt-sleeves.

"What have you done with my knickerbocker suit?"

"They've taken it away," said Mrs. Chrystal, pausing in her operations, and looking at her husband with a sad smile.

"What on earth do you mean? Who've taken it away?"

"The police."

"The police? God in Heaven, woman, what do you mean?"

"I've been trying to tell you, Walter," answered Mrs. Chrystal with dignity, "but you wouldn't let me. The sergeant I mentioned just now was a police-sergeant. Sergeant Thunderbolt or Backbone or some name like that. From the Chesworth police station. Quite a respectable man and . . . and he called on business."

Chrystal had turned white. His knees shook. "What was it all about?"

"It was about Mr. Bonar's murder."

"He wanted to see me about Bonar's murder?"

"Yes. He said you might be able to tell them all about it."

At this innocent perversion of the sergeant's words, Chrystal staggered back and dropped into the armchair. He looked very small and feeble and hunted.

"Well, and . . .?"

Mrs. Chrystal arranged herself on the sofa, unchecked.

"I told him you had gone away and didn't know when you would be back. He asked me a lot of questions, but I don't think I said anything I ought not to. Then he went away and . . ."

"Yes?" asked Chrystal, haggard.

"Two of them came back later with a thing they said was a search-warrant, and they took your knickerbocker suit and tied it up in brown paper and went away with it."

Chrystal looked at her helplessly.

"But, Daphne, I. . . I didn't. . . Really, it's extraordinary. Preposterous!"

"They said, would you please let them know as soon as you returned."

The shrunken little man looked round at the window as if he were calculating his chances of escape. He turned his head back, placed his hand on his forehead, and sought comfort at last from his wife.

"Really, Daphne, I don't know what to do. What do you think I ought to do?"

"Why not ring them up and tell them you've come back?" she suggested brightly. "It would look as if you were innocent."

"But, my God, Daphne, I am innocent."

"Of course you are, Walter dear. But they want convincing, don't they? And I think you may as well speak to them, because they're bound to find you sooner or later, aren't they?"

He winced, rose from his chair, hesitated, looked at her appealingly, and stumbled out to the passage. He stood for a minute beside the telephone and could not summon up courage to take the receiver from its hook. He came back, hanging his head in the doorway, then, with a gesture of desperation, went into the passage again. She could hear his thin, quavering voice as he spoke on the telephone . . . so greatly changed from the tones in which he had bragged and boasted and threatened on his return from town.

"Would you give me the police, please? . . . Thank you. . . . May I speak to the officer in charge? My name is Chrystal. . . . All right. . . . Oh, no, really I couldn't. I couldn't do that. I . . . I caught a chill last night and can't possibly leave the house. Couldn't you make it convenient to come here?. . . Where am I? Oh, at home. . . . Yes Very well."

He came back into the sitting-room looking, thought his wife, like a little old man. He seemed to be about to sit down by her side on the sofa, but he thought better of it, and returned to the armchair.

"Daphne, they're coming. They'll be here very soon. You'll stay with me, won't you, when they come?"

"Why, of course, dear," she said soothingly. "Why shouldn't I? You'll find Sergeant Waterbottle such a nice man. He's tall and slim and fresh-complexioned and his face is covered with freckles. Such a healthy, country sort of looking person."

Chrystal groaned and buried his face in his hands.

His wife looked at him through vague but motherly eyes. It would have been difficult to guess at the thoughts that were passing through her mind. Indeed, there were people who maintained that Mrs. Chrystal never had thoughts at all, but only instincts and emotions. If this were so, it is likely that those emotions now included a certain sense of relief, and that her instincts told her it was no longer necessary to fear being turned out of bed at the intemperate hour of six the next morning.

Her violet eyes were fixed upon her husband. He was not an impressive figure now that he had shrunk to his normal size. He looked even less important, she told herself, when he was in bed in his pyjamas. . . .

2

Rumour, presented with plenty of material to embroider upon, had a busy morning. People knew that Sergeant Whalebone had interviewed Mrs. Chrystal; that he had come back with another officer and left the house carrying a brown paper parcel, on which speculation was rife and varied; and that late in the evening two men from Scotland Yard had called at the semi-bungalow and spent a long time there.

Michael heard all this through the usual channels. It unsettled him. His spirits, which had been high, dropped heavily. If Chrystal were arrested for the murder, as seemed possible . . . Michael, at the expense of the work he was supposed to be doing, considered what he secretly knew in the light of whether it would help Chrystal. It might be necessary to come forward with a true story, and then . . .

"But, damn it all," he told himself, walking up and down his study, "it couldn't have been Chrystal. The idea's absurd. He hasn't the strength. Surely the police will see that."

For the thousandth time Michael cursed the impossibility of confiding in his wife. . . .

Lunch found him in a wretched state. He came into the dining-room to hear Hugh, aged nine, and Kenneth, aged seven, chattering with zest about the details of Bonar's murder.

"They hit him over the head with a great big spanner and then they threw him in the river."

"It wasn't a spanner: it was a spade."

Michael winced.

"It was a spanner."

"Fat lot you know about it: it was a spade."

"Wasn't."

"Was."

"Wasn't."

"Stop quarrelling, and don't talk about things like that," said Mary.

She watched her husband covertly. Michael had nothing to say and was scarcely eating. He caught her glance and made an effort to behave normally. Mary turned away.

"Another potato, Hugh?"

"That's O.K. with me, chief," said Hugh, extending his plate.

Mary frowned.

"Why do you say such things? You know your father doesn't like it."

"What's that?" asked Michael, hearing himself mentioned.

"Oh, just Hugh favouring us with another choice specimen of his talkie slang."

Michael grunted.

"Dennison," said Kenneth, in a laudable attempt to change the subject, "has got a moustache."

"Call that thing a moustache?"

"Of course it is. If you rub it with a match-box you can hear it grate."

The precocity of the head boy at the prep, school did not interest Kenneth's parents. The meal went on in unaccustomed silence, to be broken presently by Kenneth pushing back his plate and chanting in a high-pitched voice: "I don't like rice pudding."

"Shut up, you little beast," said Michael, his nerves worn beyond endurance.

Mary coloured.

Kenneth gave an exhibition of this sort about once a month. It was the practice of the Holt family to take no manner of notice of it. Ignored, Kenneth would repeat his slogan in less defiant tones, and, still ignored, he would reconsider the matter and decide, without shame, that a hungry boy could, at a pinch, make shift with rice if there was nothing else going.

Kenneth was agreeably stimulated to find his father for once responding to his war-cry. Enjoying the limelight, he cheerfully pushed his plate three inches farther back, and proclaimed, *fortissimo* and *rallentando*: "I don't like rice pudding."

Michael sprang from his chair, whisked Kenneth out of his, sat down by the fireplace, turned the kicking boy across his knee, took off one of the slippers he was wearing, and, using the heel, planted six rapid stinging blows. Then he pushed the child aside and went back to his place, avoiding Mary's eye. This sort of behaviour, he was well aware, ran counter to all her theories on the bringing up of children.

Kenneth's brother, Hugh, sat frozen on his chair, staring at his father with eyes so round that they protruded from his head.

Kenneth himself relieved the tension. With crimson

face he stamped his foot and blubbered: "I'll never forgive you for that: never as long as I live. I'm like the elephant that never forgets."

In the language of Parliamentary reports, loud laughter followed, in which the honourable member who had just spoken eventually joined. . ..

Michael escaped as soon as he could and shut himself in his study, where he sat with a stubborn pen in his hand and scowled at the empty sheet of paper in front of him. After a time he left his chair and paced up and down the room. Losing patience, he cursed himself for a fool.

"Look here, my good ass," he said to himself, "if you were a bricklayer and couldn't lay bricks because you had something on your mind, the foreman would kick you out, and serve you jolly well right. If you were a doctor and neglected your practice because you couldn't concentrate on the ailments of your patients, you'd soon land in the Bankruptcy Court. Do you think you're entitled to loaf just because your tool is a pen? Does that give you any right to malinger when you don't feel up to your job?"

It was of no use.

He went out into the hall. Running into Mary, he told her casually that he was going down to the town to change his library book. She looked at him curiously, but said nothing beyond advising him to take his raincoat.

It occurred to Michael as he crossed the footbridge over the Denne that he had not yet dealt with John Rudd. This fantastic charge of embezzling twelve hundred pounds from the company's funds! Really, as Chrystal would say, it was extraordinary; but something had to be done about it, if only to throw dust into the eyes of the police. He thought he would not go and see Rudd: he would write a letter. In tone the letter would be suave, icily polite, but it would make Rudd take notice. He composed it as he went along.

"It has come to my knowledge that a rumour which is intended to do me harm has been circulated in Chesworth. Inquiries I have made seem to show that this rumour emanated from you. This I am reluctant to believe, and indeed, in such an atmosphere of petty spite and narrow-mindedness, it is necessary to be on one's guard against accepting gossip at its face value."

That was a nasty one: that was one in the eye for John Rudd.

"I need scarcely say that if you disavow the paternity of this slander I shall accept your denial with my sincere apologies for troubling you about such a wretched business. For my sake, however, I must make my position clear."

Now for the big stick.

"If you have been misled into bringing this quite unfounded charge against me, I must ask you to give me your undertaking that you will retract and deny it at every opportunity; and I desire it to be known that if the slander is repeated by anyone I shall not hesitate to take legal action."

Oh, shan't I? said Michael to himself. I may be forced into taking legal action, but shall I hesitate to take legal action? I shall.

Michael smiled, and continued: "I am sorry it is necessary to write to you in these terms, and I shall be glad to have word from you that the information I have been given is inaccurate."

That ought to do the trick.

Yet, as Michael passed the Norman doorway of the church and entered the Pavement, he mentally tore up the letter. The language was pompous and stilted. He could write something better than that. . . .

3

At the farther end of the Pavement, where the Urban District Council had so unfortunately established a car park, a tall and handsome woman was locking up her Lanchester. Her calm, sad eyes rested casually upon Michael as he approached. She looked at him more keenly, and hesitated. Michael raised his hat.

"Rose!"

"You remember me after all these years, Michael?"

"Could I forget?. . . And what are you doing here?"

"I am staying with the Tyldesleys at Rusper, and I've come in to Chesworth to do some shopping. How are you, Michael?"

"Full of trouble and full of care," said Michael, his eyes resting on the car. "No need to ask how you are."

"I'm fourteen years older," said Rose with a smile.

"If your eyes are as good as ever, you must have noticed a moment ago that I have grey hairs."

"Not many?"

"Not many. It's very pleasant to see you again, Rose. How's Gerald?"

"Still flourishing."

Michael remembered that there were no children.

"Glad to come back to these parts?" he asked.

"I always loved them."

"Chesworth hasn't changed much, except to acquire three cinemas, innumerable bus routes, one-way streets and car parks."

"Cars everywhere," said Rose. "But no doubt Chesworth remains the same under its skin."

"I suppose you are full of errands?"

"Yes, but there is plenty of time for them."

It seemed rather stupid to be exchanging banalities at a first meeting after fourteen years.

"Come up to Father Time's Tea Rooms," said Michael. "We can talk there, and the buns are not so old as the sign would lead one to suppose."

They turned into the High Street and climbed the stairs next to the bicycle shop. Michael always liked the little café. It was a homely place, full of gear without being overcrowded or untidy. The tables and chairs were all of different sizes and patterns. Room was found for everything, from written notices of dancing lessons to ash-trays which bore, incongruously, advertisements of someone's shag. From a seat near the window one could, by twisting one's head, look down into the High Street and see the long line of cars parked all down one side, without a break, by people who had come in to do their shopping. At this early hour of the afternoon Rose and Michael had the place to themselves, apart from the two waitresses and the white-haired proprietress.

"The flowers are different on every table, just as they used to be."

"And it's still one of the few places where they know how to make coffee," added Michael.

Rose smiled at him. Had they come there for that? "I have read all your books, Michael. It was one way of keeping in touch with you."

"Sometimes I thought of writing to you, but . . ."

"I know," she said quietly. "I felt the same. Still. . . I have heard a great deal about you. You are back in Chesworth for good?"

"I shouldn't like to prophesy."

The waitress brought the coffee. They welcomed the interruption. It was a difficult meeting for both of them.

"You have been in the north?" asked Rose after a pause.

"Yes. I was in Newcastle first. Where the flower-girls say, 'Pennies each,' and call you 'hinny.' Drifted into journalism. Got a regular job afterwards on a Manchester paper. Wrote stories in my spare time. Met my wife there. Worked like a nigger for nine years: then found myself in a position to give up journalism and concentrate on novels. Bought the Vineyard here in March, my wife having fallen in love with the place when I brought her down last summer. Two boys: Hugh and Kenneth, nine and seven respectively. I think that's all."

Rose nodded.

"We have been very fortunate," she said. "Gerald has built up a big business from small beginnings. I did very well for myself, as they say."

Michael was surprised by the last remark, and

wondered whether he detected irony in her tone.

"Oh, Stevens & Company is a household word," he said idly. "I always thought a lot of Gerald: knew he had the makings of a successful man."

There was another pause.

Rose admired the tulips in the tall vase.

"Why did you say just now that you wouldn't care to prophesy?"

"Oh, I don't know." He offered Rose a cigarette: she shook her head. He lit one himself. "It's a little strange coming back to a place after a number of years."

"There must be still plenty of people you know here?"

"Oh, there are heaps of people I used to know."

She looked at him quickly, but said nothing.

"Rose, do you remember John Rudd?" asked Michael suddenly.

"Of course I do. Father's trusted right-hand man. A pillar of honesty, but a dry old stick. A grim person. Very chapel. I can't say we were ever great friends. As a girl I was rather afraid of him. . . . Why do you ask?"

Michael wondered whether to confide in her. Was it fair?

"I imagine he could be a spiteful old man," Rose added intuitively.

"He could. . . . Rose, you remember I left Chesworth rather suddenly? Did you ever guess why?"

She blushed.

"Perhaps"

"I doubt whether you know the whole reason," he said doggedly. "There was a silly sort of romantic notion involved: the sort of romantic notion one has at twenty-one. Gerald would . . ." He checked himself. "You drove up from Westhampton alone?"

"Yes. I like driving. Shall I tell you how many miles the Lanchester does to a gallon?"

"It wouldn't interest me," said Michael gloomily. He resented being laughed at.

Rose leaned forward slightly. Her face was serious.

"If you think I could be of any help . . ."

He looked at her inquiringly.

"You said when I met you that you were full of trouble and full of care."

"And you feel that I wasn't joking?"

"Well, Michael . . ." She smiled at him. "You never were successful in concealing your emotions. Seriously, as an old friend, now sufficiently detached to be able to take impartial views . . ."

"It was never any use trying to hide anything from you, Rose. You understood me too well." Perhaps, he reflected without bitterness, that was why she had married Gerald. Well, all that belonged to the past. They could talk, as she had hinted, like old acquaintances, with something in common, but not too much. He put his cigarette down on the ash-tray advertising someone's shag. Abruptly he found himself blurting out the whole story. "I left Chesworth without saying good-bye to a soul. Cleared out just as quickly as I could. A few days after I had gone, the firm discovered that there were twelve hundred pounds missing. Rudd, I remember, had been down with 'flu and away for several weeks, or such a thing could scarcely have happened. He must have found it out as soon as he returned to the office. The inference was obvious. I had gone off with the money. For some reason they hushed it up. I heard about it for the first time yesterday. I had known there was something in the wind, without knowing what it was. It puzzled me. Many of the old friends you mentioned just now were turning the cold shoulder. Yesterday I went to see someone and asked him point-blank what it was all about. He told me. Rudd has been talking. Apparently," concluded Michael bitterly, "he thought it such brazen cheek on my part to come back and calmly settle down at the scene of my crime that he couldn't hold his tongue any longer. He has dropped the hint to his acquaintances that I am a dangerous person to know, a common thief who by rights ought to have been in gaol." He had said all this without raising his eyes. He looked up now to see that her face was troubled. "I apologize," he said, moving uncomfortably. "I ought not to have inflicted my private affairs on you."

"Have you been to see Mr. Rudd?"

"No."

She was silent for a full minute. Presently he saw her sober eyes reading his face.

"What do you intend to do?"

"Write to him, I suppose, and threaten an action for slander."

"I think, Mr. Rudd. . .. I wonder. He was such a very strict man, a sort of Roman father. He might feel it his duty . . ."

"To fight it out in court?"

"That is not exactly what I meant." She bowed her head. "I am so sorry, Michael. It's a wretched thing to happen. I can't understand how people could ever believe. . .. It is all so unpleasant. Even if you got Mr. Rudd to take back what he has said. . . ."

"People would still go on believing it?"

"I didn't mean that either." She smiled faintly. "Chesworth people are surely not so bad as that?"

"Perhaps they're not."

"No one whose friendship is of any value, Michael, would believe such a thing of you."

"That's rather an idealistic view. As a matter of fact"—Michael was thinking of Sprague: the talkative Sprague with his two splendid daughters—"there are some people I like who . . . who can't help themselves. They dare not run counter to public opinion."

"No, I suppose they can't. . . . It's difficult to know what to say. Of course you must protect yourself, Michael, but . . . but making sure of your ground, and going carefully. I should be inclined to wait a little. The truth is bound to come out."

"And in the meantime. . . ." He bit his lip. "Rose, I'm sorry. I ought not to have worried you with all this."

She did not answer, but after a brief pause began to collect her belongings.

"Must you be going?"

"I'm afraid I must."

"You'll be in Chesworth again while you are staying at Rusper? I should like you to meet my wife."

"It would be a great pleasure. But I am not sure. . . . You see, I am staying with friends and am not a free agent." She was embarrassed. "I can't promise definitely, but I will if I can."

"I should like you to meet Mary," he repeated.

He paid the waitress and they went downstairs into the narrow, crowded street.

"I am supposed to be changing my library book."

"Then you are crossing the way. I'm bound for Shilling & Mapp's."

"Remember me to Gerald."

"I will," she said abstractedly. "Good-bye."

He stood watching her thread her way along the congested pavement before he crossed to Boot's.

4

The meeting between Michael and Rose after so many years left each of them with plenty to think about. Michael, for his part, as he left the massed cars behind him and came again into the quiet stretch of the Pavement, relived the mad year in which he had reached the age of twenty-one.

Most men in the middle thirties can remember with an indulgent smile the ups and downs of their adolescence, its heavenly ecstasies and its cimmerian despairs.

Michael never willingly recalled that fever. He would gladly have wiped the twelve-month from the record. He had done things that clouded the whole of his later life. He was singularly fortunate to have escaped the full force of their consequences . . . if indeed he had.

There was nothing unusual, Michael was thinking as he passed Miss Perks's house, in young men going off the handle when they were turned down by a girl. It was a common thing. They looked somewhere else for consolation, and either made a hasty marriage which they would repent at the proverbial tempo, or went on the loose. Just a commonplace of psychology. They had to find a vent somewhere. . . .

Gerald Stevens had been twenty-one in the same year. Michael and he had been fast friends. It was the attraction of opposites. Gerald, athletic, debonair, very much one of the gayer young men of the town. Michael, quiet, interested in intellectual things, reserved. They sat together in Nichol & Company's office; openly cursed, secretly admired, and certainly worked like horses for their rough-spoken boss; feared the dour secretary of the company, John Rudd; and, in the best tradition, worshipped their master's daughter. . . .

Rose had changed. She had parted with her gaiety: she had grown sad and wise. Fourteen years before she had been a frank, laughing, mischievous girl. Michael could not wonder that she had preferred Gerald Stevens. Yet how he had felt that blow! It had thrown him completely off his balance.

There was a September evening of fourteen years before that he would never forget. He had been to a concert at the Town Hall and was sitting in his room with Emerson's *Essays* in his hand. He meant to read for half an hour before he went to bed. Chandos, then a curate in the town, had strongly commended Emerson: stuff for men, he called it. Michael thought Emerson dull and rather priggish: he still did. He willingly dropped the book when he heard Gerald dashing up the stairs.

Gerald blew into the room like a strong wind, and flung himself full length upon the bed. Michael occupied a bed-sitting-room: chromolithographs of landscapes on the walls, giving an odd Teutonic aspect to famous English beauty-spots; above the bed, a picture of a young woman in a voluminous green frock who clung to a cross erected on a wave-washed rock in a stormy sea, with a couple of verses of *Rock of Ages* printed underneath. . . .

"I've had a day," said Gerald, propping up his tennis-shoes on the brass bed-rail, and he was silent for at least thirty seconds.

Michael tossed him a biscuit. He caught it neatly and crammed it into his mouth.

"Where've you been mouldering to-night, Michael?" he demanded, with his mouth full.

"Concert at the Town Hall."

Gerald made a face.

"I say, Michael, you ought to get out more, see life, have a good time. Enjoy yourself while you are still young: that's my motto." Then, with a noticeable change of tone: "God!" he groaned, "it's hell."

"Have another biscuit."

"Look here," said Gerald fiercely, ignoring the invitation, and swinging himself round so that he sat on the edge of the bed with his feet on the floor, "is it to be you or me?"

"What on earth do you mean?"

"Damn it all, Michael: you know what I mean."

"Well, perhaps I do."

"You know damned well what I mean. . . . All right, you needn't look at me like that. I'm not going to challenge you to a duel. . .. A fair fight and no favour, and may the better man win. If it's you, good luck to you."

Michael had thought him melodramatic, talking like that.

"It may be neither of us."

"Rot!"

"In any case, there's the old man to be considered. He's not likely . . ."

Gerald smiled knowingly.

"She can twist him round her little finger. . .. Besides, she told me only yesterday that the old man was all in favour of early marriages. Said that if a couple were hard up to start with, so much the better. They had something to work for. That's how he began."

"Rose told you that?"

Michael remembered how grave doubts about the wise ordering of the universe had seized him at that moment.

"It doesn't follow, you know, old man," said Gerald, kicking his heels as he answered the unspoken question. "She may have meant me to pass the information on."

"That doesn't sound likely."

"Why not? She knows we're pals." Gerald bent down to fasten a shoelace. "We are pals, aren't we . . . no matter what happens?"

"Of course we are."

"Good egg! And so, as I said before, may the better man win." Gerald swung his feet back on to the bed-rail and studied the ceiling. He was choosing his next words carefully. At length he went on: "All the same, Michael, do you know what I feel like doing if . . . if Rose turns me down? I shall clear out of Chesworth and go to Canada or somewhere and start again."

"I suppose I should feel like that, too."

"There must be plenty of openings in a place like Canada for anybody who understands the motor business. You know, Michael, I'm keen on starting on my own. I've got any quantity of ideas. No use putting them up to the old man. He's too old now, too conservative. There are improvements I could suggest. . . . But what's the use of talking about it. If Rose marries me, I suppose I shall succeed to the business. If she doesn't, then I shall shake the dust of Chesworth off my shoes and be off to Canada with my bundle on my shoulder." He stretched himself and yawned, and made the bed creak. "Damned embarrassing if she married you, and I had to go on working in the office."

"And how do you think I should feel, if she married you, and I had to go on working in the office?"

"Yes, there is that," conceded Gerald. "You know, Michael . . . honestly, old man . . . I feel that if she married either of us, the only decent thing for the other to do would be to buzz off."

Michael smiled to himself as he remembered that remark. At the time, as he recalled quite well, it had seemed to him, on contemplation, that Gerald was magnificently right. He said so.

"Then it's a gentleman's agreement?" Gerald spoke eagerly, nailing him down. "If she marries you, I go to Canada. If she marries me . . ."

"I shall get out of this damned place, and I don't care a hang where I go," said Michael. . . .

It was all very romantic and chivalrous and proper to that stage of life. . . .

"So that's that," said Gerald, in a tone of relief. He dragged himself off the bed and yawned again. He slapped Michael on the shoulder and looked at him with kindly eyes. He picked up the book that Michael had been reading and glanced at it.

"Emerson. Any good?"

"Not much in my line."

"Looks pretty heavy going."

He chucked the book into a chair.

"I've been given a good tip for the three o'clock tomorrow," he remarked casually. "Dropped a packet last week. With any luck shall get on the right side again." He wandered round the room, examined the picture of the green-garbed girl in the stormy sea, made a suitable comment, ate one of Michael's biscuits, filled and drank from the tumbler on Michael's washstand, flung a pillow at Michael, grinned, and said: "Well, I mustn't keep you from your beauty-sleep any longer. Good night, old man." He sprinted down the stairs and a moment later the front door banged; and Michael heard his landlady grumbling underneath. . . .

Two days later Gerald had invited congratulations. Michael whole-heartedly wished him the best of luck; and, returning to his lodgings, manfully packed his suitcase, left behind an extra week's money for his landlady, and took the train to London without saying good-bye to anyone.

One did do things like that when one was twenty-one. . . .

Michael's thoughts passed involuntarily to the misery that followed: the struggle with poverty in the north, and that episode in which he was entangled with a common little hussy in Newcastle. He shut his mind on that: he did not want to recall it. . . .

After all, he had emerged very luckily. He had Mary; he could think now without a regret about Rose; he had met and talked to her without too much embarrassment. He had had his share of happiness . . . not without fighting for it. But who didn't have to fight? One had to be constantly armed and alert: never relax, or the enemy would be across the frontier. And he resolved to go on fighting, with whatever weapons he could use. . . .

He had passed the church and come to the Garden of Remembrance. He stood for a moment to watch the scene. It was Saturday afternoon, and the place was full of children, wading in the pond, riding their miniature bicycles, climbing about the limbs of a fallen tree and jumping from it into the sand spread beneath. The children liked this garden: there was an absence of regulations that appealed to them. Yet it had been a bone of contention in the town since the Chesworth woman who owned the place had thrown it open as a memorial to her son killed in the war. Her plans had at first included the making of a swimming-bath in the meadow beyond, and as a preliminary she had erected a long oak fence to serve as a screen. When the Council decided to build their own swimming-bath, she abandoned that part of her plans, but the fence remained. The fence ran for some distance along the Denne in a pretty spot, and many people thought it an eyesore and wished to have it taken away. So there was a petition and a lot of fuss: a typical small-town squabble. "The fence will remain," said the good lady to all representations; and there it still was, serving no purpose, and therefore an artistic error and a blot on the landscape.

"Women," thought Michael, "are like that. You have to be so jolly careful or they do exactly what you don't want them to do."

He grinned as he found himself arriving at this epoch-making discovery, and by a natural sequence his thoughts went back to Rose. He pondered her troubled face as he confided in her. Why had he bothered her about that ridiculous story of the twelve hundred pounds? What did *that* matter?

In the meadow by the Denne, an elderly cow was automatically whisking her tail to and fro. She knew very well that her tail was not long enough to deal properly with the flies on her flanks, but she went on trying. Michael saw in that cow an analogy to himself. . . .

Rose had seemed more upset than she had any need to be. Could . . .

Michael stood still and looked down into the well-filled stream. He had been visited by a strange idea. Twelve hundred pounds had been stolen from Nichol & Company's funds. He had not stolen it. Who then had?. . .

The more he thought of it, the queerer the business seemed. When Rudd discovered the deficit, why did not Nichol send for the police? There was no reason why the old man should wish to shield Michael. On the other hand . . .

Michael had often wondered why Nichol left his business to Rudd instead of his son-in-law. Rose had been provided for, but her money was tied up. Gerald could not touch a penny.

Where had Gerald found the capital to start in business for himself, even in a small way? He had never saved. . . .

There was only one satisfactory solution to the problem. . . .

Michael kicked a stone into the water. "I shall not write to Rudd," he said to himself as he moved on. Then:

"I wish I had never said a word to her, but it is too late now: she knows."

He left the path and came out into his lane, and there, strolling moodily along, Chrystal met him.

"Hallo, Holt. Been to the inquest?"

"Was it to-day? I didn't know."

"Purely formal, I suppose," said Chrystal. "An adjournment to allow the police to continue their inquiries: that's the usual thing, isn't it?"

"I believe it is."

Chrystal turned and walked along with Michael.

"They suspect me!" he blurted out. "Of all the extraordinary things! Really, I . . ."

"It's ridiculous, old man," said Michael kindly.

"All very well for you to say so. I have to go through it." The little man was plainly in a very bitter temper.

"We might be in Russia! They catechize my wife, they come and search the house in my absence, they make a third visit and cross-examine me until midnight. Trying to catch me out, I suppose."

"It's too bad."

"Really, I . . . What do you think? I tell them the very idea of my killing a great strapping fellow like Bonar is absurd. In reply they suggest a way I might have done it. Extraordinary! If I were standing on the wall, they said"—Chrystal indicated the low stone wall that bounded the Denne—"I could bring down a spade with sufficient force to crack anybody's skull. Isn't it extraordinary?"

"Why a spade?" asked Michael. He found the question irresistible.

"Why a spade?" echoed Chrystal gloomily. "Why not a stick or a spanner or a hatchet? That's exactly what I asked them."

"And what did they say?"

"They said they took a spade to serve as an example. It's extraordinary. It really is. You've no idea, Holt, what it's like to be put through it. If there's any justice in this country, I'll get an apology from the Home Secretary for this persecution. . .. As if I could have done it! . . . And they didn't try to explain how I could lift that ox of a man and throw him into the water. Extraordinary!"

He trotted along, mumbling to himself, and from time to time looked up at Michael as if he were about to ask a question. He came out with it at length.

"Talking about spades, Holt, did you get yours back that night?"

"Yes. I found it in my garden in the morning."

"Where? In your garden? How do you mean, you found it in your garden?"

"Why," said Michael good-humouredly, "when I went out into my garden in the morning, there it was. Back among the wallflowers."

"You mean it. . . What an extraordinary thing! How did it get there? Who brought it back?"

"I have no idea."

They had reached the gate of the Vineyard. Chrystal stood indecisive.

"It's not there now," he said foolishly.

"No. It's been taken away from me."

"Whatever . . ."

"The police seemed interested in it. I suppose they've taken it away for blood tests or something of that sort."

"Good heavens! Well, really, I . . . I can't make head or tail of this business at all, really I can't."

Chrystal shambled away down the lane, with his hands clasped behind his back and his head bowed: the picture of a perplexed and harassed soul.

VII. Miss Perks Offers Advice

Thornhill's car swung out of the endless line of Saturday traffic on the Worthing road, inserted itself between the main gates of Forest Park, and passed up the celebrated double avenue of lime trees.

"Miss Martindale is in, sir," said the untidy old butler of the seventeenth-century mansion: himself a museum-piece, as Thornhill thought. "If you will step into the drawing-room I will inform her of your arrival."

Thornhill parted with his hat and coat.

"How is Miss Martindale?"

"Naturally she is a little upset, sir, as we all are, but otherwise I think she is in robust health."

"She arrived yesterday?"

"That is so, sir."

"And what is she doing at this moment?"

"I believe," said the butler stiffly, "she is in my poor master's study, but if you will kindly . . ."

"Which is your late master's study?"

The butler looked at Thornhill and met his eye before answering the question.

"It is the room immediately overhead, sir, and I will go up at once and . . ."

"Don't bother," said Thornhill.

The butler watched Mr. Thornhill, that well-known Chesworth bachelor, sprint up the stairs. Shaking his head, he hesitated for a moment; and then, grumbling to himself, went away to his own quarters.

Kate Martindale stood at the window, looking down the drive. She turned sharply at the sound of someone entering the room. Thornhill came slowly towards her.

"How now, Kate?"

"Frank! You startled me."

"I'll startle you again, my lovely charmer."

He caught her in his arms, lifted her until her face was on the level of his, and planted a smacking kiss on each cheek.

"Frank! Behave yourself."

"Is that how you greet your devoted lover? I'll give you two more kisses for that."

He did, and set her down: then regarded her ruefully. "It's no use, Kate, it's no use," he said. "I cannot help myself.

Man may escape from rope and gun . . .

Do you know that song from *The Beggar's Opera?*" He broke into a snatch of it:

"But he that takes woman, woman, WOMAN, Ruin meets!

Escape you . . . never!" he added sardonically.

Kate had retreated to a chair, her face flaming. She was patting her costume into place.

"Neat but not gaudy, a sober black," remarked Thornhill. "Well suited to the melancholy circumstances."

"Which is more than I can say of your behaviour, Frank," she retorted.

"Why, oh why, my beautiful one, did they make you a schoolmistress?" demanded Thornhill ironically.

"And why not?"

"You who should never have wasted your sweetness on the classroom air! You . . . and there's the rub, Kate, one of the rubs . . . you the heiress to thousands!"

"And why shouldn't I be a schoolmistress? Our family were plain ordinary people. My uncle rose from the same class. He was as poor as a church mouse when he started life."

"The characteristic common sense of the profession!" exclaimed Thornhill. "I am abashed."

"That is very unusual," said Kate calmly. She inspected her lover. "You have a button off your waistcoat."

"That is not so unusual. Anyhow, it's one I never use. We weren't allowed to fasten that button at school, and youthful habits cling, you know, Kate."

"That's no reason why you should have it off."

"I am a poor bachelor, and buttonlessness is the badge of all our tribe."

"What do you pay your housekeeper for?"

"Because she is a good cook. Can good cooks sew on buttons? And is this a moment for talking of buttons? I see you again after many dreary Kateless months, I clutch you to my bosom in an ecstasy of desire, and you tear yourself away and talk about buttons."

"Buttons are symbolical," said Kate good-humouredly. "When a child is ill cared-for, I am never surprised if its behaviour leaves something to be desired."

Thornhill groaned.

"There she goes again!" He called the gods to witness with a tragic gesture. "These schoolmistresses! It gets into the blood. They go round spotting things wrong everywhere, and have to scold someone. It's an occupational disease. Even time brings no cure. Once a school-mistress, always a schoolmistress. It's sad."

"If you object to schoolmistresses," retorted Kate with spirit, "there's no reason why you should marry one."

"No, indeed," he said soberly. "I thank you, Kate, for reminding me." Then, as she looked at him oddly, he went on: "Ah, but I shall try to reform you, my dear. I know it will be a task of almost insuperable difficulty, but I shall have a shot at it. I shall be your Petruchio, Kate. I shall tame the pretty shrew. I shall be the schoolmaster to your schoolmistress. I shall send you to bed without your supper, and stand you in the corner, and make you stay in on sunny afternoons to write out a thousand times, 'I must not be a cross old schoolmistress,' and . . ."

"And beat me, I suppose?" suggested Kate acidly.

"You shall be black and blue with my . . . kisses and caresses. I shall stick at nothing, Kate. I am determined to drive the schoolmistress out of you."

"Well, I shall know what to expect."

Thornhill went to the window and looked down the great avenue.

"It was only by accident I heard you were here. You didn't tell me."

"Really, Frank, I had so many things to think about, and, besides . . ."

"The time is not propitious for love-making? It may be you are right, Kate. Truly, Kate, I wrestled with myself before I came, but I fell. You are my lodestone.

Man may escape . . ."

"Don't start all that over again, please."

"Well, if you'd really rather not. . . What made you come? Did old Thimbleshanks send for you?"

"You mean my uncle's lawyer? Yes, he said he thought I ought to be here. I suggested staying at an hotel, but he told me I ought to come to the house. . . . It's a great, gloomy place, and, Frank, it's been shockingly neglected by the servants."

"There she goes again," said Thornhill mockingly. "She lifted the ornament from the mantelpiece and, 'Mary Jane,' she said, 'you have not dusted here. You are a very naughty girl. Go and fetch the cane from my private room.'"

"You are ridiculous," said Kate coldly. "And after all, Frank, my uncle is lying dead."

"You never loved him, Kate. No one did. Your sorrow is assumed, simulated, conventional."

"You're outrageous, Frank. In any case, there is a good deal to be said for the conventions. At least they make one behave with ordinary common decency."

"A nasty one for me, that," said Thornhill cheerfully. "Well, I'll be good: please, teacher, I really will. . . . Do you remember what a glorious time we had in the Mediterranean? I believe you forgot all about your musty old school in the Mediterranean. Not to mention the conventions. . .. But I will be good, Kate. What are you supposed to be doing here, and can I help you?"

"Really I suppose I have nothing to do at present. The funeral is on Monday. After that I expect to be busy putting affairs in order, going through my uncle's papers, and so on. I believe he's left stacks and stacks of papers. If you like going through papers I should value your kind assistance next week, so long as you can bring yourself to behave. . . . But at the moment I am only the nominal head of the house, whose instructions the servants dutifully ask and obey if it suits them."

"How that must annoy you!. . . Kate, are you really going to try to run this enormous mansion?"

"I shall have to try. It's a condition of the will."

"I thought wills were not read until after funerals."

"The lawyer told me in advance."

"But, Kate, how are you going to run a house and estate like this?"

"It's just a matter of common sense."

Thornhill looked at her admiringly. "I believe you domestic economy experts are prepared to tackle anything. When one of you becomes Prime Minister, this country will be so well organized that it won't know itself."

"I dare say," said Kate complacently, "we should make a better job of it than the men."

She was sitting in the chair at Bonar's desk and had turned to face him. Thornhill left the window and sat down in an opposite chair. He leaned forward with his hands on his knees and looked at her with a whimsical expression.

"Kate, I have a jolly little house of my own, complete with all the usual offices, and standing in its own small but highly eligible grounds. The garden is well-stocked and matured. It's all mine, no instalments to pay off, or anything."

"Yes, you've told me so before."

"Kate, I have no occupation, profession or calling, but entirely through the exertions of my 'forebears, whom I daily remember in my prayers, I have an income of a thousand a year, derived from gilt-edged securities."

"So you said in the Mediterranean. Why are you bringing all this up again?"

"Because these things look different in the light of certain happenings. My little house is a minnow compared with this Triton. In your eyes an income of a thousand a year must seem very small beer, and practically no cheese at all."

"You must think I am very stupid."

"On the contrary, Kate, I am overwhelmed by your intelligence and practical sense. If anyone can face facts with a clear eye and no prejudice, you can. That is why I am drawing attention to a deplorable truth. People will say I am marrying you for your money."

"Are you marrying me?" inquired Kate, lifting her pretty eyebrows.

"I certainly heard some rumour of the sort. . . in the Mediterranean."

"I may change my mind . . . in Sussex."

"That's exactly what I am afraid of. . . . By the way, Kate, I omitted to mention that I have a perfect darling of a car, which has been known to do seventy-five."

"I shall certainly never marry a road-hog," said Kate, tossing her nicely-tended head.

"But I don't, Kate. I mean I'm not. I never hog it. Thirty is about my limit. I told you that because some girls have a craving for speed: that's why young men go wrong and buy motor-bikes. I see you're not that sort of goil."

"Thanks."

"It's Jennings," added Thornhill explanatorily, "who gets seventy-five out of it."

"Who is Jennings?"

"My housekeeper's husband, poor fellow."

"Why do you call him poor fellow?"

"Because he'll be out of a job soon."

"How is that?"

"I shall be selling the house when I come to live here."

"I shouldn't sell it just yet, then. . .. Oh, Frank, can't we be serious for one minute?"

"I have never felt more serious in all my life."

"You don't show it. . . . Do you think, Frank, the police will find the man who killed my uncle?"

"Do you want him caught?"

Kate frowned.

"I really think you'd better go, Frank. Plainly you're not in a frame of mind to discuss anything sensibly."

"How should I be, dearest Kate? The delight of seeing you again has gone to my head like wine."

"Then you'd better go and sleep off the effects of your intoxication."

"She has a sharp tongue and a dry wit, i'faith. . . .Kate, I am now sober. I am prepared to talk like a magistrate and an elder of the kirk. In reply to your inquiry of even date, I understand that the police may make an arrest at any moment. The only difficulty is that they are not sure which man to arrest."

"That, of course, makes it harder for them."

"They suspect a man called Chrystal."

"Who is he?"

"A neighbour of mine. He lives in an architectural miniosity—is that the diminutive of monstrosity, Kate? — called a semi-bungalow, which, in the language of house-agents, does not mean half a bungalow, but a bungalow and a little bit more. He is a little man, a human shrimp, a tiny little fellow in knickerbockers, a ninth of a tailor, without muscle or thews . . . oh, it is only the eagle eye of the police that would spot him at all, Kate."

"He doesn't sound much like a murderer. Why do they suspect him?"

"The old, old story of the eternal triangle, Kate," said

Thornhill sadly. "They think he was overwrought by
passion and jealousy, which temporarily gave him
courage and some semblance of strength. . .. He ran away
to London by the first possible train after the murderer.
He came back again later the same day, as a matter of
fact. . . Oh, the whole idea's absurd, Kate. It's as if the
circus dwarf in a sudden fit of frenzy knocked the strong
man down and brained him. There's nothing in it. It's just
the sort of funny notion the police get into their heads. . . .
Oh, and that reminds me. I've got to call in at the police
station myself."

"You, Frank?"

"There is no cause for alarm, my dearest one. I merely
have to return a gold brooch which I think must be the
one described in a police notice I saw in town last night."
He drew Miss Perks's little gold brooch from his waistcoat
pocket. "It caught my eye in our lane this morning before
breakfast. For I must tell you, Kate, I am not one of the
idle rich who come down to breakfast in their dressing-
gowns: I always take the dog out every morning at dawn,
or soon after, or not so very long after . . . at any rate, at
quite an early hour. I haven't told you about my dog,
Kate. His name is Chin, and he's a Chow, and he has a
blue-black tongue and an Oriental pride. If you want
Chin to take the slightest notice of you, I am afraid you
will have to marry me. Even then you will have to play
second fiddle in his affections. However . . ." He handed
Kate the brooch. "An old-fashioned thing, I think: a
trinket of sentimental value."

"Some old lady's relic of her girlhood, I should
imagine," said Kate. "It's very dirty."

"It would be, after knocking about for a day or two. I
found it in a crack at the foot of the wall, probably kicked
there unwittingly by some passerby."

"What's this stain on it? Frank, I believe it's blood."

He examined it.

"You may be right in your horrid surmise, Kate. The
old lady pricked her finger with the fastening, perhaps . .

. or . . . strange thought! Can it be a ker-lue? This will interest the sleuths of Scotland Yard, Kate."

"It doesn't seem likely," said Kate, in matter-of-fact fashion, "but you can do no harm by pointing it out to the police."

"Shall I?" said Thornhill thoughtfully. "I suppose I should. It will amuse them." He put the brooch back in his pocket. "And now, will you come and dine with me to-night?"

"Most certainly not."

"Not even to see my house and Jennings and Mrs. Jennings and Chin the Chow? And I'll bring you back in the car at twenty-five miles an hour."

"You know I couldn't dream of such a thing."

"Then when will you come and dine with me?"

"After our engagement has been announced."

"That's better, Kate. That's spoken more like my own true lass."

"And that won't be until a decent interval after the funeral," said Kate coldly. "And if you go on behaving as you are at present . . ."

"Like this, for instance," he said, lifting her from her chair and kissing her with gusto.

"It won't be at all," she finished, breaking away as he set her down, and biting her lip.

"I'll give you six more for saying that," declared Thornhill.

She tried to evade him, but he fulfilled his threat. Breathless, she sank into a chair. Thornhill went to the door of the room, turned, stood for a moment, regarded her sadly, seemed to be on the point of coming back, turned on his heel abruptly, and went downstairs. She heard him humming the tune from *The Beggar's Opera.* She crossed to the window and watched him get into his car. He caught sight of her, waved his hat, and started slowly down the famous avenue.

Half-way to the gates, he pulled up sharply to avoid some of the Park deer which had taken it into their heads to seek fresh pastures. While he waited, he was suddenly seized by the beauty of the view that opened to the north, where the Surrey hills lay clear in the afternoon sunshine. Then his eyes fell on the notice-board which requested the public to keep to the footpaths. There were rights-of-way on this side of the Park with which even Bonar had not ventured to interfere. The notice added, with sinister implication:

The keepers cannot be responsible for
gun accidents if the Public subject themselves to being off the Paths.

He grinned; and found himself wondering what the Forest Park estate would be like when it had been subjected for a year or two to the dominion of Kate Martindale, ex-headmistress of a domestic economy centre. She would correct its English style, certainly; and probably bring its feudal notions more into line with modern thought.

His face changed, and soberly he re-started his car and drove down the lime avenue.

2

Thornhill turned into the main road, and caught sight of a familiar small figure in black standing irresolutely on the grass verge at his right. She seemed to be hesitating in front of the steep stile which straddled with many steps across the tall fence of the Park. He drew up.

"At your time of life you've no business to go gallivanting over Jacob's ladders," he called out cheerfully.

Miss Perks turned.

"Oh, it's you, Frank Thornhill."

Thornhill grinned at his old schoolmistress. Another one of the tribe! But Miss Perks was of a former generation. She had belonged to a different school.

"These buses are very inconvenient," said Miss Perks sourly. Her tone suggested that she held him responsible for the deficiencies of the Southdown service. "I have just missed one and there won't be another for an hour. Very well, I say, I will walk back by the short cut and save twopence. But what, I ask, is the use of providing short cuts to the town, if the stiles can only be climbed by those effigies who walk about the country in their drawers?"

"Not drawers, Miss Perks!"

"Don't pretend I'm shocking you, Frank Thornhill," rejoined Miss Perks. "They're on the short side even for drawers, some of them."

"You object to them on the score of immodesty?"

"Stuff and nonsense!" said Miss Perks, quite angrily. "I object to them because girls look so ugly in them. A girl ought to have more sense than to put on short drawers and go about exposing her knobbly knees. If I had my way, I'd . . ."

"Yes, I know exactly what you would do to 'em," remarked Thornhill quietly.

"I must say they look no better in long trousers," added Miss Perks balefully. "The rotundity of the feminine form behind is somehow brought out very unpleasantly in long trousers. And in plus fours they look bigger sights than the men, and that's saying a great deal."

"Better let me give you a lift," suggested Thornhill kindly.

Miss Perks peered distrustfully at the car.

"How many miles an hour does that contraption go?"

"Seventy-five."

"Oh, thank you. In that case, I prefer to break my neck at my own speed," and Miss Perks placed a determined foot on the lowest rung of Jacob's ladder.

"But only when Jennings is driving," explained Thornhill.

"Jennings? Is that your giant of a man who brings me books?"

"Yes, Miss Perks. I hope they meet with your approval."

"If one has to waste one's time reading novels," said Miss Perks, "it matters very little what sort of novels one reads. . . . Jennings was kind enough to set up my new wireless."

"I expect he did it properly."

"I have only listened to the thing for five minutes, and I must say that the type of programme provided by the broadcasting people came as a complete surprise to me. But," added Miss Perks generously, "I suppose it would be hardly fair to blame Jennings for that."

"Good Lord, no. His shoulders are broad, but not broad enough to take upon them all the shortcomings of the B.B.C. . . .. I was about to say, Miss Perks, that my own driving pace is a timorous twenty-five."

"In that case, I'll risk it," grunted the old lady. "But no tricks, if you please, Frank Thornhill."

Thornhill assisted her into the front seat.

"And now," he said, as he returned to his place and started the car, "Please talk. I like a continuous flow of conversation when I'm driving. I find it soothing, and it keeps me from attempting wild flights of speed."

"I don't know that there's anything I wish to talk about, but if talk I must to save you from playing the fool like other people who have these dangerous machines, talk I will. You had better suggest a topic."

"There is only one topic at present, surely. One subject alone engrosses the Chesworth public. I should be interested to know what your views are on this all-engrossing subject. Who do you think killed Douglas Bonar?"

"I know Mr. Chrystal didn't," said Miss Perks' curtly.

"Now that's very interesting," said Thornhill, with his eyes on the road. "Several people think he did. I suspect that the police are of the same opinion. What makes you think otherwise?"

"Well, look at the man," said Miss Perks

contemptuously. "I should not suppose him capable of hurting a mosquito, let alone a great hulk of a fellow like that man Bonar."

"Exactly," agreed Thornhill cordially. "Just what I was saying to . . . nasty little bridge, this Tarn Bridge."

"As for the police," went on Miss Perks, "I doubt whether they would lay their hands on the murderer if you gave them a month of Sundays. Which is a comforting thought for somebody. . .. If they could perform the elementary duty of stopping mad bicyclists from maiming peaceful people in the lanes after dark, I might think more highly of their efficiency. If they found my little gold brooch, I might give them credit for a little intelligence."

Thornhill pulled up the car with a jerk which pitched Miss Perks forward in her seat.

"What's possessing the man?" she demanded indignantly.

Thornhill took something from his pocket.

"Here's a thing, and a very pretty thing. . . ."

Miss Perks calmly stretched out a hand and took possession of her brooch.

"As it happens," she said, "I am the owner of this pretty thing."

"Then you must pay a forfeit. I believe the usual penalty is a . . ."

"Frank Thornhill," said Miss Perks frostily, "don't behave like a fool. Where did you find it?"

"In our lane."

"Whereabouts?" asked the old lady sharply.

"In the immediate neighbourhood of the architectural error of judgment that the Chrystals call their semi-bungalow."

"Oh!" Miss Perks considered. "I don't know how in the world it got there. . . . However, I've got the thing back, and there's no sense in holding an inquest on it."

"Perhaps not. Inquests are unpleasant things."

A pause.

"Is the man going to stay here all day?" asked Miss Perks of the dashboard.

"I was just wondering whether . . ."

"Whether what? Don't leave your sentences unfinished in that stupid way."

"Sorry! I was just wondering if you had noticed. . . .However, it doesn't matter,"

The old lady scrutinized the brooch.

"It's very dirty, but it doesn't appear to be damaged, if that's what you mean. This looks like a spot of rust."

"That's what I was thinking of. How do you account for that? Gold doesn't go rusty, does it? I suppose you were not misled by the man who sold it to you, were you? You should have gone to old Bisgood. He's a pattern of probity. He would never have let you down like that."

"What a fool you can be when you feel like it, Frank Thornhill," said the old lady with frankness. "This spot. . . . Now I come to look at it, I think it must be blood."

Thornhill echoed the word in a sepulchral tone, giving it two syllables.

"Yes, blood, or however you like to pronounce it, and," added Miss Perks with vigour, "don't sit there like a ninny. A perfect pair of idiots people must think us, sitting in a stopped car in the midst of all this traffic. For goodness' sake, drive on."

"To the police station?" asked Thornhill innocently.

"In the name of all that's sensible, why?"

"I thought they might be interested. They might like to have the blood analysed. You see, if it happens to be Bonar's blood, it will at least give them an idea of the spot at which the crime was committed. And so," concluded Thornhill meekly, "I thought perhaps I ought to drive to the police station."

"You'll do nothing of the sort, Frank Thornhill," declared the old schoolmistress sternly. "You'll drive me straight back to my house."

"Very good, Miss Perks." Thornhill obediently restarted the car.

"I've got my brooch back without the assistance of the police," muttered the old lady, as they were held up for a moment by the automatic traffic signals at the entrance to the town, "and that's enough for me. No one but a fool troubles the police unless he is obliged to."

Thornhill did not reply to this remark. The light changed to green, and he was fully occupied in driving through the Saturday afternoon congestion in the Chesworth High Street.

Set down at the door of her house in the Pavement, Miss Perks paused a moment.

"Frank Thornhill," she said, "it's a pity you never married a sensible young woman who could look after you properly."

"I have often thought so myself."

"I suppose it is even yet not too late, if you can find a suitable person who has the advantage of knowing nothing about you."

"That's just the snag."

"I'm afraid you'll have to look beyond Chesworth," added the old lady grimly.

"I thought of trying one of these Mediterranean cruises," murmured Thornhill.

She looked at him and, with no further comment, went into the house. Even as Thornhill reversed his car, he could hear her slamming the two bolts home.

VIII. Miss Perks Makes A Call

On Monday morning the Reverend William Chandos, rector of Chesworth, sat in his study writing letters. He was a man of abundant energy and never suffered from those after-effects of Sunday which afflict most of his cloth, and have added a word to the English language. Not for him that Mondayish feeling.

He glanced at the clock and laid down his pen. In the afternoon, he remembered, he was to officiate at the funeral of Douglas Bonar. There would be a large crowd. Probably all Chesworth, and many people from outside. It was rather disgusting, the avid curiosity which was shown on these occasions, and yet very natural.

He wondered whether Miss Martindale would attend her uncle's funeral. He wondered a good deal about Miss Martindale. He had heard that she was the favourite niece of Douglas Bonar; and report named her as the sole heiress to all her uncle's money and estates. It appeared that she was to live at the Park. She therefore automatically became one of his most influential parishioners. It would be his duty to console her in her affliction. He had never met her, and, indeed, had only become aware of her existence during the week-end. She was said to be both handsome and intelligent. He hoped she would attend the funeral. He had meditated a letter of sympathy, but if she were present at the ceremony, he would probably have an opportunity of speaking to her, and his condolences would come better by word of mouth.

The rector crossed to the mantelpiece and filled his pipe. He was inclined to think highly of Miss Martindale in advance. She would be a distinct acquisition. . . .

"Mr. Rudd to see you, sir."

The grim little housekeeper's announcement took the

rector by surprise. John Rudd was a pillar of nonconformity. He had never called at the rectory before. What could he want now, and on a Monday morning?

"Show him in."

Rudd came in, balancing his bowler hat a little nervously. He was a tall, loose-limbed man. He wore a blue suit. A black tie testified his enduring loyalty to the memory of Mrs. Rudd, who had died many years before. His hair had been dark, but was turning grey. His moustache was still jet-black.

"Good morning, Mr. Rudd," said the rector, shaking hands, and using the effusive manner he adopted towards those he would have avoided socially if he had not been obliged to meet them professionally. "Do sit down."

Rudd's eyes dwelt for a moment upon the crucifix that hung above the rector's desk. His face twisted in distaste, and he took the offered chair as reluctantly as though he had been offered a front seat in the house of Rimmon.

"And what can I do for you?" said the rector genially. His mind sought for possible motives of Rudd's visit. "About Sunday games, is it?" That seemed likely. . . . Rudd was coming to suggest a united Christian front, thought the rector. He must be headed off. "It looks, Mr. Rudd," he went on quickly, "as if the matter had been taken out of our hands. The Council have already decided to open the new swimming-bath on Sundays, and at their next meeting, I understand, they are to discuss Sunday play on their tennis-courts and putting-greens. They will probably feel that if they have allowed the one, they must logically allow the other."

"And where is it to stop . . . Mr. Chandos?" demanded Rudd, too proud to bring himself to address the other as "rector." "We have cinemas on the Sabbath, and now we are to have public bathing by both sexes on the Lord's day, and, it seems, tennis and golfing as well. Tell me, Mr. Chandos, where is it to stop?"

"Why, you know, Mr. Rudd," said the rector, looking down his nose, "I think in all probability it will stop there for some time. Won't you smoke? Let me pass you the tobacco-jar. Or you will find some cigarettes in the box on that little table."

"Thank you," said Rudd stiffly. "I do not indulge in tobacco in any form."

"I am afraid I am wedded to the vice," said the rector. He blew out a cloud of smoke in evidence. "Yes, we are cautious people in Chesworth. We do things by degrees."

Rudd resented the rector's taking it upon himself to speak for the people of Chesworth.

"If you think, sir, there is not a strong body of opinion in Chesworth opposed to this profanation of the Sabbath, you are very much mistaken."

"Oh, undoubtedly. Undoubtedly. There is a great deal to be said on both sides."

"There may be much to be said on both sides," said Rudd dourly, "but you, sir, should know there is only one side that can be taken by people of religion."

"Oh, I don't know, Mr. Rudd." The rector jibbed at the suggestion that he must be taught his duty. "The Sabbath was made for man, you know, not man for the Sabbath."

"Made so that he could rest," retorted Rudd. "And what sort of a Day of Rest can it be with young men and women chasing balls about, and showing themselves off in bathing-costumes? Not to think of the attendants who are robbed of their seventh day so that . . ."

"Oh, come, Mr. Rudd," interrupted the rector. "There's no need to"—the metaphor unconsciously suggested itself—"to go in off the deep end about it. These things are only to be permitted during certain hours. There will be nothing to hinder the attendants, and the bathers and tennis-players, for that matter, from attending church or chapel."

"And in a pretty frame of mind they would be to profit by it!" Go in off the deep end, indeed, thought Rudd: that was a nice way to be spoken to! He glared at the rector. "Then, if the truth were known, Mr. Chandos, I suppose you are in favour of these fine goings-on on the Sabbath day?"

Chandos knitted his brows. He had been willing
enough to propitiate his caller. It was so much pleasanter
to remain on friendly terms with everyone. Yet Rudd's
tone nettled him.

"For some little time," he said, "I have been giving
earnest thought to this question of Sunday games, Mr.
Rudd. Obviously, circumstances are different here from
those obtaining in the large industrial towns; and I was
just a little in doubt whether the innovation was suited to
Chesworth. However, events have shown that a large
number of people in Chesworth want Sunday games. The
Council has swung round, too. After all, Mr. Rudd, one
must move with the times."

"I had rather be in the right with two or three . . ."
began Rudd.

"Oh, come, Mr. Rudd, what possible harm can there
be in people enjoying a swim or a game of tennis before
coming to church? None at all." Indeed, if it would annoy
persons like Rudd, the rector was ashamed to find
himself thinking, he would go the whole hog and have
Sunday cricket and football, and dancing in the Square
on Sunday nights, and fairs and carnivals in the streets
on Sunday evenings during festive seasons . . . ox-
roasting, perhaps, and Marathon races and chasing the
greasy pig.

"Then we must agree to differ," Rudd was saying; and
he added, ill-advisedly: "I for one am not going to trim my
sails to catch the wind of popularity."

"Really, Mr. Rudd!" The rector bridled. "That is an
offensive suggestion. You must at least give some of us
credit for trying to be Christians even if we do not think it
necessary to pull long faces and behave like hide-bound
Puritans."

Rudd clutched his bowler hat and rose convulsively
from his chair.

"After that," he said, "I shall have the pleasure of
wishing you good day."

The rector's long legs reached the door first. He held it open with a courteous smile.

"I'm sorry if you really must be going, Mr. Rudd."

"I'll not stay in this house a moment longer," declared Rudd, marching out. He crossed the hall. On the threshold he stopped with a puzzled expression. After a few moments' consideration he turned back.

"Yet there's something else I have to say to you," he said, standing in the doorway of the study. "As a matter of fact, it was not in connection with Sunday games that I came to see you at all."

"Then come and sit down, man," said the rector heartily. "Let me offer you a . . . a glass of wine. Perhaps we were both just a little . . ."

"No, thank you, I will not sit down. Nor do I touch intoxicants." The rector retreated to his hearthrug and glanced dubiously at this uncomfortable visitor. "I will just say what I meant to say and go," went on Rudd. "It's about Mr. Michael Holt."

"About Holt, eh?"

Rudd glared at the rector with a sternness born of the embarrassment he himself was feeling.

"It is my duty to contradict the unpleasant rumours circulating about him in the town."

"Rumours?" said the rector automatically. "What rumours? Are there any rumours?"

"There are, I am sorry to say."

"And who started these unpleasant rumours?"

"That's beside the point," said Rudd, Hushing. "The important thing is that the rumours are quite unfounded. Mr. Holt is perfectly innocent of the charges brought against him. I should like this to be generally known."

"And why do you come to me to say this?" asked the rector blandly.

"Because," retorted Rudd, with the suspicion of a smile flickering over his grim jaws, "I wanted it to be generally known."

With this parting shot, he walked swiftly out of the

house before the rector had a chance to reply.

He paused on emerging from the shabby rectory gates, and saw Sprague strolling down the Pavement under the pollarded trees.

Rudd did not suffer bores gladly. As a rule he fled when he saw Sprague in the offing. He could summon up no interest in Sprague's Splendid Daughters. On this Monday morning he looked about instinctively as usual for means of escape, then hesitated, smiled sardonically, and deliberately courted the encounter. Sprague was delighted to meet him.

"We've just heard from Polly. She sent her mother the jolliest little toy dog. At least I thought it was a toy dog, but my wife laughed at me. She said it was a lady's nightdress case. Rather embarrassing, eh? But it's made up to look just like a Peke. With a zip fastener in his tummy. Very cleverly done. Buttons for eyes. Almost a human expression. Clever the things they have in the big stores nowadays. Polly bought it at Selfridge's. I suppose you could keep pyjamas in it too. Most ladies nowadays would, eh?" Sprague tittered. "But that's like Polly. She always was generous, though how she manages to exist in London on her salary as a dispenser and still constantly send her mother little presents, I can't understand. I think she must be a very good manager, don't you? One thing, though, is certain, though perhaps her father is not the right person to say it, and that is she will be a prize for a man some day. Perhaps the day is not so very far off, either." A chuckle. "Polly's very guarded in what she writes home. Girls will be, won't they? But my wife has all the intuition her sex is credited with, and she's positive there's something in it. A most clever fellow too, reading between the lines. Almost any post would be open to him, but he's content to slave away at the hospital on an absurd wage to get all the experience he can. Very sound, don't you think? Still, it means they will have to wait a bit before they can get married. Not a bad thing, perhaps. I don't approve of long courtships, but hasty marriages are just as foolish. Somehow, for Polly's sake, I hope it won't be too long. She's very domesticated. Una is a different kind of girl altogether. You would almost think she had no use for young men at all. I dare say she'll grow out of that. Not natural, eh? But at present it's nothing but athletics with her. She's taken to golf with amazing enthusiasm, and she looks like being as good at that as she is at badminton. I told you, I think, that she played badminton for the ladies of Sussex? It wouldn't surprise me in the least if she represented her county at golf too. I can tell you this. Her poor old dad won't be able to go on giving her a stroke a hole much longer. Oh, dear, no! The boot will soon be on the other foot." Sprague laughed heartily.

Rudd resolutely cut in.

"I wanted to speak to you about Mr. Michael Holt, Mr. Sprague."

Sprague turned suddenly grave.

"Oh, Holt? Yes?"

"And about that deficit we found in our accounts shortly after he disappeared so suddenly from Chesworth years ago."

"Yes," murmured Sprague sympathetically. "A painful business for you, but I think you acted quite rightly. As you said, since he had been so injudicious as to return quite openly to Chesworth . . ."

"Never mind what I said. It was a mistake. I wish to withdraw it. There is no imputation on Mr. Holt at all. I find he was perfectly innocent in the matter."

Sprague stared, deprived miraculously of speech.

"I wanted to tell you that," said Rudd, with a wintry smile. "Good morning, Mr. Sprague."

He was off, threading his way swiftly among the parked cars. Sprague was left gazing in bewilderment at his disappearing back.

Rudd walked on towards his works. He was thinking of Mrs. Stevens. She had come to see him on Saturday afternoon, and her visit had left his mind in a state of confusion. The one thing about which he had remained in no doubt was Rose's firm conviction of Michael Holt's innocence. She assured him, positively, that Holt had not taken the money. Then who had? How was it to be explained, Rudd asked himself, frowning involuntarily at a display of bathing-costumes in Shilling & Mapp's windows. Had old George Nichol secretly withdrawn the money for some occult purpose of his own? Was Rose herself involved in the mystery? But that was absurd. Then there remained Gerald Stevens. . . .

Rudd instinctively sheered off such dangerous ground. He had had enough of rumours and scandals. He meant to be mixed up with no more of them. Better forget the whole business. It happened a long time ago. Let sleeping dogs lie. Hush it up. . . . He would do a great deal more than that for his old master's daughter. . . .

Well, he had eaten his words. He had humiliated himself. He had told the rector . . . and he had told Sprague. A pity he had not thought of Sprague first. That would have spared him the interview with the rector. Sprague was certainly the proper person to go to.

If he had stood in a white sheet at the bull-ring in the Square, thought Rudd, and shouted his retractation to the assembled populace, he could not have spread the news more effectually. . . .

He entered his office quietly and surprised the rosy-faced office-boy with feet propped on desk and head in a copy' of *Motor Cycling*.

The rosy-faced office-boy received a dressing-down that he remembered for a month.

2

Michael, who usually took exercise in the afternoon, stayed at home that Monday because of Bonar's funeral. The weather was fine and he worked in the garden. Presently a car drew up at the gate of the Vineyard, and Thornhill's voice was heard giving a cheery hail.

"Come for a joy-ride, Michael?"

"I should like to," said Michael, coming to the gate, "but I don't want to run into the gaping crowds who'll be making holiday."

"I thought of that, but it's all right. They'll be at the cemetery now, at Hillside, and the coast will be clear. Perhaps Mary would like to come too."

"Thanks. I'll ask her."

He returned with a message of thanks from his wife who, however, begged to be excused. He himself climbed into the seat next Thornhill, and the car picked its way through Chesworth northward. At Roughey it left the main road and took a lane on the edge of the forest, a lane bordered with ancient trees twisted into humorous shapes. They turned southward along the main London to Brighton road at Pease Pottage, and Michael watched the speedometer quiver quickly up to fifty.

"That's unlike your usual style of driving, Frank," he said.

Thornhill laughed and decelerated.

"I'm a moody devil to-day."

They took to the lanes again at the entrance to Handcross. More ancient trees, bowed and twisted into Rackhamesque attitudes. Thornhill was unusually quiet.

"Miss Perks has been advising me to go away," he said at length.

"Oh! Why?"

"She thinks I need a sensible wife, and my best chance of finding one is in some place where I am not so well known."

Michael laughed.

"How very Miss Perks!. . . But . . ."

"Yes, I know what you mean," said Thornhill. He paused at a fork in the road before committing himself to a right-hand branch. "I'm not sure that anything is coming of that. The Mediterranean invested our meeting with a false glamour. In the paler light of Chesworth we see more plainly. Miss Martindale," he added, steering carefully round a woman cyclist, "is . . . Well, I suppose the honest truth of the matter is that she's too good for me in a number of ways."

"Oh, nonsense," said Michael encouragingly.

Privately he had come to think it might turn out an excellent marriage. Miss Martindale, as an exheadmistress of a domestic economy centre, had qualities that Thornhill lacked. Thornhill, as Thornhill, had accomplishments not usually in the repertory of headmistresses. They could atone for one another's deficiencies.

"It isn't nonsense," said Thornhill gloomily. He said nothing more for five minutes, and then he said, "Damn!" The narrow road was almost entirely blocked by a steam-engine attached to an enormous lorry bearing the painted inscription, "Sylvester's Galloping Horses. Fairs attended. Healthy and Harmless Recreation for All Classes." An elderly man in his shirt-sleeves sat, chewing at a straw, in the driver's seat. The engine was stationary. To judge from the elderly man's expression, like that of Patience on the monument, it had been stationary for some time.

"Now what are we going to do?" said Thornhill.

"Want to get past?" inquired the elderly man, removing the straw from his mouth.

"I had some idea of the sort."

"Sorry." The elderly man grinned pleasantly. "You'll have to wait, I'm afraid, till Sam comes back. Shouldn't be long now."

"Had a breakdown?"

"Just a little matter of a bolt or something," said the elderly man vaguely. "I'm an old-timer and I don't understand these things. Sam he knows. Sam he puts a bit of her works in his pocket and off he goes to a smithy we passed up the road. He'll put her to rights in a brace of shakes as soon as he gets back."

"Well, it's a nice afternoon for loitering," said Thornhill good-humouredly. He held out his tobacco-pouch.

"Thankee, but I don't smoke a pipe. Somehow I could never master a pipe. It always got the better of me. It always turned me up, a pipe did."

Michael produced a cigarette-case.

"Ah, thankee, sir. That's more within my capabilities."

"Did I hear a gentleman say something about a cigarette?" A younger fellow with a gaudy scarf round his neck and a twinkle in his blue eyes strolled leisurely up from behind the lorry.

"Hullo, me lord," said the elderly man facetiously, "where you been to? Hiding from the police?" He chuckled: his allusion appeared to be topical.

"I missed my usual after-luncheon cigar, and I could do with a cigarette if there's nothing better going."

He looked at Michael and winked. Michael, who had recognized his voice at once, silently held out his cigarette-case. The man with the scarf helped himself and winked again.

"Did you get your spade back, sir?" he asked.

"Yes, thanks," said Michael.

Thornhill glanced at him curiously.

The man with the scarf turned to the philosopher on the engine seat.

"This will interest you, Henry. It's what you might call a coincidence."

"It don't matter what I call it," said the elderly man, lighting his cigarette. "Either it's a coincidence or it isn't.

"Well, it is, Henry. Here am I, a couple of hours ago stopped by the police in East Grinstead, and invited to explain what part I took in standing up for the public rights in Chesworth the other night, and particularly what I did with the spade. Here am I, now, accepting a cigarette and, I hope, a light—I am much obliged, sir— from the gent I borrowed the spade from. Is that a coincidence, Henry?"

"It is a coincidence, James," said Henry solemnly.

"The police have been interviewing everyone who was up there that night," said Michael.

"That's a comforting thought, sir."

"And I suppose," said Thornhill, lazily intervening, "you told them the exact truth?"

The man with the blarneying voice winked again.

"I always do, sir. The police and I are on very confidential terms. I told them I'd done my bit for democracy with the spade, and then, not seeing its owner, gave it up to a skinny little gentleman in knickerbockers —begging your pardon for the description, sir, if he's a friend of yours—who promised to see that it got back to the right quarter."

"And was that all they wanted, James?"

"That was not. They wanted to know if I saw anything or heard anything that could throw any light on something that happened later on."

"And you hadn't, James?"

"I couldn't oblige them at all, Henry."

"Ah, you wouldn't, James." The elderly man chuckled a second time.

"So we parted with best wishes on both sides. . . . That sounds to me like Sam."

Sam wore oil-stained overalls and had a dirty face. He carried a bit of machinery under his arm.

"Got the doings, Sam?"

Sam did not answer a word. He took a spanner and busied himself with nuts. After two minutes, during which Henry and James watched him with mild interest, he stepped back, sighed, and said: "I reckon she'll do now."

Henry retired from the driver's seat to a less prominent perch, and Sam took the wheel. "Back her a bit into the gate," said Henry.

James took up a watching brief in the rear and with some difficulty Sylvester's Galloping Horses made way for Thornhill's car to scrape through.

"Give my love to the Chesworth police," called James as they drew clear.

On the return journey Thornhill deliberately set

himself to talk with animation about nothing in particular. It was Michael's turn to be mute. He thought all the more, and the spade was the centre around which his thoughts revolved. This latest revelation seemed to implicate Chrystal more deeply. Why had he said nothing about returning the spade? What was he concealing? There was some secret. Like Michael, Chrystal had strong motives for a lack of frankness. . . . And that is putting it pretty mildly, said Michael to himself. We are a pretty pair of dissemblers, Chrystal and I.

3

When he parted from Thornhill at the gate of the Vineyard, Michael was not surprised to see a familiar bicycle propped up inside the little drive. Sergeant Whalebone was standing at the door.

"Oh, here you are, Michael," said Mary. "The sergeant wishes to see you."

She spoke curtly, as though she were out of patience with all these proceedings.

"I shan't keep you a minute, sir," said Whalebone. He spoke the formula cheerfully enough, but he looked tired and worried. Evidently a murder case was not proving such exciting and fascinating work as he had hoped. The sergeant had indeed been working overtime on seemingly interminable and almost always fruitless inquiries.

A twinkle came into Whalebone's eye. He had thought of a joke. "That's what it is," he told himself. "Spadework. Nothing but spadework."

"Come along in, sergeant," said Michael wearily.

Whalebone put his cap on the carpet at the side of his chair, and brought out his notebook.

"It's about your spade, sir. I just want to check up on one or two particulars. I think you said you lent the spade to a stranger on the hill and that you saw nothing more of it until the following morning?"

Michael knew he was treading on dangerous ground.

What story had Chrystal told Scotland Yard? Had he said anything about the spade? If so, did his account square with Michael's?

"That is so," said Michael quietly. He had decided that there was nothing for it but to stick to his original statement.

"In the morning you found it in your garden?" continued Whalebone. "You have no idea who returned it or how it got there?"

"None at all."

The sergeant made no comment.

"With regard to the spade, sir, I am afraid we may have to keep it a little longer." He looked up from his book. "There are no traces of its having been used for the purpose we had in mind."

"That's a comforting thought," murmured Michael.

"But we have a sort of idea that it had been carefully cleaned before being stuck in the soil. We think sandpaper might have been used."

The devil they did, thought Michael.

"I suppose you know nothing about that, sir?" said the sergeant.

"Nothing at all."

"Well, sir, I am sorry to have bothered you and thank you," said Whalebone, rising. "I hope I shan't have to trouble you again, but you never know."

Michael smiled politely, for the sergeant evidently intended his last words as a jest. He saw Whalebone to the gate, and lingered casually until the bicycle was out of sight. After that, he went into the tool-shed. It was not the first time he had examined it closely since the fatal night. He assured himself again that everything was in order. The burnt rag and the burnt sandpaper had left no traces. If the police took it into their heads to search the premises—as well they might if Chrystal had blundered—they would find nothing at all to interest them.

Mary was calling from the door of the house.

"Come and have your tea, Michael."

"Already? I haven't heard the boys come back."

"They've gone out to tea with some friends."

Michael went upstairs to wash and to compose himself for a *tete-a-tete* with his wife. He had seen a certain look in Mary's eyes and he understood it. She was not sorry that the boys had gone out. She welcomed this opportunity of having him to herself for a quarter of an hour. She was going to ask questions. He made a grimace and saw it reflected in the mirror. "I'm getting into this pretty deep," he told himself. Could a dilemma have three horns? This one had.

Thinking of horned creatures, he recalled the cow which kept swishing her tail though she knew it could not reach the most troublesome flies. He had behaved like that when he had whipped himself into indignation about that absurd charge of Rudd's. Changing the simile, he compared himself to a man who chases away a small boy with a pea-shooter, well knowing that two stout desperadoes close in on him meanwhile with intent to kill.

He went downstairs.

As soon as he came into the drawing-room, Mary asked him what the police had wanted.

"It was about that damned spade again." He had told her on the previous occasion exactly what he had told the police. "I think," he added, "they have found the man I lent it to; but they don't seem to attach much importance to it."

"Who is he?"

"A man attached to a travelling fair. I suppose he was with those shows on the Jews' Meadow last week."

"They don't think he did it?"

"Apparently not."

She said nothing more until she had poured out the tea. Michael put his cup and his plate on the little table next his chair, and made no attempt to eat or drink. Mary began her attack.

"There's something worrying you, dear. I wish you would tell me what it is."

Michael looked down his nose.

"It's not money, is it? Because if it is . . ."

"No, it isn't money. At any rate, not more than usual." He forced a smile. "I'm a bit under the weather, I think."

"Caught a chill? You were out on that awful night when . . ."

"I don't think it's a chill. It . . ." He caught at the first reasonable explanation that suggested itself. "The book's not going as it should."

"Is that it?" She smiled. It was the rather sad smile of a woman who had been married to an author for ten years. Writers were difficult people to be married to: a woman who made a success of it, she was accustomed to tell herself, deserved a medal. "I might have known," she added. "I thought you were concealing some dreadful secret from me."

Michael moved his head uneasily. Mary did not appear to notice the movement. Her own head was tilted to one side. It was her characteristic gesture when she was thinking seriously.

"Why not drop everything," she said suddenly, "and go right away for a fortnight?"

"By myself?"

"Well . . ." She looked at him mischievously. "I haven't arrived at that stage yet," protested her husband. "You're not getting on my nerves. I'm not hating the sight of you."

"Nice to know that. . . . Still, I think you need a change. We can go together if you really prefer it."

"And the boys?"

"Take them with us. After all, the prep, school will contrive to bear up. It's not as if they were Council school children. We shan't have a summons from the attendance officer. . .. Or we might pack them off to that farm near Wisborough Green which we liked so much when we stayed there last year. It would do them no harm to run loose with the village boys for a fortnight, and Mrs. Drake would look after them like a mother."

"They would pick up worse words than 'guts.'"

"Perhaps they would." Mary's smile meant that she was prepared to take the risk in a good cause.

"And shocking habits."

"I shouldn't think so. If they do return to us picking their teeth or forgetting what handkerchiefs were made for, we can cure them while they are still young."

"I believe for once you are thinking of me instead of the boys," said Michael with a propitiatory grin.

"I believe for once I am."

"Very well. We'll send Hugh and Ken off to Mrs. Drake asking her to feed them well and be a mother to them in all respects. If I remember rightly, she has a good stout arm."

Mary refused to be drawn.

"I think it's a very good idea," she said placidly.

"Very well, then . . ."

Michael hesitated. He had been visited by a ridiculous vision. He saw himself taking tickets at the Chesworth booking-office window. A detective tapped him on the shoulder. "I beg your pardon, sir, but where might you be off to?" "I am going away for a short holiday," said Michael in his vision. "Oh, you are, are you?" The visionary detective went up to the booking-office window. "Give me a ticket to the place that gentleman has booked to." Michael, in his vision, saw the detective making himself comfortable in a corner of the same compartment. . . .

Was that how it would happen?

No. It was impossible to run away from Chesworth at this moment. He would have to stay and, if necessary, face the music. . . .

"No, old woman. It can't be done. Funds won't run to it. Besides, I must get that book finished. A contract is a contract. I can't overrun the date. I shall be all right in a day or two. I'll make an effort and pull myself together. It's only a question of sticking to it. You mustn't fuss over me like this. You'll be persuading me next that I have an artistic temperament."

She made a little face.

"Which, of course, is the last thing you possess. . . . Have a sandwich? If you want to convince me that you are normal, you must eat your tea."

He made an effort to consume reassuring quantities of food. He caught Mary's eye regarding him speculatively from time to time. She was only too obviously full of an unsatisfied desire for information; but she said nothing more. Ultimately Michael was allowed to escape into the garden without any spoken protest. Mary remained behind, and thought steadily for several minutes before she stirred herself to ring the bell for Susan.

4

Mary remembered she had to go to the High Street before the shops closed. She took the footpath way along the Denne, and as she crossed the river she met Miss Perks. Miss Perks was standing on the little bridge and regarding the Garden of Remembrance with a jaundiced eye.

"That fence!" she exclaimed in her deep tones. "Why don't they pull it down?" She turned her critical look on Mary. "What have you got to worry about?"

The question surprised Mary. She had not suspected Miss Perks of so much insight.

"Do I look worried? I've nothing at all to worry about." She added involuntarily: "Michael is not too fit. That's all."

"I should have thought that was something to worry about," said the old lady caustically. "What is the matter with Michael?"

"He's feeling a little bothered."

"Bothered? What about?"

"The book he's writing. He thinks it's not going well."

"H'm," said Miss Perks. Her gaze made Mary

uncomfortable. "Are you looking after your husband properly?"

"I hope so," said Mary good-humouredly.

"H'm," said Miss Perks again. "Well, I must be getting along."

She took the path along which Mary had come, and presently she gained the Vineyard and turned in at the gate.

Michael was digging furiously near the tool-shed. He had prescribed himself the exercise as a prophylactic. Thornhill, he knew, would have quoted:

The cure for this ill is not to sit still
Or frowst with a book by the fire:
But to take a large hoe and a shovel also
And dig till you gently perspire.

He grinned at the "large hoe and shovel also." Gallant fellow, Kipling! He would shove in anything to fill a line up. There was nothing wrong with the philosophy, however.

He heard a deep voice at his elbow.

"Kipling, I think?"

"Hullo, Miss Perks. I didn't know I was reciting the piece aloud."

"There's no harm in reciting Kipling aloud. If it had been one of those milk-and-water pretty fellows who pass for poets nowadays, you might have blushed. But there's no shame in a man knowing Kipling."

"Thornhill would agree with you."

"Frank Thornhill!" There was something in Miss Perks's tone that suggested she did not attach a high value to the literary judgments of her former pupil.

Michael leaned on his fork and smiled at the dour little figure in black.

"I see you're using a fork."

The fact was so obvious as to require no comment. Michael wondered: it was not Miss Perks's habit to make unnecessary remarks.

"Are you looking for Mary? I'm afraid she's gone down town."

"No. Oddly enough, I'm looking for you." Miss Perks's eyes wandered down the path. "You have a large garden. There's a seat under the tree yonder. Shall we sit there?"

Michael, puzzled, put on his coat, and accompanied her to the rough wooden bench.

"I'm afraid it's not very comfortable. Let me fetch you a cushion."

"Thank you. I carry a very useful little cushion about with me," said Miss Perks, sitting down plumply without a smile. "We are not likely to be overheard here, are we?"

"How very mysterious you are! No, I should think we are quite safe."

"Where are those two rascals of yours?" demanded Miss Perks, looking suspiciously up into the boughs of the oak.

"Hugh and Ken? Oh, they're not up there. They've gone out to tea."

"I'm glad to hear it. Well, I've come to set your mind at ease."

"Splendid," said Michael. He wondered what on earth the old lady was driving at. He gave her a side-glance and could make nothing of her grim smile.

"I believe in cutting the cackle," said Miss Perks. "In the first place, there's that little question of the reason for your leaving Chesworth . . . when was it?"

"Fourteen years ago."

"John Rudd said you took with you twelve hundred pounds from the company's funds."

"I know. I'm thinking of taking legal action about that."

"You needn't bother. John Rudd has eaten his words. He now says it wasn't you who took the twelve hundred pounds."

"That's the sort of man he is," said Michael warmly. He still found it easy to whip up a show of indignation over this matter. "He airily flings a charge of embezzlement against me, and then just as airily withdraws it."

"Not very airily. If you knew John Rudd as well as I do, you would never accuse him of doing anything airily."

"Perhaps not," said Michael. "Airily is the wrong word. I'll substitute . . ."

He could not think of the word he wanted to substitute.

"I shouldn't worry, if I were you," said Miss Perks.

"It's an irresponsible sort of thing to do. Yes, that's the word: irresponsible. I shall make Rudd advertise a public apology."

"He has."

"I don't understand."

"He's told Mr. Sprague," said the little old lady dryly. "That is as good as advertising it in the *Chesworth Chronicle*. Better, in fact. Mr. Sprague is our local broadcasting-station. And then," added Miss Perks thoughtfully, "as if it were not enough to tell Mr. Sprague, I believe John Rudd has confided in the rector too. You can't say the poor man hasn't done his best to spread the news."

Michael was somewhat mollified.

"In that case, perhaps the best thing will be to let the matter drop."

"That's magnanimous of you." Her tone was sarcastic. Michael looked at her. She returned his look. "Michael Holt," she said sternly, "is that all there is on your mind?"

Michael wriggled under her inspection as if he were one of her small pupils again and had done something he should not have done.

"No," he said.

"I thought not." Miss Perks turned her face away. "Well, you're behaving very stupidly. You have nothing to worry about."

"I really don't understand you, Miss Perks."

"Surely you do. You're not so stupid as you pretend.

Don't think I don't understand your character, Michael
Holt. You're secretive and you're inclined to be obstinate,
but you're not. . . and nobody will make me believe it . . .
you're not . . ."

She paused.

Some people said "anyone" and "no one" while others
said "anybody" and "nobody," reflected Michael. They
were two distinct camps, like those who put the tea into
the cup first and those who first put in the milk. Did
everyone (or everybody) notice such things at the oddest
moments, or simply writing people like himself?. . . Could
Miss Perks have that moustache removed by some
painless process, and, if so, why didn't she? Perhaps she
wilfully cultivated it, to add a little extra grimness to that
already sufficiently alarming countenance. . . .

"Make you believe what?" he heard himself saying
aloud.

"Make me believe. . . Well, it's not a question of what I
believe. I know. I know you didn't kill that man Bonar."

Michael came back to the wakeaday world, like a man
coming out of gas.

"Of course I didn't kill Bonar," he said.

"Equally, of course," retorted Miss Perks, "you are
afraid that you may be suspected of killing the man."

"Well . . ." He made a gesture of helplessness with his
hands.

"And I tell you," said Miss Perks firmly, "that it's
nonsense to be afraid. You may be suspected: probably
you will be. Very likely you haven't told the whole truth
to the police . . ."

She waited. Michael said nothing.

"That doesn't matter. The important thing is that you
didn't murder that man Bonar. Get that into your head,
Michael Holt. If you didn't do it, what need is there to
worry about it?"

Michael faced her.

"How do you know," he asked slowly, "that I didn't kill
Bonar?"

Miss Perks rose.

"Michael Holt," she said, "I have given you some good advice. You'd better take it: for your own good and the sake of your wife and family. And now I must be going." Michael walked mechanically beside her. "You don't do much watering, I see. Perhaps you're wise: once you start you have to keep on. It's like paying blackmail. We need rain. I don't know what's come over this climate of ours; but the world's been turned upside down since the war, and if you turn the world upside down you must affect the atmosphere, I suppose." With this original contribution to meteorological theory, Miss Perks reached the gate. There she paused just long enough to add: "I doubt whether the police will ever find out who killed that man Bonar. That's a comforting thought for somebody. You will be kind enough to treat what I have said to you as confidential, Michael Holt. Good-bye."

Her sturdy little figure clumped away towards the town.

Michael went back to his digging. He was very thoughtful. He had been visited by a flash of intuition. He knew now who had killed Douglas Bonar. . . .

5

One thing puzzled Michael considerably as he dug. Miss Perks was wearing a little gold brooch. He could not understand why that little gold brooch should have been lying on the scene of the crime. . . .

"Oh, there you are, Holt!"

"Hullo, Chrystal," said Michael coldly. He did not trouble to stop digging or to look up at the sound of that thin, metallic, peevish voice.

"Really, Holt, it's too bad. It's . . . it's not English. It's like the Inquisition. Really, I had no idea such extraordinary things could happen in our country."

"What's been happening?" asked Michael, pausing with his foot on the fork.

"Why, I . . . I say, do you mind if we sit down, old chap?"

"Is that how you feel?" thought Michael. He glanced at Chrystal. The little man was obviously in a pitiable state. Michael dropped his fork reluctantly. "There's a bench under the oak." He walked with Chrystal to the bench on which Miss Perks had been sitting.

Chrystal dropped on to it and sat huddled up, with his face in his hands. Michael stood watching him.

"Really, I wish you'd sit down," Chrystal exclaimed irritably. He added: "I'm sorry. Really I don't mean to be rude, but I hate people watching me. It seems to me I'm being watched all the time now."

"Well, if it's any comfort to you . . ." Michael sat down beside him. "How's Mrs. Chrystal?"

Chrystal brightened.

"Oh, she's very well, thanks. I think really she's better now than she has been for some time. She's not really strong, you know. Housework knocks her up. I've been pressing her to get a daily help for some time. Extraordinary how she would insist on doing all the work herself."

Michael smiled in his sleeve. He had seen the interior of the semi-bungalow under Mrs. Chrystal's management.

There was a pause.

"Holt," said Chrystal suddenly, "I've just come from spending two hours at the police station."

"Oh! Hence your reference to the Inquisition?"

"You don't sound very sympathetic, Holt. I hope you will never have to go through it yourself."

"I hope I never shall." Michael kicked a pebble away from him. "Seen the Scotland Yard men?"

"Seen them? I've been cross-examined by them for two hours. Really, I scarcely knew at the end of it what I was saying."

"I hope you said the right things. What are they after now?"

"I suppose," said Chrystal bitterly, "they're trying to convict me out of my own mouth. They've made up their minds I killed Bonar. I really do believe they think so. If it wasn't for one thing, I'm sure they would have arrested me there and then."

"Oh, and what was that?"

"When they searched the house they took away the suit I was wearing on that night. I believe they expected to find blood-stains on it."

"And didn't they?"

"Of course they didn't."

"Did they say so?"

"They wouldn't admit it, but they would have been quick enough to say so if they had. You see, the inquest report said that the blow severed an artery. Bonar must have bled like a pig. So they expected to find blood on my clothes."

"I see."

"Then, again," said Chrystal truculently, "could I possibly have lifted Bonar's body and thrown it into the river?"

"Not without assistance."

"Who was going to assist me? Really, Holt, the whole idea's absurd."

"It doesn't follow that the person who threw Bonar's body into the water was the person who killed him."

Chrystal stared.

"But who else would want to do such a thing?"

"That's an interesting question," said Michael.

Chrystal looked at him and was silent. He scowled.

"You haven't told me why Scotland Yard wanted to see you again," suggested Michael.

"I believe you know," muttered Chrystal suspiciously.

"I? Why should I know?"

Chrystal drummed with his fingers on the seat. "It's that damned spade of yours. . . . Holt, what did you tell the police about that spade of yours?"

"Just what I told you. Naturally."

"You see, I . . ." Chrystal was very unhappy. "Really, I suppose it was my fault partly. I left it out of my first account."

"What do you mean?"

"I mean I didn't say anything about the spade when they first saw me."

"Why should you?" asked Michael.

"Because I brought it back from the hill for you."

"The devil you did!"

"The fellow you lent it to on the hill asked me to bring it back because he couldn't find you."

"That's true enough," thought Michael, smiling.

"But . . . but I dropped it on the way."

Michael waited. Things were turning out more or less as he expected.

"And naturally the Scotland Yard people wanted to know why I didn't say anything about it before."

"Naturally. And how did you explain it?"

Chrystal looked at him defiantly.

"I told them the truth."

"Always the best way, as Miss Perks used to tell us."

"I wasn't one of her pupils," snapped Chrystal.

"No. You missed that experience. It was your loss."

"Really, I . . ." Chrystal resented Michael's manner. Nothing but the irresistible desire to confide in someone induced him to go on. "I suppose," he said, somewhat aggressively, "you're wondering why I didn't tell the police in the first place." He changed his tone. "Holt," he asked nervously, "do you mind if I tell you this in confidence?"

"I am a specialist in keeping secrets," answered Michael solemnly.

"Thanks, Holt. I had to tell Scotland Yard, but . . . but really I shouldn't like anybody else to know. I came down from the field, carrying your spade, which I'd promised to bring back for you, and when I was outside our house . . . The hell I went through that night, Holt!"

"Go on," said Michael encouragingly.

"The light was still on in our sitting-room and . . . and I saw the shadow of a man on the curtains."

Michael looked at him curiously.

"Well, what of it?"

"Well, really . . . It was eleven o'clock at night and . . . Oh, hang it all, Holt, you would never understand. You've never . . ." The little man was almost crying.

"I'd noticed several little things in the last few weeks. I was rather wrought up about them. Probably without any reason. . . . But at the time I thought . . ."

"I see," said Michael.

"I was quite unjust to her." Chrystal lifted his head and looked fiercely at Michael as he said this.

"I understand. What did you do?"

"I waited until the man came out. It was Bonar. . . . As a matter of fact," added Chrystal hastily, "he had only been using our telephone. But . . . but I didn't know that. I . . . I spoke to him angrily."

"What did he say?" asked Michael, picturing with grim amusement the ill-assorted encounter in the dark lane.

"He . . . he was very angry. He said I was a . . . a fool and a liar."

"Both of which you are," thought Michael unkindly.

"Then he . . . he walked away."

"And you went into the house?"

"No. Not then. Really, I could not trust myself. I was in an extraordinary state of mind. I went for a long walk to . . ."

"To cool down?" suggested Michael. "A very sensible thing to do. And what happened to the spade?"

"Really, it . . ." Chrystal was confused. Michael reflected that he must have cut a poor figure under interrogation by Scotland Yard. "It slipped my memory altogether. I suppose I must have put it down while I was waiting for Bonar, and then, in the excitement and nervous strain, forgot all about it."

"And this is what you told Scotland Yard this

afternoon?"

"Yes, and I explained I had said nothing about it before because I did not care about discussing my wife."

"Were they satisfied?"

"I've told you they weren't," said Chrystal irritably. "They asked me an extraordinary number of questions. Really, they seemed reluctant to let me go. And I believe I'm being shadowed."

"Then they know you are talking to me now?"

"Probably."

Michael was thoughtful.

"Who put the spade back in your garden, Holt?" asked Chrystal suddenly.

"The police would like to know that too," said Michael carelessly.

"Have you had much trouble from them?" asked Chrystal eagerly.

"They've been here once or twice." Michael fished his pipe and pouch out of his jacket.

"Extraordinary about your spade. The whole thing's extraordinary." Chrystal glanced moodily towards the house. "Out there, I dare say, there's a man watching. It's a pleasant feeling to be suspected of a murder! I suppose they'll be digging up all my past history."

Michael paused in filling his pipe.

"Yes," he said gloomily, "I suppose they would do that in the case of anyone they suspected of murder."

He grinned with an effort, and added: "It's to be hoped your past will bear being looked into."

"Oh, I've no fears on that score."

Michael yawned, and disdained to conceal it.

Chrystal rose.

"I must go and . . . I don't know what I shall tell Daphne. She'll be wondering."

"Oh, I should be quite frank with her," advised Michael. "She'd better know." To himself he added: "It will do her the world of good."

"Really, I think I shall," said Chrystal. "At any rate, I

can depend on her understanding and sympathizing."

"That makes all the difference in the world," said Michael.

He lit his pipe, saw Chrystal off the premises, cast an eye in search of the attendant sleuth, could not find him, and went indoors to write a letter to a solicitor in Liverpool.

IX. A Nice Way To Behave

Thornhill did not attend Bonar's funeral, and a week passed before he saw Miss Martindale again. He received a note from her saying that she had begun the task of going through her late uncle's papers: the accumulation was enormous and she would value the assistance Frank had been kind enough to offer. It was formal but evidently designed as an olive-branch. Thornhill thought at first of drawing back. Eventually he responded to the call, but only after considerable hesitation: and he was full of misgivings when he got out the Standard and drove up to Forest Park.

As he entered the mansion he remarked that the butler, whose untidiness had been painfully obvious on his previous visit, was looking a little smarter, though not yet by any means so spick and span as a well-regulated butler should be. The difference, thought Thornhill, was such as might be observed in a small boy who, after neglecting his personal appearance during a week's holiday in the country, had been met by his mother at the station and hastily subjected to an impromptu tidying-up. Thornhill saw the hand of Kate in this and speculated upon the probable course of the butler's evolution under the modifying influence of that capable ex-schoolmistress.

"A great change for you here," he remarked sympathetically.

"You are right, sir," said the man gloomily. He seemed to be willing to say something more, but stopped in time. Thornhill guessed that his schooling had included a lecture on the proper reception of visitors. "Miss Martindale is in the upstairs room where you saw her before, sir. I was instructed to show you up at once."

"There is no need to show me up, thank you," said Thornhill, smiling. He cut short the man's murmured protest, and went up the stairs. Kate was seated at a table piled high with red-ribboned bundles of letters and documents. A desk near by carried a similar burden.

She looked up and frowned.

"I must speak to Johnson. I told him to . . ."

"Don't blame Johnson," said Thornhill. "I took the bit between my teeth." He stood in the doorway and regarded her quizzically. "Is this purely a business meeting, or may I . . ."

She calmly lifted up her face to be kissed. Thornhill found himself unable to put his whole heart into a caress which was accepted in such a matter-of-fact way. Ruefully he felt that it was rather like kissing an aunt.

"I am so glad you have come," said Kate absently. "There is a great deal to be done, as you can see."

Thornhill surveyed the stacks of red-ribboned bundles.

"Burn 'em, Kate," he advised.

Kate was shocked.

"They must all be gone through. There may be papers of the highest importance amongst them. I have left those on the desk for you. Put on one side everything you think ought to be kept. If there is any doubt, of course"—she looked at him as if she distrusted his discretion—"you must ask me."

Thornhill made a grimace; then, like a well-behaved pupil, sat down at his allotted task.

Bonar had recently attended to his correspondence himself, but for many years he had employed a secretary, and it seemed that the secretary had been a conscientious Kate-like person who had filed everything. Even begging letters had been solemnly docketed and preserved. Thornhill saw that most of the papers could go without loss to the bonfire. Yet here and there he found a good deal that interested him.

"Kate," he said, "I am glad you put me on to this job. It is good training for me. It is at least equal to a correspondence course on how to succeed in business in twelve lessons."

"I have always understood," said Kate, "that the secret is to buy in the cheapest markets and sell in the dearest."

"What a remarkably intelligent woman you are," said Thornhill in admiration. "No wonder you were your uncle's favourite niece. You express in a nutshell what was evidently the secret of his success."

"I am at present a very busy woman," retorted Kate, "and do not wish to be interrupted unless it is absolutely necessary."

"Sorry, Miss Martindale. None the less, I think you would be interested in knowing How To Make A Pickle Factory Pay."

"Did uncle have a pickle factory?"

"Amongst many other enterprises. It was the Nova Zembla Pickle Company, Limited, to the world at large, but Bonar was the guiding spirit. There's the whole history of it here in a long series of reports. Confidential, most of them: especially the later ones. The Nova Zembla Pickle, it appears, began by being a first-class pickle, one of the best pickles on the market. There was only one thing against it on the market. I mean its druggishness on the market. No one would buy it. So your uncle took over the company. Naturally it was going cheap. He amended the recipe by omitting all the expensive ingredients and substituting cheaper ones. It became a sadder and wiser pickle by the time your uncle had finished with it. I should imagine it contained constituents altogether novel in the history of pickles. I gather from a guarded reference of the sales manager to the wholesale market-price of mangel-wurzels that these played a large part in it. Bit by bit the cost of production was chiselled down by seventy per cent. But here your uncle showed his genius. Your captain of commerce must be no mere niggler and scraper. Niggling and scraping have their place and time, but he must know when to fling caution to the winds and plunge. He plunged on the glass jar and the label, Kate. He had these redesigned until they brightened any table on which they stood, and leapt straight to the housewife's heart from any shop window in which they were displayed. Notwithstanding this extravagance, your uncle was able, by sternly economizing on the materials, and also by contriving to make the jars look as if they contained rather more than rival brands, whereas in cold fact they contained at least an ounce less . . . he was able, I say, to sell his pickles at a halfpenny less than any competitor. The rest of this epic of commerce is mainly a record of extensions at the factory. A great man, your uncle, Kate, and a keen student of feminine psychology."

Kate had long since ceased to listen. Thornhill's voice sounded to her like the distant babbling of the weir in the ears of an attentive fisherman. With her pretty face clouded by an unbecoming frown she was trying to make head and tail of a curious letter connected with the purchase of a vinegar works. Her uncle's interests had been many and various. Some of his financial transactions were beyond her ability to understand, and for some unacknowledged reason she was rather glad of it.

Thornhill put on one side the papers relating to the pickle factory, and he became absorbed in a saga of strawberry jam. Apparently mangel-wurzels entered into the strawberry-jam industry also. This was a novel idea to Thornhill. He was certainly learning rapidly. . . .

The butler came upstairs with visiting-cards on a silver salver. Kate picked them up and read the names aloud.

"Mr. and Mrs. Herbert Goodbody. Miss Cora Champken. Do you know these people?"

"Two of the most virulent females in Chesworth," said Thornhill cheerfully, "and one of the most cantankerous husbands. They have probably come to spy out the land."

"They are in the drawing-room, madam," volunteered the butler.

"I will come down in a minute," said Kate.

She waited until the door had closed, and then turned sharply on Thornhill.

"Frank, I wish you wouldn't say things like that in front of the servants."

"Sorry, Miss Martindale."

Kate resented the mockery. She looked at him: more in anger than in sorrow, thought Thornhill.

"Really, Frank!"

His eyes twinkled. He thought her flushed cheeks became her. He turned in his chair and was tempted to jump up and hug her and kiss her. Evidently she suspected as much, for she composed herself and, glancing in a business-like way at the papers on the desk in front of him, inquired:

"How are you getting on?"

"I am blazing a trail through the forest of files. This lot can be burned without hesitation . . . these must be kept in the archives . . . and these are doubtful and I have set them on one side for you to look through."

"That's excellent. Thank you very much, Frank. Shall I leave you to it, or have you had enough of it for the time being?"

"I'll carry on for a bit."

"That's very nice of you."

She smiled and went downstairs. Thornhill chuckled. He felt very much like a good little schoolboy who has been praised by his teacher. He pushed back his chair and lit a pipe. What, he wondered, would it be like to have Kate for a wife? She would be constantly trying to correct him: partly from habit, and partly because there was so much to correct. He would find it difficult not to be as constantly pulling her leg. Things might degenerate into a scrapping match, a sort of guerilla warfare. He sighed and returned to his task.

He grew more and more interested. Three letters to Bonar from Newcastle, two of them typewritten on plain paper, one written in a feminine hand on fancy paper,

particularly held his attention. . . . He was reading them
through for the second time when the butler reappeared.

"Miss Martindale's compliments, sir, and tea will
shortly be served in the drawing-room."

"I suppose, Johnson, I shall have to show up?"

"I think it is expected of you, sir."

"Give me two minutes."

The butler bowed and retired. Thornhill glanced again
through the letters from Newcastle. He sat back with a
curious expression in his eyes. Then he folded the letters
neatly and put them in his pocket, knocked out his pipe,
and, like a lamb to the slaughter, made his way
downstairs to the drawing-room.

2

Thornhill knew Mrs. Goodbody and Miss Champken
very well, for in Chesworth everyone knew everyone very
well. He knew them so well, indeed, that he was in the
habit of giving them as wide a berth as possible, though
in the narrow waters of Chesworth this required
considerable skill in steersmanship. He was not surprised
to find that they were Kate's first callers.

The ladies of Chesworth had been much exercised in
their minds about the etiquette of the occasion. No one
seemed to know what was the interval that should be
allowed to elapse before calling on a new resident whose
uncle had been murdered. The usual authorities were
silent on the point. Mrs. Goodbody and Miss Champken,
thinking independently, had decided that a week was
ample. At any rate, since no one was likely to call at
Forest Park without waiting at least a week, they were
sure of the satisfaction of getting in first. The only
opposition to this proposal came from Mr. Goodbody, who
opposed everything. He was overruled by his wife, as
usual, and had come in a very bad temper.

As Thornhill entered the drawing-room, Kate looked
up at him soberly, almost apprehensively, as though she

feared that she might be kissed in front of these comparative strangers. A light in her eyes warned Thornhill not to behave as a lover: reminded him that their engagement was as yet private and confidential, unannounced and unavowed. Thornhill understood the signal, and winked. Kate frowned, and looked round anxiously to see whether the indiscretion had been noticed. Mr. Goodbody was examining his nails and grumbling to himself. Mrs. Goodbody and Miss Champken were beaming. They had vied with each other in being effusive to their hostess, and they were now priming themselves for a campaign of cordiality towards Thornhill. A thousand a year and that nice house of his, they both agreed in estimating, made him a person of consequence in Chesworth: and if it were true that he drank rather a lot, that was a venial fault in a lonely bachelor, who might well be expected to feel desperately bored at times. Miss Champken especially was ready to overlook this vice, if vice it were. She felt that all Thornhill needed to make him an unexceptionable citizen was the refining influence of a really good wife. Mrs. Goodbody might have taken the same view some years earlier, but she was now provided with a husband, though not a very satisfactory one. She looked with favour upon Thornhill for another reason. Her foible was to ingratiate herself with the well-to-do. If the well-to-do, like Thornhill, had been to a public school and one of the senior universities, so much the better. That kind of training gave a man a sort of hall-mark, mused Mrs. Goodbody. Or a *cachet*. Yes, that was the better word: a *cachet*.

As for Thornhill's reactions to these feelings, they were simple. He thought Miss Champken an old hag. He thought Mrs. Goodbody a snobbish old cat. He was sorry for Goodbody, in that he was married to Mrs. Goodbody: but Goodbody was a cantankerous old ass. He sat down, and Mrs. Goodbody fired the first shot.

"We were just saying, Mr. Thornhill," remarked Mrs.

Goodbody, "how romantic it is to have a woman as *chatelaine* at Forest Park. After generations of bluff old English squires—I suppose I might call them squires— squires whose sole interests were fox-hunting and *la chasse* . . ."

"What's the difference?"

The growl came from her husband.

"*La chasse* is what we call shooting, Herbert," said Mrs. Goodbody graciously. "The chase of birds and animals that are killed with a gun: not foxes."

"English is good enough for me," said Mr. Goodbody.

"After generations of hunting squires," continued his wife, unruffled, "it is strange to think that one of the gentler sex now reigns within these ancient halls."

"And jolly good for the ancient halls," broke in Miss Champken, who prided herself upon being a downright, practical and modern young woman; and had indeed so prided herself ever since the end of the war. "The ancient halls could do with a bit of a woman's loving care. I expect Miss Martindale will do what I should do if I were in her shoes: roll my sleeves up and give the ancient halls a dose of spring-cleaning."

"That is Miss Champken's jocose way of putting things," remarked Mrs. Goodbody with an indulgent smile. "Of course it will be quite unnecessary for Miss Martindale to roll her sleeves up. She will devise the new schemes of decoration, and the usual firms will carry them out under her supervision."

"And if you ask me," said Mr. Goodbody, "you can't supervise 'em too closely. Workmen take a lot of watching nowadays."

Kate thought Miss Champken a rather forward person.

"I know there's a great deal that should be done," she admitted, good-humouredly enough. "My poor uncle put in six new bathrooms, but there he seems to have stopped."

"Good for the old lad," said Thornhill cheerily. "First

thing I should have done myself."

Mrs. Goodbody looked at him as though she were not quite sure whether this breezy way of speaking about a man who had so recently been murdered was quite nice; but she remembered this was Mr. Thornhill, and she smiled.

Miss Champken cut in swiftly.

"But naturally, Mr. Thornhill, if you were a married man, you would expect your wife to stir up the paperhangers and decorators."

Thornhill looked at her with some distaste. Suddenly she reminded him of the centre court at Wimbledon.

Thornhill had once been persuaded to spend an afternoon at the centre court, watching the somewhat neurotic gods and goddesses of the racket disporting themselves before the rapturous applause of the other spectators. He had been wedged, hopelessly bored, in a place from which he could not escape; and he had suffered from a phobia about Wimbledon ever since. Miss Champken was watching him intently, as if he were a tennis idol and she were a suburban woman in the front rows of the centre court at Wimbledon; and as in the case of, alas, too many of the enthusiasts at Wimbledon, her concentrated stare, combined with a too lavish use of cosmetics unskilfully applied, made her look sulky and stupid. (Thornhill sometimes wondered whether he had been unjust to the kind of women who desperately followed lawn tennis at Wimbledon, but whenever he saw a photograph of spectators watching an important match, he realized that he had not.)

"Do you play lawn tennis, Miss Champken?" he asked involuntarily.

"Oh, yes. Rather! I'm frightfully keen. I went to Wimbledon last year. Had a marvellous time. Do you play, Mr. Thornhill?"

"No," he answered laconically. "Hate the game."

He saw Kate glance at him sharply, but Miss Champken's withers were unwrung.

"Ah, I expect that's because you haven't seen it at its best. At Chesworth, you know, it's only a kind of patters people play. You ought to see some of the real wizards. You should look in at Wimbledon sometime."

"Waste of money," growled Mr. Goodbody. "Absurd the charges."

"I have been to Wimbledon," said Thornhill grimly.

"Yes," inserted Kate quickly, "I know there's a great deal to be done. The place has not been cared for as it should have been. But it will all take time."

"My dear Miss Martindale," said Mrs. Goodbody, "nobody expects you to concern yourself with such things at a time like this."

"Oh, I don't know," said Thornhill. "It's good for her to have something to think about. As a matter of fact I wouldn't mind betting that K . . . that Miss Martindale has already taken things in hand and impressed her personality on the domestic staff; and from what I have seen of them they needed it."

The vulgarity of Thornhill's remark was not redeemed by its truth. Kate's training had made her impatient of slovenliness and remissness of all kinds: she could not see anything done badly without feeling an irresistible impulse to set it right and admonish the offender. She had already found occasion to utter winged words to every individual member of the indoor staff: from the butler and the housekeeper to the boy who cleaned the knives and boots. They had not taken kindly to it. They were not used to being spoken to like naughty school children, and some of them had pointedly said so. The ancient halls were on the verge of a domestic mutiny.

Kate bit her lip. She found herself blushing, which annoyed her. She caught the glances exchanged by Mrs. Goodbody and Miss Champken when Thornhill nearly blurted out her Christian name, and her blush deepened, which annoyed her still more. She rose to ring the bell for tea, and while she was on her feet crossed the room to draw the curtains of a window through which the sun shone rather awkwardly: she was used to doing things for herself and had not yet acquired the habit of letting her servants perform such offices for her. Thornhill leapt to her side and drew the curtains.

"Kate," he whispered in her ear as they stood together by the window, "send these dreadful people away. I want to talk to you."

"But how can I, Frank? Don't be absurd."

"Then leave them to guzzle their tea by themselves," he murmured urgently, "and come for a walk across the lawn, or through the shrubbery, or in the walled garden or somewhere. Show me the greenhouses or the stables."

"You're being ridiculous," remonstrated Kate with annoyance. "It's impossible."

She was uneasily conscious of three pairs of eyes determined to miss nothing of this interesting interlude.

"If you don't," whispered Thornhill savagely, "I'll tell the Champken-hag that she's Fifty If She's A Day and old enough to know better than to prink herself up like a silly little typist in the City; and I shall commiserate with the Goodbody-cat on having a pig of a husband who spends all his spare time in deceiving her with the cook."

"Frank!"

The tone that would have petrified the whole assembly of the County Council Domestic Economy Centre, staff and pupils included, merely made Thornhill grin.

"You naughty puss! If you dare to speak to me again like that, I'll kiss you *coram populo*."

"And what may that mean?" asked Kate, with considerable coldness.

"It means in front of the Champken-hag and the Goodbody-cat."

With perfect precision which was the result of many years of discipline, and disconcerted even Thornhill for the moment, Kate turned on her heel and sailed back, with heightened colour, but serene dignity, to rejoin the three guests whose ears ached with the strain of trying to hear something of this conversation.

"I have just been telling K . . . Miss Martindale," said Thornhill, recovering his aplomb as he returned to his chair, "that in my judgment a pale green would be good as the predominant tint in a new colour scheme for this room."

Kate looked almost grateful. Mrs. Goodbody tried to look as if her one desire was to believe this report of what had passed by the window. Mr. Goodbody looked down his nose. Miss Champken looked as if she were much annoyed, but she tried to conceal it.

The moment could not have been more tactfully chosen for the arrival of tea; and no sooner had this been set out by a footman under the supervision of the butler than the Reverend William Chandos, by a miracle of timing which did him great credit, dropped in to join the party.

The rector had been bicycling along the Worthing road wondering whether the hour was yet ripe for a formal call at the Park. In front of him he saw the Goodbody's car turn down the famous avenue, and a moment later the bus overtook him and dropped Miss Champken. He made a swift deduction, a sudden resolve and a lightning calculation. The last informed him that if he visited a certain parishioner in Salisbury Road and stayed a certain time, he would arrive at the Park at the most likely moment for a cup of tea. His programme had gone through exact to schedule, and he was in the best possible temper.

3

Indeed, the rector was getting on splendidly when something happened to put him off his stroke. Although as a rule he preferred the society of men to that of women, he exerted himself on this occasion and did his best to make a favourable impression on his hostess. He contrived at one and the same time to show that he condoled with Kate on the death of her uncle while rejoicing that the unhappy event should endow her with riches; and he gave her to understand that a capable and sensible young woman, in a responsible position such as hers, would be a great gain to the parish. He chipped Miss Champken about her tennis and, more decorously, agreed that in the matter of Sunday games . . . how weary the rector was of that subject!. . . one must move with the times: it did no harm to get up early on Sunday morning and enjoy a bathe before going to church. Indeed, it was a good thing. Mrs. Goodbody showing herself a little anxious lest the extension of the principle should lead to all kinds of games going on all through the Sabbath, the rector added that of course it was necessary to show moderation in all things, and one must not act too precipitately. The pace set by Brighton or a Socialist County Council in London might not be the correct *tempo* for Chesworth. To Mr. Goodbody, who said the trouble with Chesworth was that it did not move fast enough, he answered amicably that so far as some matters were concerned he often felt the same.

Thornhill, who was an old friend of the rector, sat silent and enjoyed this exhibition of casuistry, this skilled ecclesiastical balancing on the fence. It bored him after a little, and when a slight sensation was caused by the unexpected arrival of Miss Perks, he welcomed the diversion. Why she had taken it into her head to call he could not imagine, but she might be expected to enliven the proceedings. In the presence of the rector Miss Perks, to speak metaphorically, kept her dagger unsheathed. Some feud existed between them of which the origins were clouded in the past: possibly it had begun many years ago when the rector was a little boy at Miss Perks's school in the Pavement. Miss Perks was the only person in Chesworth with whom the rector consistently quarrelled: or, to put it more generously, and, indeed, more accurately, Miss Perks was the only parishioner who flatly refused to have anything to do with the rector.

Thornhill saw her wrinkle up her great hooked nose when she found the rector among the company, and fully expected to hear her snort like a war-horse, but she disappointed him. She ignored the presence of the Reverend William Chandos. She concentrated on her hostess, and began, characteristically, with blunt questions.

"So I do not find myself alone? I was half afraid that my visit was premature. . . . Two, please, and put the milk in first."

"I always do," said Kate placidly, "unless otherwise instructed."

"That's something in your favour," said Miss Perks, nodding her black bonnet. "You have sense enough not to put the milk in last. So you are the new owner of Forest Park?"

"I suppose I am," said Kate, smiling.

"Why suppose?" demanded the old lady. "You must know one way or the other. If you are, I hope you'll do something about Jacob's Ladder. A ridiculous thing it is. Replace it by a sensible stile, or, better still, a gate. Of course, you won't be able to keep the place up properly, will you?"

"I hope to try."

"Depend upon it," said Mrs. Goodbody, "a woman's hand . . ."

Miss Perks interrupted Mrs. Goodbody.

"Death duties," she said saturninely. "Even a woman's hand has to stump up those. I believe they take half the money. You can't do it on what's left, can your

Miss Perks did not know that it was the wish of Douglas Bonar, expressed in his will, that Kate should live at the Park, and that he had arranged things so that she should be able to do this without difficulty, indeed with ease and luxury. Kate did not feel called upon to explain all this. She was inclined to resent Miss Perks's open curiosity. She thought she was not very fortunate in her visitors, with the exception of the rector and, possibly,

Frank Thornhill. She felt, and with justice, that they did not offer a fair cross-section of Chesworth society.

"I shall have to exercise economy," she said.

"Of course you must. Everybody ought to. There's far too much of this mad spending nowadays."

Miss Perks ignored Mr. Goodbody's contribution to the discussion.

"How have you been earning your living hitherto?" next demanded Miss Perks. She softened the asperity of the question by adding: "I suppose that like all the modern young women you have had a profession of some sort."

"I was teaching."

"H'm," said Miss Perks. She had been a teacher herself and she had met a good many teachers in her time. She had no great opinion of teachers. "A bad preparation for any other walk in life. It tended to sap the intelligence even in my time, when teachers remembered their dignity and at least tried to behave like adults; but now, when they slap their pupils on the back and call them by their Christian names, it is demoralizing. I am afraid you will find you have taken on a big task in trying to manage an estate like this."

"If I fail," said Kate quietly, "it will not be for want of advice."

Miss Perks chose to miss the implication.

"Lawyers and agents, I suppose you mean." She grunted. "They will swindle you right and left. I know them. No, you must marry, my dear. Get yourself as soon as you can a sensible husband."

"Exactly," said Thornhill. "That's just what I've been telling her. Thanks for rallying to my support, Miss Perks."

Kate looked very angry indeed. Miss Champken and Mrs. Goodbody raised their eyebrows. They were annoyed, not so much with Thornhill as with Miss Perks, who had waded in and seized with both hands the information for which they had been fishing without success for half an hour. Mr. Goodbody looked glum. He thought marriage an overrated institution, but did not care to say so in the presence of his wife. The rector, feeling that the atmosphere was somewhat strained, hastily launched into the relation of an amusing incident that had attended the last choir treat. . . .

"I doubt whether we mean the same thing," said Miss Perks, ruthlessly interrupting the rector. "I said a sensible husband. You overlooked the adjective, Frank Thornhill. I would advise Miss Martindale to look for a man of energy and experience, who has shown himself to be of some use in the world, and has not simply vegetated in idleness on the income bequeathed to him by foolish forebears."

Thornhill was not at all abashed.

"You don't know my capabilities," he hastened to say before the rector could make another tactful attempt to change the subject. "I have strong business instincts. Indeed, I am thinking of going into trade almost at once. Then, through my knowledge of the ropes, acquired by careful study, I shall make a large fortune."

"How?"

"By distilling strawberry jam from mangel-wurzels. It is the latest process and there is a great deal of money in it. You buy mangel-wurzels in the cheapest markets and sell the strawberry jam in the dearest."

While Kate bit her lips with vexation, and the rector made hasty inquiries after Mrs. Goodbody's tulips, Miss Perks looked at Thornhill as she had been accustomed in past days to look upon some especially wayward and ill-conditioned little boy.

"Frank Thornhill," she said, "I should advise you to give up all thoughts of marriage. A person like you ought not to marry at all. That is, unless you are prepared to put your back into some decent form of hard work and redeem your wasted years. At present you are merely playing ducks and drakes with your opportunities, and no girl who was not a fool would look at you . . . no girl in

Chesworth, where it is known the sort of man you are. If you have any sense left, you will go away and start again."

"You said so before."

"I say so again."

"Miss Perks is my old schoolmistress," said Thornhill, beaming upon the company. "She delights in telling me off. I always feel about schoolmistresses that . . ."

"I hear," said the rector, in a voice of valiant loudness, "that the new swimming-pool will not be ready for opening until July."

"What Chesworth really needs," said Thornhill, "is a sun-bathing centre. That is another plan I have for making money. I propose to open a sun-bathing centre on the outskirts of Chesworth."

Mr. Goodbody woke up.

"You mean one of these nudist places?" he demanded.

"Certainly."

"We shall have to be thinking about going," said Mrs. Goodbody, "so don't start one of your long arguments, Herbert."

"What sort of fettle is your tennis-court going to be in this year, rector?" inquired Miss Champken.

"Do let me give you another cup of tea, Miss Perks," said Kate.

"And where do you propose to have your nudist what-d'you-call-it?" growled Mr. Goodbody.

"There's a little property I have on the edge of St. Leonard's Forest which would do admirably for the purpose," said Thornhill. "It is a natural arena: grassland surrounded by a thick belt of trees. It occurred to me the other day that it's the very thing for a sun-bathing centre. Not much use for anything else, as a matter of fact. But admirable for sun-bathing. The trees will keep off the draught and the prying eyes of hoi polloi, and there, as Milton said, you can sit clad in your virtue and enjoy the bright day."

"Don't say 'you'," muttered Miss Perks. "I have no

wish to sit clad in my own virtue and presumably nothing
else. Still, no doubt there are fools who do." She
remembered the unfortunate affliction of her brother
Robert, and bit her lip. She accepted Kate's offer of
another cup of tea and took no further part in the
conversation, but during the rest of the proceedings sat
watching Thornhill with malevolent eyes.

"It doesn't look like being too good, I'm afraid," said
the rector. "I really must do a bit of grubbing among the
plaintains when I can find time."

"You'll never make a thing like that pay in
Chesworth," said Mr. Goodbody contemptuously.

"Oh, I don't know," said Thornhill. "People will come
from miles around. They'll be glad of the opportunity. In
these overcrowded days there are not so many places
where one can go back to Nature without taking the risk
of being run in."

Mr. Goodbody grunted.

"And you think you will get them to pay heavily for
the privilege of making an exhibition of themselves to one
another?"

"Yes, rather," said Thornhill. "I shall fix the
subscription at a very high figure. Only the best people
need apply. Obviously, a centre of Nachtkultur would be
nothing if it were not select. Refinement will be our
watchword."

"If you call that sort of monkeying about without any
clothes on refined," said Mr. Goodbody.

"Herbert," said his wife, "we mustn't forget that we
have to find time on the way back to call at the iron-
monger's before they close."

"Miss Martindale," said Miss Champken, "I do hope
you will play tennis. It will be really too marvellous if the
courts at the Park . . ."

"I must say," admitted Mr. Goodbody grudgingly,
"that I cannot see that the expenses of running such a
place would be very heavy."

"That's just what I've been wanting to do," said

Thornhill with enthusiasm. "Talk over that side of the scheme with a practical man. You can give me some valuable advice. I suppose in the first place I should have to engage a respectable person to watch over the morals of the place and see that everyone is properly undressed."

"Did you say a respectable person?" asked Mr. Goodbody. "Was respectable the word you used?"

"Or do you think," murmured Thornhill musingly, "that it would be advisable to employ two respectable persons for the purpose? One of each sex?"

"My dear Thornhill," the rector was heard at this stage to murmur.

Kate, falling back weakly on the obvious gambit, offered another cup of tea to Mrs. Goodbody, who showed signs of being interested in Thornhill's plans in spite of her better self.

"No, thank you, Miss Martindale," said Mrs. Goodbody. "What do these people do?" she went on, incautiously speaking her thoughts aloud. "Do they merely sit or stand about in their skins? I have often wondered when I have heard of these nudist places. It must become rather dull, I should imagine, after the sensations of the first few minutes."

She saw the rector looking at her askance. She blushed brilliantly.

"I think, if you don't mind," she said hastily, "I will change my mind and have another cup of tea, Miss Martindale."

"Yes, what do they do?" echoed Mr. Goodbody in more aggressive tones.

"I am not an expert myself," confessed Thornhill, "but I understand that they do p.t.—physical exercises, you know—and play games."

"Leapfrog, I suppose," said Mr. Goodbody with another of his characteristic snorts.

"No doubt," assented Thornhill politely. "Then, of course, refreshments are served. Afternoon tea and possibly light lunches. Meals *al fresco*. It would give the

scene a pleasant, picnicky touch, besides being an
additional source of handsome profit. We could charge
whatever we liked, you see. They couldn't very well pop
across the road to a pub. Not without forfeiting the
untrammelled liberty it is their whole purpose to enjoy."

"I don't think my tennis days are over," said Kate
wearily. "I hope later on to play a little."

"That will be too marvellous," said Miss Champken.
"Of course most of the players in Chesworth are pretty
lou . . . not much class, but there are a few who are not
too bad. The rector is positively a wizard."

"My dear young lady," said the rector indulgently,
"you overrate . . ."

"And who are going to serve these refreshments?"
demanded Mr. Goodbody.

The same thought had occurred to the rector. He
paused to listen.

"I haven't gone into that yet, but surely," said
Thornhill airily, "it won't be difficult, in these hard times,
to engage a sufficient staff of competent helpers. There
must be plenty of strapping wenches in Chesworth who
would be glad of a job."

"I shall hope, my dear Miss Martindale," said the
rector thoughtfully, "to get you interested in our girls'
club. With your experience . . ."

"And what costume are these strapping wenches to
wear?" pursued Mr. Goodbody implacably.

"Why, naturally, since this is to be a centre of nudist
culture. . . ."

Mr. Goodbody snorted very loudly indeed.

"You won't get Chesworth girls to do it," he declared.
"Not if I know anything about Chesworth girls. Their
morals are perhaps not all they should be. . . though," he
added, catching a glance from his wife, "of that I cannot
speak from experience. But this is an old-fashioned place.
This is not Paris. This is not the Folies Bergere."

"You don't think," returned Thornhill in a tone of mild
surprise, "that the damsels of Chesworth would consent

to serve tea, clad only in lipstick, face-powder and chastity?"

"There may be brazen young hussies in Chesworth," said Mr. Goodbody, apparently unaware of the horrified silence in which his words rang out so clear, "perfectly willing to do as you suggest; but unless their mothers have entirely lost the strength of their right arms . . ."

"You think the daughters may be dissuaded? Then I suppose I must give up the idea. It will be a pity to spoil the general effect, but if it is as you fear . . . However, perhaps some simple Greek costume . . ."

"You will never get decent women to wait in such surroundings," said Mr. Goodbody. He grunted again, and his manner showed that he refused to waste any further time in the discussion of such a ridiculous project. Mrs. Goodbody and Miss Champken rose abruptly and simultaneously.

"If I go now, I shall be just in time to catch the jolly old bus," said Miss Champken.

"Oh, do let me give you a lift in my car," said Thornhill.

"Thank you very much, Mr. Thornhill, but in the circumstances I couldn't possibly think of putting you to the trouble," said Miss Champken frostily.

"You can have a seat in ours, my dear," said Mrs. Goodbody, with the air of a mother hen stretching out a wing to protect a chick whose modesty was in danger of being assailed.

"Oh, thanks awfully. That will be top-hole."

"How about you, rector?" asked Thornhill.

"Thank you, Frank," said the rector sadly. "I have my bicycle."

They went into the hall. Kate accompanied them. To judge from the little nervous scraps of talk that floated through to the drawing-room, conversation was somewhat embarrassed. Thornhill followed after a pause during which he sat smiling sardonically at his own thoughts.

The Goodbodys' car started off. The rector leapt into his saddle and, waving a friendly farewell to Miss Martindale, whom he privately hoped soon to see under less congested and more congenial conditions, pedalled down the drive. Kate turned to find herself facing Thornhill.

"*Au revoir,* Kate."

She did not reply.

"Give me a kiss, Kate. A fond kiss, and then we sever."

Her face was noticeably cold.

"I have never felt so ashamed in all my life," she said. "Please go."

Thornhill stood still and looked at her with a queer smile. He was humming a tune. Kate knew the words very well:

I attempt from love's sickness to fly: in vain,
Since I am myself my own fever,
Since I am myself my own fever and pain.

She turned her head away.

"I think somebody was offering people a lift," said a deep voice behind them.

They both started. They had forgotten Miss Perks.

"Delighted," murmured Thornhill.

"I shall expect to see you soon at my little house in the Pavement," Miss Perks said to her hostess, in the manner of one delivering an ultimatum.

Thornhill helped her into the car. He sat down beside her. Miss Perks spoke:

"That's a nice way to behave, Frank Thornhill!" she said.

Thornhill looked at her oddly.

"That's exactly what you used to say to me when I was a little boy," he said after a pause.

"And you've needed having it said to you more than

once since," said Miss Perks.

Thornhill was silent. He started the car.

"Some of those silly-looking hussies in their short drawers," Miss Perks exclaimed as they approached the place where the right-of-way crossed the avenue.

Thornhill slowed down to let the ramblers pass, and glanced at the notice-board. The minatory reference to the possibility of gun accidents had been erased, and in its place appeared:

Please do not pick the wild flowers or leave any litter behind. Do not mar the enjoyment of those who come after you by your own thoughtlessness.

The schoolmistress was abroad in the land, he thought.

Miss Perks heard a curious sound escape from the lips of her companion. It might have been a chuckle. It might have been a sigh.

X. A Bit of Larceny

Chrystal was walking after tea in the lane. He was not going anywhere in particular: he was merely walking up and down, savagely, like a caged animal. He carried a stick and struck furious blows at the heads of the tall grasses growing under the Park hedge. His whole demeanour was bitter and resentful, expressing hatred of mankind.

Thornhill's man Jennings, walking down towards the town, touched his cap pleasantly.

"Lovely afternoon, sir."

"Using your feet for once," said Chrystal sarcastically. "Where's the bicycle? You're usually tearing along on that, when you're not scorching in the car. Really, I never saw such a fellow as you for being in a devil of a hurry. Extraordinary!"

"I'm afraid the bike wants a new pair of tyres."

"Really, I'm not surprised. . . . Do you go to the pictures much, Jennings?"

"Why do you ask, sir?" said Jennings defensively.

"Oh, I just wondered. . . . What time do they come out as a rule?"

"They're all over by half-past ten."

"That's what I thought. Difficult to find anything to do in Chesworth after half-past ten, I should think. Extraordinarily difficult, eh?"

"I suppose it would be," said Jennings coldly. "Can't say it worries me much. I must be going on now, sir. Good evening."

Chrystal's eyes followed the tall fellow with a brooding expression. He furiously whipped the grasses with his stick. He stood thinking hard, with bowed head, and did not notice the approach of another person.

"What is this world if, full of care, we have no time to stand and stare?" inquired a gentle voice behind him. Chrystal, looking up with a start, saw Robert Perks.

"It's a hell of a world," he said with conviction, "but really I don't know what difference standing and staring makes. It's a poor world in any case."

Robert murmured something in which Chrystal caught the word "loitering." A knight-at-arms was also alluded to.

"I'm afraid I didn't quite get that," he said crossly.

"It's of no consequence. I was quoting Keats. It's a bad habit of mine, alas, to quote from the poets. It rarely seems to go down well anywhere." Robert smiled agreeably. "I must give it up. Why so pale and wan?"

"Really, I ask you! Who wouldn't be pale and wan who had gone through all I've gone through in the past few days? To be treated by the police as a suspected murderer, and examined and cross-examined again and again. It's not pleasant, I tell you. Really, it's not pleasant at all."

"I should imagine it's extraordinary unpleasant. But why should they suspect you?"

"Exactly. Why should they suspect me?" asked Chrystal warmly. "Do I look like a murderer? You saw me that night. Did I look then as if I had just committed a murder?"

"Under the greenwood tree," murmured Robert. "You are referring to our nocturnal encounter near the Sun Oak. I thought at the time that you were singularly preoccupied and ill at ease, but it didn't for one moment occur to me to think that you had just committed a murder."

"Nor had I," said Chrystal indignantly.

"Of course you hadn't, my dear fellow," said Robert soothingly. "I shouldn't dream of suggesting such a thing. Nor would anyone else."

"Except these crass fools from Scotland Yard."

"Oh, well," said Robert tolerantly, "the dyer's hand,

you know. It's the business of those fellows to suspect everyone. I should not be in the least surprised if they suspected me."

"They might just as well," said Chrystal gloomily. "Really, I don't know why they haven't."

"I have not altogether escaped the net," mentioned Robert. "Sergeant Whalebone inquired into what I was doing on the fatal night. He was quite nice about it."

"Do you always know," asked Chrystal savagely, "what you have been doing?"

Robert raised his eyebrows.

"What do you mean?" he said.

"Oh, nothing. That is . . . Oh, really, I don't know. I shouldn't have said that, I suppose. Everybody knows that you are not really aware . . ." Chrystal bit his lip. "I'm talking a lot of nonsense. That is, I'm saying things I ought . . . Oh, don't take any notice of me. I'm in an extraordinary state of mind. When you think of what I've been through . . ."

Chrystal stood swinging his stick. Robert watched him rather anxiously in silence.

"Do you know," burst out Chrystal suddenly, "what I shall do when I have found out who killed Bonar?"

"So you think you will?" asked Robert, interested.

"I'm sure I shall. Really, I think I could tell you now. Extraordinary how it hasn't occurred to Scotland Yard. I should have thought it was as plain as a . . . as a what-d'you-call-it."

"As a pikestaff?" suggested Robert.

"As plain as a pikestaff. I only want to make quite sure."

"And then what will you do?"

"I shall announce it publicly, and let people see how the police can waste their time in badgering decent citizens and miss what lies under their very nose."

"Oh," said Robert. He looked at the angry little man and changed the subject. "How is Mrs. Chrystal?"

"Oh, very well, thanks." Chrystal answered brightly

enough, but did not seem willing to enlarge upon the topic.

"I must be getting along," said Robert. "I am taking a book back to Thornhill."

"You'll find him out. He went along the lane in his car before tea, and I haven't heard it come back yet. That man of his," added Chrystal, decapitating a thistle with deliberation, as though he had tried it and found it guilty, "is out too."

"Then I shall have to leave the book with Mrs. Jennings."

"Thornhill drinks, you know," said Chrystal irrelevantly.

"It is a matter of common report in Chesworth. It is understood that he keeps a rare store of Cyprus and Malvoisie: also of sack and Canary. Chesworth has little doubt that all the year round there would be brewing of ale, too, if there were not a brewery so handy in the town." Robert smiled. "I fear I am being frivolous. Chesworth gossip has that effect upon me. You think it may render him a dangerous driver?"

"I'm not suggesting that it has any effect on his driving," answered Chrystal testily. "But he does drink. He drinks more than ever. Extraordinary the amount he drinks. Really, I don't think it can do a man any good to drink as much as he does."

"One would give him credit for a pretty sound constitution."

"Oh, extraordinary! Really, I think he is the most powerful man I have ever met. The rector runs him pretty close, but Thornhill lives a healthier life."

Robert looked surprised. One did not as a rule asperse the rector's moral character.

"Oh, you know what I mean," said Chrystal. "Thornhill is in the open air all day, while the rector has to go and call on old women and sit in stuffy houses. . . . But I do think Thornhill drinks too much. I'm not a teetotaller, but really, I shouldn't care to take half as much as he does."

Robert was unwilling to discuss Thornhill's habits.

"I should imagine," he said, "talking of powerful men, that Jennings runs his master pretty close."

"Oh, Jennings!" said Chrystal, and decapitated another thistle. A motor horn caused him to look round. "Talk of the devil!" he muttered.

Thornhill stopped and waved to them cheerfully.

"Hallo, Robert, I've just been taking your sister home. We enjoyed an interesting afternoon together at the Park. Quite a nice little tea-party. Hallo, Chrystal, how are your friends of Scotland Yard? I see they are getting into hot water with the Press. The popular papers think something ought to be done about it. No doubt the criticism has stirred them into renewed activity. Not, I hope, at your expense?"

"Oh, don't talk to me about it," said Chrystal. "I'm sick of the sight of a detective. Really, they can't let me alone. I never had much opinion of the intelligence of the British police, and now I have less than ever. Fools!"

"Don't be too hard on them: it's a difficult case." Thornhill looked at the little man and saw on his face signs of all he had been going through. For the first time he felt sympathetic towards his nearest neighbour. "I admit it's rough on you, Chrystal. Why don't you go right away and take a holiday?"

"How can I?" demanded Chrystal crossly. "They'd follow me and be more suspicious than ever. . .. Besides, I've got something to do in Chesworth. Something I've got to carry through for my own satisfaction."

"Dark words," murmured Thornhill.

Chrystal flushed.

"I want to make Scotland Yard a laughing-stock, and show them up for the bunglers they are."

"I wish you luck."

"I believe you're ragging me, Thornhill," said Chrystal with dignity, "but I mean exactly what I say. Indeed I do. Really, I think Scotland Yard are extraordinarily dense.

"Oh, come," said Thornhill.

"But I do. They suspect me, and I believe they suspect Holt, and, for all I know, they may suspect you and Perks. And all the time . . ."

"Yes?" asked Thornhill eagerly.

"Oh, never mind."

"You disappoint me," said Thornhill lightly. "I thought you were on the verge of a revelation. . . . Well, we shall hear no doubt, in good time? We shall be duly staggered?"

Chrystal did not deign to answer.

Thornhill smiled, and glanced at Robert. Robert, having dropped out of the conversation, had been left to his own devices. He was standing very still under the hedge, and a dreamy look had come over his face, but his fingers were undoing the top buttons of his waistcoat. Thornhill spoke to him sharply.

"Robert!"

Robert came back slowly from a world of his own. His face resumed its normal expression.

"Oh, hullo, Thornhill. I'm glad I've met you. I was bringing back the book you lent my sister."

"Excellent," said Thornhill heartily. "Jump up, Robert, and come along to the house. It's cocktail time, and we'll have one together. . . . You, too, Chrystal?"

"Thanks," said Chrystal curtly. "I'm off the drink."

"Well, all the best. I hope to hear you have duly done down the police."

As the car slowly made way, Thornhill glanced quickly round. He saw Chrystal standing in the lane, swiping idly with his stick. Thornhill gained the impression that the little man was waiting: waiting for someone or something.

2

Michael had been almost himself again since the beginning of the week. On Monday, when Thornhill had so sadly misbehaved himself in front of Kate's callers,

Michael had written as many as three thousand words of his new book. On Tuesday he wrote three thousand more. He was by no means sure that all these words were the best available words arranged in the best possible order, but there was something comforting in the sight of the steadily rising pile of manuscript. Now he could press on to the last page and then take a day or two off before he revised. The book would need a good deal of re-writing: his first drafts always did. (Was not the secret of composition to write down the first thing that came into one's head, and then tear it up and write something else? Repeating the process as often as necessary.)

Michael's characters had a deplorable habit of taking the bit between their teeth: they would behave on page 200 in a manner altogether belying the portraits he had made of them in the earlier chapters. That had to be set right. Critics were so particular about that sort of thing. Michael's plots, too, suffered a similar change. They arrived at conclusions which would have considerably surprised any intelligent reader who had been allowed to peruse the work in the original manuscript. Well, Michael would see to that also, in the revised version. Such trifles no longer worried him. He was feeling happier than he had felt for days as he pottered about in the front garden after tea. Hugh and Kenneth, victims of a sudden passion for horticulture, were digging strenuously, or, at any rate, redistributing the soil, in a private patch allotted to them at the back of the house. Michael had left them to it.

Thornhill came up the lane, bareheaded, carrying a stick. His shoes were muddy.

"If you've got a few minutes to spare," he said, grinning over the Vineyard gate, "come and join me in a cocktail."

Michael hesitated.

"Do come," urged Thornhill. "Have pity on a lonely soul."

Michael joined him and they strolled up the lane together.

"I have been to Ditchling," said Thornhill. "I took tea at the Old Forge, in the garden, under the cherry tree."

"Did the car break down?" surmised Michael, with a glance at the muddy shoes.

"Car? My dear Michael, when one wants to think, one does not take one's car. If one has personal problems to resolve, one does not carry them out motoring. If one mixes the consideration of one's troubles and cares with the dangerous adventure of driving on the modern highway, one courts sudden death, which is certainly an issue out of all one's afflictions, but not as a rule the exit to be desired. . . . But do not fear, when I refer to my preoccupations, that I am about to unload my troubles on you."

"The world is full of troubles," said Michael thoughtfully. "My publishers have just sent on a letter from Australia. A woman in New South Wales saw my name in a book review and wrote to ask if I were her long-lost brother."

"And are you?" asked Thornhill with interest.

"I am not."

"To a person desirous of avoiding personal publicity," said Thornhill thoughtfully, "the business of authorship must have its drawbacks."

Michael glanced at him.

"Yes," he said curtly.

"It must have," repeated Thornhill. "Oh, well, there are disadvantages in every calling. . .. As I was saying, I left the car at home to-day. I walked. I told my staff at luncheon that they would be rid of me until the evening, and I walked across country, over the hills and far away. To arrive at Ditchling is pretty good going, as you must admit. True, I bussed the major part of the way back. But I have walked many miles, I have faced my problems, I have resolved on a course of action, and I am relieved in mind, as fit as a fiddle, and ready for a cocktail and a bath before dinner."

"Hugh thought he heard your car pass about an hour

ago."

"So he has an ear for the note of engines? A typical sprout of the younger generation. . . . That would be Jennings. He had some things to fetch from the station."

They passed the Chrystals' semi-bungalow.

"That fellow Chrystal," said Thornhill, "has something on his mind. He lurks in the lane and utters dark sayings. He thinks that he, unaided, will find and denounce Bonar's murderer, and so cover Scotland Yard with shame. I fear that the gruelling they've given him has affected his brain, as it has palpably affected his body. It seems absurd to say that he is merely the shadow of his former self. You would think it impossible for him to shrink, since he was already a homunculus, a pigmy, a mannikin, a duodecimo, a wraith, an ambulant skeleton: yet I could swear that he has lost flesh. From him that had not has been taken even that which he had. He will soon be an impalpable presence. I cannot say I ever loved him, but I am sorry for the fellow. . . . Sometimes I wonder whether his real trouble is not being suspected of detectives, but simply and solely being married to Mrs. Chrystal."

"Poor devil," said Michael.

"A warning against marriage, eh? You are an exception, Michael: nearly all the other husbands I know are standing arguments against matrimony." They came into his garden. "I have been giving that matter considerable thought recently, and . . ." Thornhill stood on his lawn and contemplated the loveliness that bounded it on three sides. "There was a loose rock lying in a field near Ditchling . . . and I hadn't my car. *Sunt lacrimcs rerum*, as poor Robert would say. I know the exact spot where it would go very nicely. To-morrow, perhaps, I will take Jennings with me on a filibustering expedition. He's a good fellow, Jennings, always ready for a little larceny. He's another husband who is happily married. He and Mrs. Jennings have the air of being devoted to one another. . . . This marriage business!" Thornhill snapped his fingers. "In the language of the populace, it gets me down. . . . Oh, damn it all. Come and have that drink."

Even then, he paused at the edge of his rock-garden, and went on talking.

"Look at that little beauty: prim and self-contained, like a schoolmistress. How would you like to be cultivated like a plant, Michael? Assigned to your little patch of soil, prevented from roaming, trimmed and cared for every day, brought up exactly in the way you should go? Appalling fate! Some human beings submit to it. Not I!" He hummed a tune of Purcell's.

Michael recognized it, as Kate had recognized it. So Thornhill attempted from love's sickness to fly . . . in vain; for he was himself his own fever and pain? Then his was a parlous fate, thought Michael. . . .

Thornhill, still humming, led the way into his house through the French window. Michael heard the tune break off as a wireless set goes suddenly mute in obedience to the touch of a switch. It was succeeded by an exclamation. Thornhill stood still. Michael, coming beside him, followed the direction of his eyes. The sideboard was stripped bare. The great weight of silver which had proudly loaded it, the massive shields and cups awarded Thornhill for doughty deeds on the fields of sport . . . all had gone.

3

Thornhill lifted up his voice.

"Jennings!" he cried.

Thornhill's Chow came with dignified leisure through the open doorway from the hall, and, disdaining to notice Michael, stood in front of his master, smiling and awaiting orders, with his blue-black tongue pendent.

"No, Chin, I wasn't calling you, old chap. I was calling Jennings. Where is he, eh, Chin?" Thornhill bent down to pat the dog. He straightened himself suddenly and looked at Michael with a laugh. "What was it old Sherlock said?

'There was the strange incident of the dog during the night.' To which Watson replied that the dog had made no sound. Whereupon Holmes remarked that that was the strange incident he had been referring to. . . . In other words, Michael, this is an inside job."

"Jennings," murmured Michael involuntarily.

Thornhill did not answer. He strode into the hall. There was a letter lying on the mat: he picked it up, glanced at the writing, and put it in his pocket. He went into the kitchen. No Mrs. Jennings was there. He shouted. No answer was returned. He ran upstairs.

His voice came, calling to Michael from an upstairs room: "They've gone. Cleared out altogether, bag and baggage." He reappeared on the landing, and added, with his head out of the window: "The garage door is standing open, and the Standard is not there."

He came back and went to the despoiled sideboard and poured out two whisky-and-sodas.

"Sit down and have a drink, Michael," he said. "Good fellow, Jennings, I think I said just now . . . always ready for a little larceny. That, I believe, is what is called dramatic irony."

He drank half his whisky and added: "Well, I have only myself to blame, as the rector will be sure to point out. He always blamed me for putting temptation in people's way. So boastfulness and vainglory bring their own reward." He swallowed the remaining contents of his glass and took the letter from his pocket. "Excuse me, old man."

"Won't you ring up the police?"

"Eh? Oh, that can wait." He had broken open the envelope which he had found in the hall, and his face was grimly expressive as he followed the neat, bold handwriting. The letter ran:

Dear Mr. Thornhill,

I am writing this letter with genuine regret, although I feel that what I have to say cannot come as a surprise to you. For some little time I have been wondering, almost against my will, whether we are really suited to each other, and I have now come reluctantly to the conclusion that we could never be happy together. Those wonderful days in the Mediterranean, when everything was viewed through rose-coloured spectacles in an atmosphere laden with romance, will always be a poignant memory to me. Alas, that such a happy dream should be shattered in the dull light of everyday!

About your strange behaviour in my house yesterday I can bring myself to say nothing, except that you will realize how it has made any further friendly relations between us utterly impossible, unless perhaps at some future time, when we may resume the ordinary intercourse of neighbours.

I will ask you (and I regret that it should be necessary) to accept this letter as final and irrevocable. Please spare me the pain you would cause by writing to me or attempting a meeting, for I can neither read your letters nor conse'nt to see you. Good-bye and may good fortune attend you.

Believe me
Yours truly,
Kate Martindale.

"So that is that," murmured Thornhill, stuffing the letter into his pocket.

He went back to the sideboard and refilled his glass.

"What! all gone?" he apostrophized the mahogany. "All my pretty ones? . . . At any rate, my Jennings friends have been good enough to leave me a fire." He went to the grate, poked the smouldering embers, and on a sudden impulse crumpled Kate's renunciation into a ball, and committed it to the flames. He came back to the table, lifted his glass, gave the toast, "Confusion to all criminals," gulped down the whisky, and went into the hall to telephone to the police.

When he had finished telephoning he mixed himself a

third drink.

"You're getting on very slowly with yours, Michael. You go carefully before dinner? Perhaps you're right. Perhaps I'm being immoderate, but it's a special occasion, Michael."

He sat down on the edge of his chair and winked.

"I'm not referring to the loss of the pots. I am not referring to the loss of Jennings, which is still more to be regretted, for, notwithstanding his obvious faults, he had the supreme merit of being married to a first-class cook. No, Michael. I am referring to something else. Something final and irrevocable."

"Well, what?" asked Michael.

"A marriage, Michael, which had been vaguely arranged, will now definitely not take place."

Michael saw that he was smiling.

"I must say, Frank, you seem quite pleased about it."

Thornhill looked at him sharply.

"Do you remember when I used those same words to you?"

"Yes. When you told me that I was accused of stealing twelve hundred pounds."

"I could not understand at the time why you were so confoundedly cheerful about it," said Thornhill. "Most people would have been distinctly peeved. However . . ." He obviously hesitated before continuing. His eyes were very thoughtful. "However, one never knows what reasons people may have for . . ." He broke off again and grinned at Michael. "You haven't told me whether I receive your condolences or your congratulations."

"It's rather difficult to say, isn't it?" returned Michael. "On the whole, perhaps, I think you . . . I think it is a matter for congratulation. I'm afraid I am putting it rather clumsily, but I do feel that it would not have done."

Thornhill followed with an indulgent smile Michael's efforts to express himself tactfully.

"You're quite right, Michael. Kate and I would have been an ill-assorted couple. If she had caught me earlier she might have made something of me, but I am now beyond reforming. She would have tackled the job gallantly . . . and broken her heart in the process. Still, it's all very sad.

> *Had we never loved sae kindly,*
> *Had we never loved sae blindly,*
> *Never met—or never parted,*
> *We had ne'er been broken-hearted.*

When I was a sentimental youth—yes, I was once a sentimental youth, Michael—I copied those lines into my diary and invested three of the words with the additional poignancy of red ink. I need not tell you which are the three words I incarnadined. If I kept a diary now—I have long since forsworn the vanity—I should probably be entering a certain well-known passage about youth's sweet-scented manuscript. . .. I shall go abroad again, Michael, and perhaps, in other seas than the Mediterranean—a stretch of water I shall avoid like the plague. Michael—a finger will beckon to me through charmed, magic casements and I shall recapture . . . I am growing maudlin." Thornhill looked at his glass. It was empty again. He crossed to the sideboard. "My fourth! But it will be a small one. No, damn it all! It will be a large one, a stiff one, a noble bumper, for I have a toast to drink."

He fumbled with the decanter and the siphon, and turned, with a brimming glass held unsteadily in his uplifted hand. Some of the contents spilled.

"To the chivalrous memory of Davy Garrick!" he exclaimed, and drank.

He flung the empty glass into the fireplace, shattering it to fragments, and dropped into his chair.

Michael watched him curiously. He wondered why David Garrick should have been chosen for this honour. He wondered also how Thornhill was going to dine in the regrettable absence of his first-class cook. Michael supposed he ought to ask his bereaved friend to dinner: yet, in the circumstances, he was reluctant to do so. He rose.

"Well, Frank, I must be getting back."

Thornhill did not reply. He was lying back in his chair with his eyes closed, and appeared to be oblivious of everything but his thoughts.

Michael left the house. As he walked down the path Sergeant Whalebone came up on his bicycle and exchanged a friendly smile. A few yards down the lane, Chrystal was hanging about by the hedge, as though waiting for something or someone. When he saw Michael, he approached eagerly.

"They've gone to Thornhill's now," he said.   "Who have?"

"Why, the police. Really, I think they might have thought of that before. Extraordinary how slowly their brains move!"

"But they haven't gone about . . . about what you thought they had. It's a case of robbery this time. Thornhill has had his cups and shields stolen."

"Oh!" Chrystal was a little dashed. Then his eyes brightened, and he added: "Who took them?"

"Well . . . Jennings and Mrs. Jennings and the car are also missing."

"Really?" The little man was quivering with excitement. "Do you think they'll be caught?"

"You know how good the police are at catching people," Michael allowed himself to say.

"Ye-es, but this is more in their usual line. Really, they ought to be able to manage this. . .. So poor Thornhill has lost all his trophies?"

"What appears to worry him still more," said Michael, "is that he has lost his cook."

"Then what will he . . . I'll ask him to dinner," said Chrystal enthusiastically. "He won't mind taking potluck. Really, it would be a neighbourly thing to do. I'll go along now . . ." He stopped and thrashed the grass with his stick. "As soon as that policeman fellow has gone," he corrected himself, "I'll drop in and ask him."

"I'm sure Thornhill will be very grateful to you," said Michael, and passed on feeling rather dubious about it.

XI. Scene in Court

Sergeant Whalebone, to his great relief, was temporarily released from dancing attendance on the nobs from Scotland Yard, and sent in quest of the Jennings couple. Thornhill's car turned up, abandoned in a sidestreet in Croydon, on the following morning. Three days later Whalebone arrested the fugitives at Southend and escorted them to Lewes goal. It was a smart piece of work on Whalebone's part, and Superintendent Strange, who presided over the Chesworth police, took an opportunity of saying so on the Sunday afternoon.

Whalebone was driving the police car at the time, for they were making a tour of inspection of the traffic conditions round Chesworth. If Superintendent Strange looked anything but dignified in the seat next the driver's—and, indeed, he was most untidily arranged and far from presenting a smart and constabulary appearance—the blame must attach to the car, which, being one of the latest popular models, was not designed to accommodate passengers of normal adult bulk. Superintendent Strange possessed considerably more than the normal adult bulk, and it was difficult to fit him into the car and still more difficult to get him out. After some practice, the superintendent had contrived to coil himself into a comparatively comfortable though ungainly posture. His half-closed eyes noticed all that went on in the road, and his sleepy speech disclosed perhaps the half of what he was thinking.

"Yes, Whalebone, you did a nice little job there. I only wish Scotland Yard showed signs of pulling theirs off. But thank God we called them in. Difficult to help ourselves, for that matter: we had to. Still, if we'd got the man, they'd have taken all the credit. As it is, there'll be brickbats about, and they'll get 'em." The superintendent chuckled. "For we don't seem to be getting any forrader.

"Look at that fool cutting in at the top of the hill. Remember his number, Whalebone. . . .

"Of course, they think Chrystal did it, but they haven't enough evidence to hang him on. A fair case against him, but not just strong enough. Tell a judge that Chrystal came down from the hill with a spade, met Bonar, whom he suspected of playing the game with his wife, and promptly crushed his head in—and the judge will look at the little weed in the dock, admit that he might have jumped on a wall to crack Bonar's skull, but tell himself that at any rate he didn't chuck Bonar's body into the water—not, at any rate, by his unaided efforts. Then there was not the slightest trace of blood on Chrystal's clothes. Obviously, some links are missing . . .

"Those two chaps are riding women's bikes: if they hadn't grinned at us so cheerfully as they went by, I should have wanted to know where they got 'em. . . .

"Do you think Chrystal did it? You don't, Whalebone? Well, at any rate, unless something else turns up, I don't quite see how the Yard are going to make a case of it. That spade's the queerest thing. It beats me. Chrystal has it and says he put it down and forgot all about it. It turns up the next morning in Holt's garden, and they say it shows signs of having been carefully cleaned. It probably did Bonar in, all right. I suppose Holt is telling the truth. There's nothing against him, except that he's a writer of fiction. Quite a respectable person: doesn't even write detective stories. . . .

"We shall have to get the County Council to do something about this corner: a thoroughly nasty place.

"Of course I know that Holt left Chesworth years ago under a cloud, but that story Bonar got hold of was just gossip. The fact of the matter is that he was in love with Rose Nichol, and skulked away because she turned him down. A foolish thing to do on account of any woman, but. . . well, I dare say we all did foolish things at that time of life. You did, Whalebone, I expect. Oh, don't bother to deny it. Returning to Holt, he went to Newcastle and got some sort of journalistic work. He was a quiet, sober, hard-working young fellow, according to those who remember him there. Then he joined a Manchester paper: was on it the whole of the thirteen years he lived there. Very well spoken of by everyone. Married the daughter of a solicitor. A respectable solicitor, the Manchester police said: I suppose they have both sorts there, too. Took to writing books, gave up his newspaper job, and returned to Chesworth to settle down. Nothing at all against him in all that. No evidence that he ever came into contact with Bonar. Must have known him by name in Newcastle, where Bonar made his money. Newcastle police don't seem greatly struck on Bonar. Admitted he was sprung from the respectable working-classes—there's a good deal of respectability in this case—and had built up an enormous fortune by his own exertions. Go on to add that he was a dominating type of man, which we knew already, and that he wasn't over popular with the people he employed, which I imagine is putting it kindly. Still. . .

"That bloke must have removed the silencer from his motor-bike, but he went past too quickly to spot his number. You get it? Well, it's hopeless to try to overtake him, and in any case if we start bothering about motorbikes that make an offensive noise we shall have our hands full. . . .

"Still, it was not known that Bonar had any serious enemies. And there you are. You know as well as I do, Whalebone, that it's the murder with no obvious motive that's the hardest to deal with. And here the only person with anything like a motive, so far as we can see, is Chrystal, and you don't think Chrystal did it. Oh, never mind what I think. If you really want to know, I think it may turn out to be a murder that was committed on impulse, on the spur of the moment. I also think that half the people connected with the business are lying for one reason or another. Still, that's pretty normal. It doesn't

make it any easier, none the less, and if Scotland Yard
don't have a rough time in the newspapers during the
next week or so, I'll eat my cap. . . .

"Good Lord, Whalebone, did you see that? That fellow
in the sports car overtaking at a bend, coming yards over
on his wrong side of the yellow line, and missing a
collision by the skin of his teeth. After him, Whalebone!
You probably won't catch him, but we may get near
enough with luck to read his number. Step on it,
Whalebone, step on it!"

3

The Jennings couple were to appear before the
Chesworth bench on Monday morning. Thornhill,
loathing the idea of making a public appearance in the
witness-box, sought out Michael and begged the
consolation of his company. Michael was most unwilling.
He wanted to get on with his work. He had had his fill of
police courts during his journalistic days in the north.
Despite the columns and columns of humorous sketches
which gave readers of the newspapers the impression
that police courts are the jolliest places of entertainment
imaginable, Michael knew better. He held that no one in
his senses would wish to attend a police court unless he
were obliged to. Nevertheless, against his better
judgment, Michael ceded to Thornhill's pleading and kept
him company. He buoyed himself up with the consolation
that it could not be a long business. It so happened that
the case proved to be the last on the list, and he was kept
in court for three hours.

Chrystal fell in with them on their way down and
insisted on joining the party. He received no
encouragement from Michael, and still less from
Thornhill, but he clung to them like a burr and refused to
be shaken off.

Chesworth police court held its sittings in the Town
Hall, a sturdy edifice of stone, adorned with turrets and

graven coats of arms, which looked as though it had strayed south from the Border country. It almost choked one of the narrow streets leading into the Pavement. The occupants of the first floors of the houses on either side could, whenever they so desired, enjoy an excellent view of the proceedings. There were car parks at front and back, and every now and then the voices of magistrates, witnesses, solicitors and defendants would be completely obliterated by the nerve-racking din of a starting motor-bicycle, reverberated by the imminent walls of the canyon-like thoroughfares; and the processes of the law would have to be held up while a constable was dispatched to admonish the offender.

The chairman of the magistrates on this occasion was a Labour man, an ex-railway servant: he had a beautiful head of white hair and eyes a little troubled by the constant study of human fallibility. Michael had hitherto known the overworked stipendiaries of the great cities in the north, who dealt out rough-and-ready justice at high speed, and were apt to turn peevish when the wheels did not run smoothly. He liked this conscientious little man, who took his time, was scrupulously polite, and erred on the side of tempering justice with mercy. On the chairman's right and left sat two ruddy-faced colleagues who looked like prosperous country gentlemen: there was only this outward difference between them, that one was a clergyman and the other was not. These three were doing all the work. Remote, at one end of the long raised bench, two other magistrates sat through most of the proceedings, but took no part in them: they appeared to have private matters to discuss. A woman J.P. dropped in when the sitting was well under way, smiled impartially on all present, stayed a while, took a keen interest in one of the cases, showed no interest in most of the others, remembered something, went out, dropped in again after half an hour, found nothing at all to interest her this time, smiled once more on everyone, and took a final departure.

"This is a pestilential place," whispered Thornhill very early in the proceedings.

"Police courts always are," Michael whispered back.

"Really, the acoustics are very bad," complained little Chrystal, cocking a hand behind his ear in an effort to hear what was going on.

"The acoustics of police courts always are," said Michael. "There's something to be said for it."

"Extraordinary!" muttered Chrystal.

If the acoustics of the court were bad, the accommodation provided for the general public was worse. They were herded in a square pen which occupied half the rear portion of the court, and no seats were provided for them. In spite of this discomfort, a number of elderly men stood watching through all the weary length of the morning. A paternity case was a *bonne bouche* for them, but they did not despise even the flat beer of motoring offences. Outside, the morning was bright: the sun shone and the air was sweet. All these men of no occupation might have been down by the river where the birds were singing. They preferred to remain in the court, where they followed everything with greedy attention; and at the end of the three hours' sitting they tore themselves reluctantly away. It was impossible not to think that they must have empty lives, thought Michael, speculating upon the kind of homes from which they came.

Cheek by jowl with the pen which enclosed these unfortunates was a railed-off enclosure provided with chairs, and here were accommodated those persons who had business at the court. Michael, with Thornhill and Chrystal, sat at the end of the front row. Immediately in front of them three steps led up to the witness-box, and they were able to enjoy a perfect view of the rear elevation of everyone who took his stand in that uncomfortable place. Thus they saw more of the witnesses than the magistrates could; and these back views were very illuminating. Shoes, for instance . . .

there could be no better testimony than a pair of shoes to the social and financial standing of their wearer. And backs could be more eloquent than faces, since faces may be schooled to mask emotion. Michael contemplated with interest the back of a very dapper motorist in a well-cut suit of fashionable cloth. He presented a bold front to the bench; but from behind he could be seen nervously fingering the seat of his trousers, like a schoolboy who has a guilty conscience and every reason to apprehend that retribution awaits him . . . and his finger-nails were surprisingly filthy. Thornhill, awaiting his own ordeal, fidgeted in his seat; and Michael, glancing his way, was not surprised to see him unnecessarily examining his carefully manicured hands.

The dock stood in front of the barrier that separated the public into sheep and goats, and Michael had to twist his neck to the left when he wished to look at its occupants; but it was little used. The motorists who formed the greater part of the offenders were allowed to stand in front of it. In the valley between the dock and the bench was the clerk's table, and here the solicitors found seats.

If there were any persons who could unreservedly bless the advent of the motor-car, mused Michael, surely the chief among them were the solicitors in country towns. To them the internal combustion engine was a providential discovery which had filled their laps with guineas. Guineas, too, which seemed easily earned. It was only necessary to ask a police-witness a question and speak two deprecating sentences to the magistrates. Thereupon a fine was duly levied, just as though their client was in exactly the same category as those who had neglected to provide themselves with forensic aid. Indeed, he was worse off: he had the solicitor's bill to foot. It was another illustration of the triumph of hope over experience that erring motorists should continue to employ solicitors to defend them.

There was plenty of opportunity for reflections of this

nature during the motoring cases, since they were very dull and mostly inaudible. Michael retained one or two pictures in his memory. There was a moment when the woman J.P. intervened on behalf of a lorry-driver who was about to be fined two pounds. She smiled very sweetly at the chairman and held up one finger, but the chairman frowned back at her and said two; whereupon she smiled very sweetly at Superintendent Strange, who watched like a fat benevolent god from a high desk against the wall on the left. There was an interesting interlude when the gentleman in the neat blue suit was taken in hand by the magistrates' clerk and turned upside down and inside out until he contradicted himself and his defence was revealed as a ragged sham. There was an indignant person, dressed rather like a Lancashire comedian, who had a cleft palate and a strong sense of injustice. . . . But on the whole the motoring cases were neither edifying nor entertaining; and it was an affiliation order which aroused flagging interest and, incidentally, first revealed the somewhat surprising fact that among those present in the court was Miss Perks

The claimant in the paternity case was a tall, angular young woman: the defendant a hefty lad of bucolic type who worked in his mother's business The youth did not deny his share of the responsibility for the child, and the question at issue was how much he should be made to pay. Whether of his own accord or by order of the court, it was not clear which, he produced his bankbooks to facilitate the judgment of the magistrates. A budding capitalist, he kept one account with Messrs. Barclay and another with His Majesty's Postmaster-General, and each showed a tidy sum to his credit. The conditions of his employment delighted the solicitors and gave them something to wrangle about. He did not receive a normal salary, but drew weekly pocket-money from his mother, who also paid sums into one or both of his banks at irregular intervals. Oddly enough, considerable importance was attached to a recent purchase of a motor-bicycle. The possession of a motor-bicycle appeared to be regarded as evidence of means. ("These proceedings are becoming more and more detached from reality," growled Thornhill.) The girl claimed fifteen guineas for medical expenses and a weekly contribution of fifteen shillings a week towards the maintenance of the child: together with her solicitor's costs. Her solicitor was the most prosperous-looking Hebrew Michael had seen in Chesworth; and he was attended by one of the shabbiest Jews whom Michael had ever seen even in Manchester. The boy's solicitor worked up some indignation in pointing out that fifteen guineas was a large amount for a girl of that social class to spend on a doctor's bill, even in the circumstances; and then, while the magistrates were in the act of putting their heads together, and the woman J.P., feeling that the opportunity had come to show the value of having feminine assistance on the bench, was called into conference, there came an unseemly comment from the rear of the court.

"Fifteen guineas!" exclaimed a deep gruff voice. "Ridiculous!"

Michael looked round and saw Miss Perks sitting in a corner seat two rows behind him.

Several policemen, scandalized by this breach of the properties, turned frowning faces in the direction of the offender. When they saw it was Miss Perks they looked away and winked at one another. The chairman, too, who had momentarily lifted his eyebrows, exchanged a grave smile with his colleagues.

The court awarded the girl twelve pounds ten towards the doctor's bill, twelve-and-six a week until the child reached the age of sixteen, and her costs. The two Hebrews promptly seized their papers and left the building, a broad smile of triumph on the good-looking one's face; and Miss Perks remarked, in a loud voice: "Preposterous!" She added, to the delight of the patient watchers in the public pen: "Well, the young man has had to pay dearly for his pleasure."

"What may you be doing here, Miss Perks?" asked Thornhill, turning round.

"Have I not as much right here as anybody else?" retorted Miss Perks. "Don't talk, Frank Thornhill, or the policemen will turn you out."

"I wish to God they would," said Thornhill, and turned back to continue his weary wait.

3

It was not until one o'clock that Jennings and his female partner in crime appeared in the dock. Michael, twisting his head, stole a sideways look at the erring pair. Jennings had lost the dashing air with which he had been used to drive Thornhill's car at the rate of seventy-five miles an hour. It could not truthfully be said that his tall figure showed a tendency to droop: it was borne up by a framework too substantial to allow of that; but he was evidently very ill at ease. The stout woman at his side wept silently. Jennings put his arm round her.

"Damn it all," murmured Thornhill, "the blighters are fond of each other, anyhow."

They pleaded guilty.

Sergeant Whalebone went into the witness-box, took the oath, and began to rattle off his evidence at great speed. At such-and-such a time on such-and-such a day he went to a certain house in Southend and saw the prisoners, whom he charged with etc., etc. He cautioned them, and the man said, "Yes, that's right." The woman said, "Well, what can I say? We took the things. It's no use denying it when you've . . ."

At this point Superintendent Strange, shifting his great bulk slightly to glance at the clock, and reflecting that his dinner was probably spoiling, took it upon him self to say to the sergeant: "Why don't you cut it short? There's no need to go into everything. They've pleaded guilty."

The clerk to the magistrates looked up.

"Go on," he said curtly, addressing the witness.

The ascendancy of the judicial over the executive arm of the law having been duly vindicated, the sergeant went on to say exactly what he had intended to say: while the superintendent, digesting the snub, smiled affably at the ceiling.

The sergeant might have said a great deal more, reflected Michael. He had omitted a number of things that it would be interesting to hear. Even in a comparatively simple case like this, the police inquiries must have been extensive. There would be many clues to weigh and reject or follow up. Yet the sergeant modestly confined himself to informing the court that the motor-car had been found abandoned in Croydon, some of the silver had been traced to a pawnbroker's in Camberwell, and the remainder run to ground in the basement of a house at Willesden. He gave no hint of how these discoveries had been made. Unassuming fellows, the police. They were a silent service, if you liked. Highly efficient in small things. When were they going to get Bonar's murderer? The superintendent could not be feeling too happy about that. . . . Would they get Bonar's murderer? Michael, watching Thornhill step at last into the witness-box, felt that no great harm would be done if they did not. . . . A highly unethical viewpoint! He smiled and composed himself to see how Thornhill came through the ordeal.

Thornhill gave evidence and identified the recovered goods. Michael, from his observation-post at the rear, thought he acquitted himself well. He kept his arms stiffly by his side, showing that he had profited by watching the uneasy motorist. His back betrayed no idea of what he was feeling.

"Thank God that's over," murmured Thornhill, coming back to his seat.

"Have you anything to say?" The chairman of the magistrates were putting the question to the couple in the dock.

"No, sir," said Jennings. "We wish to throw ourselves on the mercy of the court."

The superintendent chipped in. He spoke in a very quiet voice, and Michael and Thornhill could not hear the half of what he said; but it appeared that he was rather sorry for the prisoners and hoped they would be let off lightly. It was true that Jennings had been sent to a Borstal institution as a boy; but on his release he had gone into service and bore a fairly good character. There had been an unfortunate lapse just two years previously, when he had decamped with some valuables belonging to his employer, much in the same way as he had gone off with Mr. Thornhill's property. On that occasion he had been bound over, and there was reason to believe that he had been trying to lead a decent life until this temptation came in his way.

"You were certainly putting temptation in people's way," said the chairman, looking at Thornhill. "It would be wiser in future to keep these valuable trophies under lock and key."

Thornhill accepted the rebuke with a bow.

"With regard to the female prisoner," continued Superintendent Strange, "it is rather a sad story. She is not married to the male prisoner."

"We might have known that," soliloquized Miss Perks audibly.

"She was very badly treated by her own husband," continued the superintendent, glancing for a moment towards Miss Perks and shrugging his shoulders. "He is now serving a sentence of penal servitude, and there is this to be said for the male prisoner, that he befriended her, and apparently is very much attached to her."

The woman in the dock sobbed, and Jennings once more stretched a protecting arm around her. Miss Perks was heard to snort.

Now the chairman consulted in whispers with the two faithful colleagues who remained. Suddenly Michael felt an abrupt movement next to him. Chrystal had risen to his feet and stood facing the bench. At first his diminutive figure attracted no attention. Then, as he persisted in his attitude, people in the public pen began to nudge one another and to point. Chrystal fidgeted self-consciously, but remained standing. Michael looked at him questioningly. Until then Chyrstal had been so quiet and absorbed that Michael had forgotten his presence.

"What's up?" he asked in a whisper, laying his hand on Chrystal's jacket.

Chrystal shook off the hand impatiently and uttered speech. His metallic voice, pitched high in his agitation, addressed the magistrates.

"May I have permission to ask the male prisoner a question?" it said.

The magistrates interrupted their conference and looked at Chrystal in surprise. There was a rustle in the public pen. The police had all the air of being shocked.

A youthful constable bent down to whisper to Chrystal in a fatherly way: "Come, come, you mustn't interrupt the proceedings." The clerk put down his pen, said, "Order in court. This is most irregular, sir," and fixed Chrystal with a professional frown.

Chrystal turned upon the young constable with the fury which the sight of a police uniform had aroused in him for days.

"I wasn't talking to you, my man," he snapped.

"I am not sure whether we ought to allow this," said the chairman dubiously. "What is it you want to ask the prisoner?"

Chrystal's voice, quavering but shrill, held the attentive court.

"I want to ask the prisoner," he said, wheeling suddenly on Jennings, "why he threw Douglas Bonar's body into the river."

For one moment there was an intense silence in the court. All looked in one direction. Many people there could not see the shaking finger which Chrystal pointed at Jennings, but it seemed that all were under the spell of this gesture as they fixed their eyes on the man in the dock. Jennings shrank back.

"I didn't do it!" he cried. "I didn't kill him!"

The woman beside him took his hand and tried to soothe him.

In the silence Miss Perks's voice rang out, harsh and clear: "You fool!" she said contemptuously. "You blundering ninny!"

It was Chrystal she addressed.

Chrystal, losing the excitement that had buoyed him up, collapsed into his chair, where he sat trembling.

A buzz of talk arose from the public pen.

"Order, order," said the clerk, rapping with his pen. "Silence must be kept. All this is most irregular." He muttered something to the solicitors: never in his experience, his manner seemed to say, had he known such outrageous behaviour in a court of law.

The chairman stroked his chin and glanced at the superintendent.

The superintendent lifted his sleepy eyes to the ceiling, and murmured: "Under the circumstances, sir, I think a remand . . ."

"Remanded for a week," said the chairman hastily; but before he could rise Miss Perks was on her feet. She hesitated for a moment, darted a venomous glance at Chrystal, tossed her head, and clumped towards the door. Such was the magnetic influence which emanated from this little old woman that the magistrates and everyone else remained as they were to watch her. For a few seconds, and it seemed a much longer interval of time, she was the sole moving object in the court-room. She walked very deliberately to the door. She reached it. The door swung behind her. There was yet another moment of silence in which all eyes stared stupidly at the door through which Miss Perks had departed. Then the spell was broken. The magistrates rose, the prisoners were removed, and policemen, solicitors, witnesses and public broke into excited conversation . . . all except Chrystal, who remained huddled in his chair with his head in his hands.

Superintendent Strange came down into the body of the court and looked ironically at the shaken little man.

"I should like a word or two with you, sir," he said.

Chrystal raised his head defiantly.

"You can have it," he said.

The superintendent smiled.

"Bass," he said, turning to the young constable with the fatherly manner, "you might send a boy round to tell Mrs. Strange that I shall be very late for my dinner. . . . Oh, Whalebone, yes. Let him tell Mrs. Whalebone too. . . . I shall want you, Whalebone. Damned nuisance about our dinners. It can't be helped, but women get into such a stew about things like that. They don't understand: no sense of proportion. When constabulary duty's to be done"—the superintendent hummed these words—"even dinners have to wait. . . . If you would be good enough to come with me, Mr. Chrystal . . ."

Thornhill put his hand on Michael's shoulder.

"Let's get out of this damned place," he said. "Let's go and have a drink somewhere."

Michael declined.

"I'm shockingly late for lunch already," he said. "I shall get into hot water as it is."

"You married men!" said Thornhill mockingly.

XII. Miss Perks Asks Questions

Kate Martindale returned Miss Perks's call that afternoon. She thought the old house in the Pavement curious, even attractive in its own way, but not to be commended from the point of view of domestic economy. In the circumstances it was highly creditable to Elizabeth that she kept it so clean. The spick-and-span kitchen earned full marks; and the bathroom merited equal praise. But a bathroom with four doors! Our ancestors, thought Kate, were promiscuous persons. Yet the bath, of course, was an afterthought: this had been intended as a bedroom. Even then . . . Still, if Miss Perks did not worry about it. . . and it did not seem at all likely that Miss Perks worried about things like that when she kept a parrot that greeted visitors with "Come in, blast you!" . . .

The first thing Miss Perks did, however, was to reach to the floor for a dark red shawl and cover up the protesting parrot.

"Ramsay MacDonald is not quite himself," she explained. "We have just installed a wireless set, and his nose is out of joint. He is not really in a fit state to meet visitors. Sit down. Elizabeth, tell Robert to come and help me entertain Miss Martindale."

She fixed Kate with her shrewd grey eyes.

"Tell me how you are getting on at the Park. Are the servants taking kindly to a purely feminine regime? I doubt it. Servants seldom do. They like to feel that there's an intelligent man in the house, even if they get their orders from the woman."

"I haven't much to complain about," said Kate guardedly, "though I expect I shall have to make one or two changes."

"I should sack the lot if I were you," counselled Miss

Perks, "and start afresh. You would be uncomfortable for a time, but in the long run it would be worth it. . . . Better still, of course, instal the intelligent man I spoke of, at the first opportunity."

"That would no doubt be the ideal plan," said Kate, with mild irony.

Irony was wasted on Miss Perks.

"You have no husband in view at present?" she demanded.

Kate raised her eyebrows.

"Not at present," she said stiffly.

"You ought to get married," said Miss Perks. "Every woman ought to get married. That's what women were meant for. I ought to have had a husband myself. I was a fool. I have regretted it ever since. It can't be helped now; but you mustn't make the same mistake." Miss Perks took up the garment she was knitting and bent over it in silence for half a minute. She continued without looking up: "It won't be for lack of suitors if you miss the opportunity. You'll have all the worthless young men of the neighbourhood pursuing you. But frankly"—Miss Perks closed her eyes for a moment—: "I cannot see that there is any young man in Chesworth or district who can be unreservedly recommended. . . . You had thought of Frank Thornhill?"

The question was shot so abruptly at Kate that she blushed.

"Mr. Thornhill and I," she said curtly, "are friends, nothing more."

Miss Perks nodded her head.

"Frank Thornhill was one of my pupils when I kept a school here. As a little boy he was quite attractive, though abominably spoilt. I did my best to correct him; but you have been a teacher yourself and you know what fools parents can be and how utterly impossible it is to undo their work. Frank Thornhill was never whipped often enough or hard enough as a child"—a glint came into Miss Perks's eye as she said this—"and the result is plain to be seen in what he is now. He still has a glib charm of manner, but he is self-indulgent and has never done a day's honest work in his life. He drinks, too. He drinks far too much. I have told him that he should go right away and find a real man's job to do. He does intend, I believe, to leave Chesworth; but as to finding a job of work—that, I am convinced, Frank Thornhill will never do."

Miss Perks, having taken away Thornhill's character, went on rather savagely with her knitting. Kate was silent.

"As to the other eligible bachelors in the town," said Miss Perks at length, "I can only think of the rector. Some people, I suppose, would call him eligible, though he is getting on for fifty. He is a man of striking appearance, and vain of the fact. His sermons are delivered in an impressive voice and much admired by some: though when reprinted, as they sometimes are in the Chesworth paper, it is obvious that they are trashy. Full of long words, but dithering about all round the place. The man doesn't know what he believes, and that's the explanation of the matter. He likes sitting on the fence and running with the hare and hunting with the hounds. He turns all ways, like a weathercock. He's a selfish, conceited fellow, and one of these days Miss Champken will land him, and he will deserve his fate."

A little puzzled by this violent attack on the rector, Kate scarcely knew what to say. She was glad when Robert Perks came in and made himself as agreeable as his sister was disagreeable, She liked Robert and thought him a distinguished, scholarly sort of elderly gentleman. She had heard nothing of the strange lapses to which he was subject, and her enjoyment of his conversation was not allayed by any private misgivings.

Elizabeth brought in tea; and Kate plunged into a discussion of books with Robert, enjoying it very much, and almost forgetting the presence of his sister, who brooded silently in the background. They had exchanged views on Dickens and Thackeray and advanced to a discussion of Hugh Walpole when Miss Perks made an impatient movement and caught the red shawl with her elbow so that it slid from the parrot's cage.

"Hell!" said the parrot, blinking at the light. "Hasn't that blasted woman gone yet?"

Robert deftly dived for the shawl and consigned the bird to decent obscurity.

Kate stood up, slightly flushed.

"It really is getting late," she said. "I must take Polly's hint and be off."

"The bird's name," said Miss Perks stiffly, "is Ramsay MacDonald."

"My sister's politics are opposed to Mr. MacDonald's," said Robert, smiling, "and so now you know what they are. Or don't you?"

"It leaves plenty of room for conjecture," answered Kate. "Well, good-bye, Miss Perks, and . . ."

"I'm coming downstairs with you," snapped Miss Perks.

She led the way through the bathroom, across the dark landing, down the winding stairs, into the kitchen and out along the stone passage. By the door she stopped.

"You are thinking, I dare say," she said to Kate Martindale, in the half-light of the space behind the carefully bolted front door, "that I am a rough-tongued, meddlesome old woman, and you're right. I am crafty and sour and vindictive . . . yes, I am all that and more. Don't you believe any of the old fools who tell you that Miss Perks has a kind heart really. It isn't true, and they don't believe it themselves. They only say it because they think it is the thing to say. But I have"—the little woman drew herself up—"a keen sense of justice, and being able to see things exactly as they are is a useful accomplishment in a far from perfect world. So, if you are not a silly woman who is frightened by a rough manner, you know where to come if at any time you feel that a little plain speaking and frank discussion of the truth would be a pleasant relief from the ordinary intercourse of Chesworth society.

Good-bye."

Whereupon Miss Perks flung back the bolts and allowed the bewildered Kate to emerge into the Pavement.

2

"For goodness' sake," exclaimed Miss Perks three hours later, "turn that thing off."

Robert obediently silenced the signorina in Rome.

"She has such a charming voice," he murmured in self defence.

"Come and sit down. I want to talk to you."

That occasional eccentricity of Robert's behaviour made his sister forget that he was normally a most intelligent man. She was accustomed to speak to him as if he were a child. She spoke so now.

Robert obediently sat down opposite her and smiled good-humouredly.

"Well, what did you make of her?" demanded Miss Perks.

"Miss Martindale? I thought she was quite a pleasant person. What made you bully her so?"

"Do I bully people?"

"Well . . ."

"Yes, I do," admitted Robert's sister. "But some people want to be bullied."

"Not Miss Martindale. I don't think those are the right tactics with her. She has a will of her own. She ought to marry Frank Thornhill."

Miss Perks dropped her knitting.

"Why do you think she ought to marry Frank Thornhill?"

"It would be a good match. They are both intelligent and they would respect each other."

Miss Perks snorted.

"I hope to goodness she never will," she said with emphasis.

Robert looked at her.

"I always thought Frank Thornhill was one of your favourite pupils. Since when have you been prejudiced against him? . . . Or is it Miss Martindale you are prejudiced against?"

"I am not prejudiced against anybody," declared Miss Perks. "You ought to know by this time, Robert, that the one thing I pride myself upon is the ability to take an impartial view of people."

"It is your characteristic trait," said Robert kindly.

Miss Perks resumed her knitting.

"Robert," she asked, with her eyes bent on her work, "does it look as if the police were going to find the person who killed that man Bonar?"

"There seems less likelihood every day."

"Murder is generally supposed to be a dreadful thing," remarked Miss Perks.

Robert looked slightly puzzled.

"Yes, Mattie, it is."

"Can you imagine yourself committing a murder, Robert?"

"My dear Mattie!"

"Answer my question, Robert," said his sister impatiently.

"Can any man," replied Robert rhetorically, "look into his heart and say that he has never been tempted to commit a murder?"

"If people are to be murdered, don't you think it is a good thing to choose a victim like that man Bonar?"

"What a gruesome conversation, my dear," said Robert.

"Can you see any reason why a person like that man Bonar," pursued Miss Perks relentlessly, "should not be put out of the way? Is not the world a better place because he has left it?"

"*De mortuis . . .*"

"Oh, for goodness' sake, don't quote that at me. No one acts on it nowadays. Read the popular biographies. . . .

Have you heard anyone express regret at the loss of that man Bonar?"

"Since you apparently wish me to be frank and natural, Mattie, I must say I have not."

"If you had murdered that man Bonar, would you feel the slightest remorse?"

"What a question, Mattie!"

"Answer it," insisted Miss Perks.

"I should be very much upset if I were found out," said Robert honestly. "Apart from that deplorable consequence . . . Well, yes, I should. It's no use my trying to live up to your ruthless standards. If I had murdered anyone, I should naturally feel remorse. It is . . . At the lowest valuation, it's an unsocial thing to do." Robert smiled. "Shall we see what the B.B.C. are up to?"

"Never mind the B.B.C." Miss Perks clicked her needles. "So that is how you would feel, is it?" she said thoughtfully. "But suppose . . . Suppose, Robert, it were not a question of your having killed that man Bonar. Suppose someone else had done it. Suppose you knew who it was."

"My dear Mattie!" murmured Robert, looking at her curiously.

"Suppose this person was . . . was somebody you knew and liked. Would you"—Miss Perks was choosing her words carefully—"would you feel it your social duty to denounce this murderer to the police?"

Robert swung round on his chair.

"Now that's a very interesting question, Mattie," he said cheerfully. "But a great many things would have to be taken into consideration, don't you think? And especially . . ."

"Yes?" demanded his sister.

"Especially, I suppose, whether any innocent person was likely to suffer."

"And if that was unlikely?"

"Well. . . Oh, I don't know. I don't think it's a very nice question for old ladies like you to have to think about."

He got up and patted her on the shoulder. "Now," he said firmly, "I'm going to listen to Rome for a little while."

Robert, listening with half an ear to the rich cadences of the young lady in Rome, wondered what his sister had on her mind. One would suppose she knew who had killed Douglas Bonar. Was it possible? Women got strange ideas into their heads at times: even strongminded women like his sister.

Ente Italiana Radiofonica. Just the name of the Italian equivalent of the B.B.C., but it sounded like a magnificent fragment of Virgil. . . .

Well, Mattie appeared to have decided that she had already said too much. Better let it rest at that. One might do more harm than good by stirring the waters.

Miss Martindale was a very superior woman. If I were thirty years younger, thought Robert. . .

From Rome came the opening notes of the overture to Carmen.

XIII. THREE LETTERS FROM NEWCASTLE

Michael Holt did not see Thornhill again until the following Friday, when an urgent scribbled message was delivered at the Vineyard by favour of the afternoon milkman:

"For God's sake, come and have tea with me."
"Frank."

The invitation being couched in such terms, Michael did not see how he could decline. He went, and found Thornhill making his own preparations for the meal. The sideboard, once so bravely cluttered up with costly trophies, was decorated by a single silver cup.

"The rest?" said Thornhill, echoing Michael's unspoken question. "The rest are locked up in a safe place. I am following the practice of the Japanese with their pictures: exhibiting one at a time. Sensible people, the Japanese." He poured some hot water from the electric kettle into the tea-pot, and emptied the pot out of the window. "Excuse my primitive methods. I feel like a man whose wife has eloped. When you come to think of it, a bachelor is familiar with all the worst experiences of the most unsuccessful husband. Every few months he comes downstairs to find that he has been deceived again and there is no one to cook the breakfast for him. I regret the pseudo-Mrs. Jennings more than I can say. She had a nice touch with grub. She is in the cells and, oh, the difference to me!"

"I understood she was remanded to an institution," observed Michael.

"She is remanded to a suitable institution and, oh, the difference to me!" Thornhill made a grimace. "Don't, in the interests of vulgar accuracy, spoil my best lines. . . . She has gone, anyhow, and, as a memorial, the unwashed dishes rise like Everest in the sink. Lunch is a sham, dinner a mockery. Breakfast, after all, is not too bad, except that one's last minutes in bed are clouded by the thought that one has to get up and cook it: I can fry bacon. Tea is a positive pleasure, the one bright spot of the day. One of my vanities is that I fancy myself a bit of a dab at making tea. You noticed how I warmed the pot? Just one of those little touches that make all the difference. Women won't be bothered about them. It takes a man to make a good cup of tea."

So Thornhill rattled on. Michael sat back in his chair and thought what a difference a Kate Martindale would have made to such an establishment. Miss Martindale, from all accounts, was nothing if not capable. She would have looked after Thornhill as efficiently as she had looked after her domestic economy centre: as efficiently as she was now settling down to look after the Forest Park estate. Well. . . that was possible no longer. Things had gone very badly wrong. It was a great pity.

"Help yourself," Thornhill was saying. "I think everything is within your reach. Just stretch out a tentacle and take what you fancy. . . . The police tell me that Jennings will get a month. Or he may merely be bound over. There's a certain amount of sympathy with him. It's a little trying to be publicly accused of murder in open court by a comparative stranger."

"But Chrystal didn't accuse him of murder."

Thornhill shrugged his great shoulders.

"It came to the same thing in popular estimation."

"Chrystal gave them no satisfaction, I hear."

"None at all. On the contrary. Refused to explain his outburst. Said if they couldn't see what was obvious, he was unable to provide them with understandings. Abused them, West Sussex police and Scotland Yard alike, for being as blind as bats and unable to notice things that lay beneath their noses. Naturally they came to the conclusion that he was a little unhinged."

"It wouldn't be altogether surprising if he were."

"It wouldn't," agreed Thornhill dryly.

"And what did Jennings say?"

"Denied all knowledge of everything. Said the accusation was such a complete surprise that it threw him off his balance. Said Chrystal must be barmy. The police, secretly agreeing with this diagnosis, put him through it all the same. They are just where they were."

"And Chrystal has gone away to the seaside to recuperate."

"Wise fellow. I think I shall follow his example and improve upon it. Go abroad, Michael."

"Abroad?"

"Yes. I shall store the furniture and shut the house up. Following this decision, as they would say in the Press, I have made no attempt to replace Jennings and the pseudo-Mrs. Jennings. I shall sell the miraculously undamaged car . . . I shall regret the garden. It will be a great wrench to leave all these lovely plants and these equally cherished rocks. I spent a long time in collecting them. But I shall soon forget them, in the excitement of gratifying a desire I have had ever since I was a boy. . . .. Another cup of tea? I see you agree with me that it's a good brew. . . . A desire, I think I said, that has been with me since I was a boy. As a boy, Michael, I used to lie on my stomach on the hearthrug and read one travel book after the other. I said to myself that one day I should go and see with my own eyes the things of which I read: watch the pilgrims bathing in the Ganges, stand on the Great Wall of China, roam among the cherry orchards of Japan—where they have such sensible views about domestic decorations—explore the Grand Canyon of Colorado, climb Chimborazo and Popocatapetl, round the Horn in a wind-jammer, eat the lotus in the South Sea Islands, shoot the tawny African lion. . . . All these things, Michael, I now intend to do."

"You will be away a long time."

"Perhaps for years. I shall come back an elderly man, tanned by the salt winds of the seven seas, and full of wondrous tales to tell to . . . other people's children."

"You are going alone?"

"I am going alone. As far as may be, I shall travel overland. I shall avoid the company of my fellow beings. I shall not risk being cooped up with them in passenger ships. I shall eschew luxurious liners and Mediterranean waters. They would bring back memories that tear at the 'eart-strings."

Michael said nothing.

Thornhill sighed.

"You see in me a man whose illusions are shattered. As one of the world's most experienced lovers put it, at the conclusion of one of his innumerable affairs:

Had we never loved sae kindly,
Had we never loved sae blindly,
Never met—or never parted . . .

Or never parted! There's the rub, Michael. There's the rub, my boy."

"You've quoted that before," said Michael coldly.

"I believe I have. I repeat myself. But you must bear with me, for it may be a long time before we see each other again.

I'm off by the morning train
To sail the seas again . . .

and that's why I demanded your presence at tea. I had to see you and talk with you before I went." Thornhill pushed back his chair. His voice changed. "Michael," he said gently, "this is going to be an awkward business, but I don't see how it can be shirked. I lay awake last night making up my mind about it. I decided it's got to be done."

He stooped to the hearth and made up the fire.

"It's on the warm side to-day for a blazing hearth, but we may need a source of combustion presently. Make yourself comfortable."

Michael moved to an armchair and waited.

Thornhill stretched himself opposite and sat for a moment in silence.

"I'm going to be brutal," he said at length. "It's the best way." He was watching Michael through half-closed eyes. "Who was it," he asked musingly, "who said that if you sent a letter to all the leading citizens of a town saying all was discovered, half of them would pack their bags straight away?"

"I don't know."

"There's some truth in the exaggeration, I imagine," Thornhill went on. "We all have our secrets. There's a skeleton in my own cupboard. I open the cupboard once a month, write the skeleton a cheque, shut the door and try to forget it again."

"For God's sake," burst out Michael, "tell me what you're getting at."

"I'm sorry, Michael. I'll cease to beat about the bush." He took two folded documents from his pocket and spread them open on his knee. Michael could see that they were typewritten letters. "I found these among Bonar's papers when I was helping my faithless Kate to go through them. I took it upon myself, having read them, to purloin them. They concern you. I propose to read them to you and then burn them." He glanced at Michael's face, and, seeing it white and set, dropped his eyes to the papers in his hand. "I think that's the best way, Michael. It may comfort you to know, as I firmly believe—for reasons I'll explain later—that your secret is safe. They are from a man in Newcastle, a certain Julius Grant, who seems to have been some sort of inferior employed by Bonar as . . . well, to put it nicely, as an agent. This is the first of his letters:

Sir,
Pursuant to your instructions, I have made inquiries

in Newcastle re Michael Holt, and am able to report as
follows. He is known to have come to this city in the
autumn of 1920. He was at first in very poor
circumstances, picking up a precarious living by free-
lance journalism, but later he obtained a staff job on a
local evening newspaper. He appears to have done very
well, and in June of the next year he was offered a better
post at Manchester and removed to that place. According
to journalists who knew him here, his personal character
was of the highest. He was a hard-working man who kept
himself to himself, and they thought he had abilities that
would take him far.

"So far, so good," commented Thornhill. "But you can
hear this unpleasant person chortling with ill-concealed
glee in his next paragraph.

I was not satisfied with this information, which, I
take it, is hardly what you would require. I took other
means of finding out about Mr. Holt, and as a result have
come into possession of an interesting fact concerning
him which does not appear to have been known to his
journalistic colleagues. It was almost an accident. A
friend of mine, asked to make inquiries, was collecting
rents in the Leazes Park district, when he happened to
meet a landlady who remembered the name. She was not
communicative, however, and I therefore went myself to
see her, and persuaded her to tell me more. According to
her, this Michael Holt was in January 1921 living with a
girl called Annette Harding, whose character was not of
the best.

"A sanctimonious scoundrel, this Julius Grant,"
exclaimed Thornhill, pausing in his reading. "Mix
yourself a drink, Michael," he added without looking up.
"You'll find the ingredients at hand.

They called themselves man and wife, but the

landlady doubted whether this was actually the case. There were constant quarrels, and eventually the girl left him. The landlady spoke very well of Holt but could not speak too badly of the girl.

I trust this will be of interest to you. Please let me know if you wish the matter further followed up.

Yours obediently,

Julius Grant.

"Bonar," said Thornhill, "evidently did want the matter followed up, to judge by Grant's second letter, which is dated ten days later.

Sir,

I must apologize for my delay in replying to your esteemed inquiries, but it has been unusually difficult to obtain all the information you desire. Annette Harding is suspicious of all approaches and refuses to answer questions. She knows on which side her bread is buttered, and if only for that reason is loyal to Holt and unwilling to let him down. However, I can now inform you that Michael Holt and Annette Harding were legally married. I have been to considerable trouble and searched many registers and have at last found a record of the marriage. Whether the marriage has been dissolved is another matter, but I believe from Annette Harding's demeanour under questioning that she is legally still Michael Holt's wife.

From inquiries in other quarters I find that on leaving her husband she returned to her former way of life. In June 1922 she was involved in a fire which broke out in some tenement houses here, and her name was at first included in the published list of those who lost their lives. Actually she suffered severe burns and was in hospital for some time. On leaving hospital she gave up her old profession and made a break with her former acquaintances, opening a confectioner's shop in Gosforth. When I saw her she had all the outward signs of being comfortably off. She could not help betraying agitation when I mentioned the name of Michael Holt, but insisted that she had no knowledge of such a person. I put certain questions which she refused to answer. Monetary inducements were of no avail. I think it is safe to conclude that she receives regular payments from Holt on condition that she keeps quiet and that she takes care to observe her agreement to the letter.

In accordance with your instructions, I am treating this matter for the present as absolutely secret and confidential, and I trust that what I have done will meet with your approval. I am obliged for your cheque. In view of the unexpected difficulties of the inquiry, I venture to suggest that an additional ten guineas would not be unreasonable.

Yours obediently,
Julius Grant.

"So much for Mr. Grant, a lickspittle and a cur if ever there was one," said Thornhill. He looked sideways at Michael, who sat with his face in his hands. Thornhill added hastily: "Now, here's a bit of unexpected luck. A bolt from the blue." He took a third document from his pocket, a letter written in pale ink on dark blue notepaper:

Dear Sir,
In reply to your letter thanking my husband for his efforts and enclosing cheque for five pounds, I regret to inform you that my husband passed away suddenly last night with heart failure.

Yours respectfully,
Angela Grant.

Thornhill chuckled. "Am I correct in reading between the lines of this letter that Angela is not altogether broken-hearted? Anyhow, it's good news for you, Michael. I should imagine Julius Grant would not have been averse to a little quiet blackmail on his own account, but he's gone where the blackmailers go. Couldn't have happened better, eh?"

Michael did not answer.

Thornhill stood up, tore the letters across, threw the pieces on to the fire, and watched them burn.

"You see, old man," he said, "no one need ever know. There go the letters. They were written by one dead man to another. No one else has seen them."

Michael lifted a white face but still did not speak.

"There's no need to worry," repeated Thornhill. "Annette Harding is keeping your secret, if only for her own sake." He went back to his chair. "It must have been pretty rough on you, Michael . . . all this."

"It's been hell for years," said Michael, his eyes on the fire. "I put it behind me when I can . . . forget it for months . . . then something happens . . . something like this."

"There's no way out?"

"I can see none. It's just a question of waiting until . . . Even now the police. . . ."

Thornhill shook his head vigorously.

"You may depend upon it the police have made their inquiries. One of the first things they would do. And they haven't heard of this. Bonar's private ferret only got hold of it by a stroke of sheer luck. It's perfectly safe to assume that the police do not know of it . . . or they would have tackled you about it before now." He got up and poured out a stiff whisky. "Here, drink this. You need it. . . . And then let's talk about something else."

But Michael began to tell his story: reluctantly at first and then almost eagerly, as though it were a great relief to be at last able to confide in someone.

"I was twenty-one, Frank. I had been turned down by a girl here in Chesworth. I left the town . . . threw up my job and didn't care what happened. Eventually I found myself in Newcastle. It was a pretty desperate existence. When I met Annette I was living from hand to mouth, and she was kind to me. You know how it happens when

one is in that state of mind: I was ready to find
consolation where it was offered . . . and I was grateful to
Annette. I was green, did not recognize her for the sort of
woman she was. . . . My landlady, good-hearted old
harridan, tried to warn me, and I told her to mind her
own business. I married Annette, and within
      a week . . . Well, it happened as you would expect. To
cut a miserable story short, we had a succession of
horrible quarrels, and then she cleared out. A year later,
in Manchester, I read her name in the list of those who
had died in the tenement fire . . . and, God forgive me, I
rejoiced. . . . I suppose a correction must have been
printed: I never saw it. . . . A year later I married Mary.
In 1928, when we had been married four years and had
two children, I received a letter from Annette. She had
written to me care of the Newcastle paper, and they had
forwarded it. She said she was in difficulties: near the
end of her tether. She asked me if I would return to her—
as if it had been I who had left her—but it was clear that
what she wanted was money. . . . You can imagine how I
felt when I got that letter."

      Thornhill nodded without speaking.

      "I had the day free. I went up on to the moors and
walked until I was exhausted, trying to face the situation
and think things out. There was only one chance. If at all
costs I had to save the happiness of my . . . It was difficult
to realize that Mary was not my wife in the eyes of the
law. But she was my wife morally and I was prepared to
risk many things for the sake of her and the children,
and— I don't want to be a hypocrite, Frank—for the sake
of my own peace and happiness. I went to a solicitor in
Liverpool, where I was not known, and arranged to send
Annette a regular allowance on the strict condition that
she remained in Newcastle and made no attempt to
communicate with me or molest me in any way." He
looked up and gazed almost defiantly at Thornhill. "What
would you have done?"

      "I fancy I should have done exactly the same," said

Thornhill promptly. "Well. . . for her part, Annette appears to have kept to the bargain."

"Yes."

"And there seems no reason why things should not go on just the same as before."

Michael shrugged his shoulders.

"I don't see why they should. My luck has been too good to last. When I consider that I am an author and write under my own name, I am amazed that I have been able to keep the secret so long. Whenever I see a reference to myself in the papers I find myself thinking that it may fall into the hands of those in Newcastle who knew Annette and myself years ago."

"They are probably not readers of gossip about authors," said Thornhill dryly.

"Once a picture paper published a photograph—a snapshot of Mary and myself—I don't know how they got hold of it . . . 'Michael Holt, the popular novelist, snapped with his wife on holiday at the Lakes.'" Michael smiled grimly. "It kept me awake for nights."

"Such is fame," mused Thornhill ironically. "Still, I don't think you need worry. Blackmail is not so popular as it was."

Michael made a wry face.

"Blackmail!" he repeated. "Bonar was not above it."

"It was his training, I suppose," said Thornhill, in the tone of one making allowances. "Big business methods. Any stick good enough to do a rival down. He wanted the Vineyard. His commercial instincts were stirred. He backed himself to succeed where his competitors had failed."

"He had offered me a price for it. . . a business price. It was within a few pounds of what I had paid for the place. I refused. Then, having got to know—from something I was foolish enough to say myself, probably— that I had lived in Newcastle, he set his jackal, this fellow Julius Grant, to make inquiries. It was a shot in the dark, but a curiously fortunate shot from his point of view."

"It was the sort of thing a man like Bonar would do automatically," said Thornhill. "He wanted to know what kind of man he had to deal with. It would suggest the likeliest line of approach. I imagine he never suspected he would find you had a . . . a secret past."

"I'm not so sure," said Michael savagely. "He was accustomed to dealing with crooks like himself. It was second nature with him to think that every man had something in his life he wished to hide."

"Oh, I don't know." Thornhill moved uncomfortably. "You may be maligning the poor devil."

"Well, whatever made him put Grant on my track, it must have seemed a happy inspiration when he heard from the fellow. Here, I suppose he said to himself, is a man, apparently a respectable citizen, leading an honourable life with a wife and two children . . . and, behold, the mask is removed and a bigamist is disclosed. This highly respectable townsman has another wife still living in Newcastle. . . . He was polite enough," added Michael ironically, "to doubt the accuracy of his agent's report. He wrote again and required definite assurances that Annette Harding was legally my wife. This fellow Grant satisfied his doubts. Bonar found all the cards in his hand. He could threaten me with perfect safety to himself. You said just now that blackmail was no longer popular. I suppose you meant that it is stamped upon by the courts. Yet here was an instance—and there must be many—where blackmail could be levied with perfect safety because the victim would never dare to prosecute. Bonar was in high feather. He saw the Vineyard already added to his estate. He came to see me again—that was on the afternoon of the day he was killed—and repeated his previous offer. I refused again. Then he told me what he had found out. . . and gave me twenty-four hours to think it over. If I refused to accept it . . . well, he left the rest to my imagination."

"Hence what he said to you on the footpaths that night."

Michael murmured the words to himself.

"'It's lucky for you, Holt, I'm a man of my word, or I might be tempted to say something more: something you wouldn't care to hear mentioned in public, eh? But I promised you twenty-four hours, and the moratorium stands.'" He looked up and smiled oddly. "I know it by heart," he said. "I have heard it in my ears many times since."

"Luckily," said Thornhill, "the police took the cryptic utterance to refer to something else."

"You can understand now why I was rather pleased than otherwise when you told me of the story Rudd had spread about me."

"It certainly puzzled me at the time." Thornhill took a drink. "All your troubles go back to one first cause," he said meditatively. "It's the old, old story. You were chucked by a girl, you cleared out of the town, you tied yourself up to the next girl who smiled at you. If it hadn't been for the girl who chucked you, you wouldn't have gone away to see life and you would never have married Annette Harding, and if you hadn't bolted from Chesworth, Rudd could never have accused you of embezzling the company's funds . . . though Rudd seems to have done you a good turn without intending it." Thornhill stretched his legs in front of him and leaned back with his eyes on the ceiling. "What a nasty piece of work Bonar was!"

"I could have murdered him," said Michael simply.

"But you didn't?" returned Thornhill, smiling.

"I didn't."

Thornhill got up and refilled his glass. He stood with his back to the fire.

"You know," he said casually, "Chrystal was right. His disordered mind leapt to a correct conclusion."

"What do you mean?"

"Why, it was Jennings who threw Bonar's body into the water."

Michael stared.

"Jennings! . . . What makes you think that?"

"Pure deduction," said Thornhill easily. He sat down and stretched out his hands in a wide gesture. "The facts are simple. Miss Perks's brooch was found on the scene of the crime, and next day, as you remember, Jennings was trying to straighten the wheel of his bicycle."

"I still don't see," said Michael. "What, for instance, has Miss Perks's brooch got to do with it?"

"Miss Perks," explained Thornhill, "was under the impression that she lost her brooch when out walking. There is another possible explanation for the loss, especially when we remember that Jennings helped on that afternoon to instal her new wireless-set, and was probably left alone upstairs for part of the time while he

was doing it. What was to hinder him from snaffling something so portable as a little gold brooch? He may well have thought it would look nice on Mrs. Jennings."

"But she couldn't have worn it."

"Later on," said Thornhill. "In easier circumstances. As for the bicycle . . . Well, I have since established that Jennings was out of the house while the rector was dining with me, and did not return until nearly half-past eleven. What was he doing? I don't know. Nothing immoral, I fancy, judging from his attachment to the pseudo-Mrs. Jennings. Possibly merely meditating a little honest burglary. However, on his way back . . . Let us reconstruct the circumstances. He comes riding furiously back from the town. On the stone bridge he nearly knocks Miss Perks down. He proceeds and suddenly hits an obstacle with such force as to buckle his front wheel. He himself is presumably flung over the handle-bars. . . ."

"And not hurt?" asked Michael incredulously.

"People like Jennings are never hurt. See statistics of road accidents. It is always the man in the way who gets hurt. Probably Jennings came down in some soft bed of grass that received him like a mother. . . . He got up, looked to see what it was he had hit, and found it was the body of a man. And promptly jumped to the conclusion that he had run him down and killed him."

"Perhaps," said Michael, only half convinced. "But why should he throw the body into the water?"

"I should have thought that was obvious," said Thornhill coldly. "A fatal accident on the road means a lot of trouble and difficulty with the police. Jennings had no wish to be embroiled with the police. People of Jennings's kidney never have. Least of all at that time, when his mind was full of evil thoughts of larceny. He had had dealings with the police before, and did not wish to remind them of his existence. So he took the easiest way out and chucked Bonar's body into the Denne."

"It seems just possible," said Michael reluctantly.

"It's the only explanation."

"I wondered about Miss Perks's brooch," added Michael after a pause. "You see, I met her that night. She came down the lane. But, as it happened, she got no farther than my gate, because, when I told her that Robert was not along this way, she went back."

"It doesn't follow," said Thornhill, rising to refill his glass, "that she didn't return. Or, for that matter, that she had not been as far as the Chrystals' place already. She may have turned when she heard you coming and walked back to meet you."

Michael hesitated. He remembered the footsteps he thought he had heard in front of him on that night. He looked at Thornhill curiously. He was on the point of asking a question. On second thoughts he refrained. It would not do. He rose.

"Well, good-bye, Frank, if I don't see you again before you go. Best of luck."

"Thanks." Thornhill shook hands. "I shall send you a picture post card occasionally. If you want to get in touch with me at any time, you can do it through the Midland Bank here. I shall keep them informed of my address. . . . And, Michael, there is something you might do for me, if you would."

"What is that?"

"Say good-bye for me to Miss Perks. I ought to do it in person, but I can't bring myself to . . ." He stopped himself, and said, "I'm afraid I can't possibly find the time. But I wish you would assure her of my best love, etcetera, because I'm rather fond of the old lady. Tell her I'll write."

"You were always her favourite pupil," said Michael.

"Through no fault of my own," repeated Thornhill gravely, "I was always her favourite pupil."

Michael walked home very thoughtfully. Among the hundreds of questions that troubled his mind, one in particular persisted. Why had Thornhill kept those letters to show to him, when he might as well have burnt them without saying a word to anyone? An answer suggested itself. It was not a nice answer. He put it away.
. . .

He would miss his neighbour. Thornhill was the complete egoist but, like so many egoists, amusing company. A pity that things should have happened as they had. He would remember the pleasanter things . . . Thornhill at work on his magnificent garden, Thornhill dawdling through the lanes in his car, with his eyes always open for a desirable piece of rock, Thornhill communicative over a glass of whisky. . . .

The whisky! That toast! To the immortal . . . no, to the chivalrous memory of David Garrick!

Michael remembered. There was a famous play about David Garrick. It showed the great actor forcing himself to behave shamefully in front of the girl he loved, so that she might be released from his undesirable addresses. Hence that toast. Thornhill had taken a leaf out of Davy's book. He had played the Garrick part at Forest Park . . . from much the same motives. He wished to save Kate Martindale from marrying a man who . . .

Michael sheered away from dangerous ground. He resolutely fixed his mind on other things. But as he opened his gate he found himself humming a snatch of a tune, and he stopped short, smiling at the corner of his garden which he could never look at without thinking of a certain spade . . . for the tune that floated in his head was an air of Purcell's.

XIV: Miss Perks to Herself

Thornhill went first to Paris but soon travelled on. He found Nazi Germany exceedingly interesting and spent a month there. Next he took a good look at Austria. In July he sent brief and hearty post cards in quick succession from Budapest, Warsaw and Moscow.

A few days after receiving a cheerful message scribbled on the back of a coloured photograph of the Kremlin, Michael opened his morning paper and read of his friend's death in Asia. It was the result of one of those unfortunate accidents that befall the modern traveller. Bandits had fired on the Siberian train, and a bullet had lodged in Thornhill's heart.

2

On a certain day, when there had ceased to be any doubt that Thornhill was dead, Miss Perks received a message requesting her to call at the Midland Bank in Chesworth. There the manager handed her a sealed letter, which, he told her, Thornhill had directed she should be given in the event of his death.

Miss Perks, showing no emotion, put the letter in her bag and walked back to the Pavement to open it in the privacy of her room.

At about the same time, Mary came into Michael's study with a letter which had been delivered by the second post.

She gave it to Michael, glanced at her husband's abstracted brows and the sheets of manuscript in front of him, made a grimace, and left the room on tiptoe with exaggerated caution.

Michael glanced at the envelope. It was from the

solicitor in Liverpool.

Miss Perks let herself into her house, navigated the stone passages, passed through the kitchen, climbed the stairs, crossed the bathroom and arrived in her sitting-room; and then, without warning, her heart began to race like one of those motor-bicycle engines that young men sometimes started up under her front windows. She could feel it pounding in her breast, a metronome gone mad. She staggered back and clutched the arms of her chair. The parrot looked on with his head held to one side and perplexity in his eye.

Miss Perks, grimly clutching the arms of her chair, said to herself: "This is the end of you, Mattie, my girl." But in another moment the palpitation was over. Miss Perks sat down and for several minutes she was perfectly still, with her head bent forward and her hands clasped in her lap.

At length she rose, looked at herself in the glass, and told herself not to behave like a fool. She went to a secret place, unlocked the door, poured out a small glass of brandy and drank it. Her bag lay on the floor where she had let it fall when the attack had come upon her. She picked it up, took out the letter which the bank manager had given her, and went back to her chair.

So, sitting in her accustomed place, with the parrot peering interestedly over her shoulder, she opened the dead man's letter, and read:

My dear Miss Perks, To-morrow I am setting off for the ends of the earth, and it behoves me, like a responsible citizen (I think I hear you snorting in derision) to put my affairs in order before I go. There is no knowing what may happen before I come back, if, indeed, I do come back; and so, in case of accidents, I want to put certain things on record and to leave the record in safe hands. I shall entrust this letter to the manager of the Midland Bank, with instructions that you are to receive it in the event of my death. Since, then, you are reading this, I am a dead man; and you may well look upon this as my Last Dying Speech and Confession.

("How the man loved to hear himself talk!" muttered Miss Perks. She broke off in her reading while she rose to get her spectacles from their hiding-place in one of the vases on the mantelpiece. She wore them sometimes now: when there was no one to see her making such an avowal of the frailty of her flesh.)

That is a tactful way of telling you that what I have seen you already suspect (indeed, I think you know it) is true. I killed Douglas Bonar. It may be that some other person will be charged with the . . .

("He's scratched out a word here," remarked Miss Perks.)
. . . with the indiscretion. If so, you will know what to do.

This is how it happened.
The rector was dining with me that night. I had a new Ditchling Press book and brought it out to show him. Soon after he had gone I saw that he had left his glasses lying beside it. I knew he was pretty helpless without them when he wanted to read or write, and so I wrapped them up, and, as it was a fine night, proposed to stroll as far as the Pavement and pop them through his letter-box. I didn't hurry: had two or three drinks first. Then I set out.
Near the architectural crime that poor Chrystal calls his semi-bungalow, I heard an altercation in progress. To put it plainly, there was the father and mother of a row going on. Two people obviously much annoyed with each other. One of the voices was Chrystal's: impossible to mistake the little fellow's metallic twang. Then a man bolted past me in the dark. It must have been Chrystal.

At the same moment something whizzed through the air, missed me by inches, and fell with a clang on the roadway. It was a spade, the property, as I have since learned, of one Michael Holt, novelist. I assume that Chrystal, in a fit of peevishness, had made to attack Bonar with this weapon. Bonar had wrested it from him, Chrystal had fled in terror, and Bonar had flung the thing after him.

I picked it up and shouted: "What the blazes do you think you are playing at?"—or words to that effect. I did not know at the moment of speaking who the other man was. It was Bonar who answered: in front of me, amazingly close, almost in my ear. "Look here," he said, "I've had enough of this." He sounded beside himself with rage. I suppose Chrystal's onslaught had come at the end of a particularly hectic evening, and he felt that the whole world was leagued against him. He lunged out furiously. I felt the wind of his fist as it went past my head. I was considerably annoyed. There was Holt's deadly weapon in my hand and I was primed pretty full with the drink. I thought to myself I would give this disorderly barbarian a tap on the head to call him to order. The whisky in me hit harder than I intended. He went down like a log. Still, at the time I had no idea I'd killed him. I flung down the spade and said: "That'll teach you to behave like a respectable member of society." Whereupon, with much dignity, I turned on my heel and, forgetting all about the rector's spectacles, walked back to the house and went to bed to sleep it off.

(Miss Perks dropped the sheets into her lap and, closing her eyes, seemed to be recalling something to her memory. She sighed and picked up the place and went on reading.)

I did not mean to kill him, but it would be humbug to pretend now that I have the least regret. It was good riddance to bad rubbish, as we used to say when we were little boys and attended your school in the Pavement.

It puzzled me afterwards when I heard that Bonar's body had been found farther down the Denne, but that is now explained. There is no need to go into that, since I fancy you know the reason.

("And that lunatic Chrystal knew the reason," thought Miss Perks, "though, like the foolish fellow he is, he jumped at the wrong conclusion. Blurting things out in the police court like that! It's lucky he didn't do a great deal of harm." She snorted loudly, and went on.)

The next day I found that my dress clothes were bespattered with blood, and I had the painful job of burning an expensive suit. It so happened that I was still engaged on this delicate operation when Michael Holt blew in to see me about something quite different, but I am sure the good fellow never for a moment suspected what I was up to.

It is necessary to tell you all this, because I want you to know, in case of need, that the whole responsibility is mine. Jennings, for example, was not an accomplice. His part in the proceedings was the result of an accident.

As I say, I have no regrets. But perhaps I ought to qualify that statement. You will understand. Yet, so far as Kate Martindale is concerned, I feel I had to do what I afterwards did: arrange for her a decent way of escape out of our engagement. I could not let her suffer the agony of finding out some day that she was married to a man accused of murder. So I behaved as I did on an occasion you will remember. It needed all my fortitude. We might have been very happy. But there was no help for it.

("Nonsense," said Miss Perks, shaking her head vigorously. "You deluded yourself, Frank Thornhill. If you had married Kate Martindale, neither of you would have been happy. She would have tried to reform you, and the hopeless task would have broken her heart. As for you . . . well!" Miss Perks left Frank Thornhill's state of mind under such a process to the imagination.)

There is just one other thing. An extraordinary business, as little Chrystal would have said. A moment after I felled Bonar with Holt's spade, the scene was suddenly irradiated with light. I suppose at the time I didn't trouble to account for this phenomenon, or thought it a manifestation of the whisky I had consumed. The whole thing, for that matter, was a kind of waking dream, a nightmare play in which I acted my part without volition of my own. But afterwards, when I was sober and tried to recall all that had happened on this not so very glorious occasion, I seemed to remember having heard a gruff voice in the background saying . . .

You remember what you used to say when you came into the classroom and caught us kids up to some mischief? . . . "That's a nice way to behave, Frank Thornhill!" . . . It came back to me that when I found myself enhaloed by that strange ring of light, I heard an old, familiar voice in the darkness, muttering, in the same gruff way as of yore: "That's a nice way to behave, Frank Thornhill!"

Did that really happen, or was it just my conscience reacting to an old stimulus? A foolish question to ask, since, by hypothesis, I am now beyond the reach of an answer. Yet, if it did happen, you probably thought at the time that you were witnessing no more than an unseemly scuffle between two grown men who were quarrelling like ill-conditioned brats in a classroom.

("Yes," said Miss Perks. "At the time.")

Later . . . well, you realized what it was you had seen, as I know from a number of hints you have dropped. I am sorry for your sake, as it placed you in an awkward position and must have rendered it difficult for you to know what to do.

("Nonsense," said Miss Perks. "I never had the least doubt in my mind about what I should do.")

I don't want you to think that I ran away abroad and left someone else to face the music. I fancy there won't be any music. This is one of those motiveless crimes which baffle the police. Had anyone been unjustly accused, however, I would have returned from wherever I happened to be; and, since it is no longer possible to do that, I have left this behind.

On reading through what I have written, and realizing that some day it may possibly have to be read in court, I feel I should have written it differently. But it is too late to start again.

God bless you.

Frank Thornhill.

Miss Perks took off her glasses.

"That's an abrupt way to end a letter, Frank Thornhill," she murmured, "and not what I should have expected of you."

She gazed into the garden, where Robert was working peacefully.

Michael's letter was much shorter. The Liverpool solicitor wrote to say that he had been informed of the death in Newcastle of Annette Harding. The payments which Michael had been making would therefore automatically cease. He begged to enclose his account.

To the Liverpool solicitor, the closing of a ledger account.

To Michael, the opening of a new chapter.

Miss Perks watched her brother working in the garden. He showed signs of growing old. He was no longer so vigorous in his movements. He rested frequently.

Miss Perks sighed. She herself had begun to feel old.

She was not able to get about so far. She could not

manage the stairs as well as she used to. Now the unruly behaviour of her heart had warned her of what lay ahead. A time was coming when she would be a prisoner in the house in the Pavement. Pottering about in an ineffectual way . . . the stairs forbidden . . . confined to one floor . . . then to one room . . . then to her bed. So, to wait . . .

William and Elizabeth would look after her reasonably well, for she had dropped hints about remembering them in her will. . . "if still in her service." (Miss Perks understood now why people inserted that condition in their wills: it was a sort of blackmail from the deathbed.)

Yes, William and Elizabeth would look after her reasonably well: but it was humiliating for a proud woman to be dependent on the services of hired dependants. One ought to pass one's last years gracefully, surrounded by the care of affectionate hands. But few loved Miss Perks. She was under no delusions about that.

Why all this fuss about the murder of that man Bonar? If ever a man were better out of the way, that was the man. But murder was a dreadful thing and brought dreadful consequences. Frank Thornhill was dead now, also. He had been a selfish fellow with little thought save for his own comfort. You could not say anything against Frank Thornhill which she had not said to herself. Yet she mourned his death, and she grudged it to that man Bonar.

She remembered now that Frank Thornhill had been kind to her in many little ways. He had come and chaffed her, brought her flowers, sent her books. She had given him the rough side of her tongue on many occasions, but he had never resented it.

Not like some others. . . .

Kate Martindale, for instance, now throwing herself with vigour into work on behalf of girls . . . a sure sign that, thought Miss Perks caustically, of incipient old maidishness. . . .. Kate Martindale, teaching little girls to guide, holding out a hand to rescue larger girls who had fallen, sending tired working girls to seaside homes . . . would Kate Martindale forgive the plain words Miss Perks had spoken to her on their last encounter? Miss Perks, whether justly or not, refused to believe that Kate Martindale would.

Miss Perks felt she was losing all her old friends and making no new ones.

Michael Holt? Michael had always been timid in her presence . . . and he was wrapped up in his wife and children. . . .

Michael Holt was sitting in his study, with his chair pushed back and his head in his hands. His release had come at last, when the suspense had grown almost beyond the point where it could still be borne. Bonar's murder, by its consequences, had nearly killed him. He had been afraid of being found out, and it is a terrible thing to be found out. The fear had been at the back of his mind for years, but in recent months, growing so formidable, it had taken away his health, his happiness and his sleep.

And now. . . was it any easier?. . . at least there were things to be done. He had to face Mary. He was free to tell her that she had lived for ten years with a bigamist. They must go through another marriage ceremony and make arrangements to legitimize the children.

He went in search of her, to break the news. . . .

Miss Perks told herself brutally that it was her own fault. She had been too fond of the truth, and people who told the truth were never loved. She should have behaved like other people, glossed over unpleasant things, made allowances, studied feelings, played the genial hypocrite. Well, it was too late. She could not change her ways at her time of life. She must settle down to face a dreary old age with such pluck as she could muster.

So Miss Perks's thoughts ran on until they were interrupted by the parrot. That bird had been watching her for some time. At length he took it upon himself to remark in his rasping voice: "Well, it's a hell of a life."

Miss Perks reached automatically for the dark red shawl.

On second thoughts she drew back her hand. There was a good deal of sense in what that bird said sometimes; and who was she to punish a parrot for speaking unpleasant truths?

THE END

Resurrected Press Books in *The Chief Inspector Pointer* *Mystery* Series

Murder at Bridge

When an afternoon bridge party attended by some of Hamilton's leading citizens ends with the hostess being murdered in her boudoir, Special Investigator Dundee of the District Attorney's office is called in. But one of the attendees is guilty? There are plenty of suspects: the victim's former lover, her current suitor, the retired judge who is being blackmailed, the victim's maid who had been horribly disfigured accidentally by the murdered woman, or any of the women who's husbands had flirted with the victim. Or was she murdered by an outsider whose motive had nothing to do with the town of Hamilton. Find the answer in... **Murder at Bridge**

One Drop of Blood

When Dr. Koenig, head of Mayfield Sanitarium is murdered, the District Attorney's Special Investigator, "Bonnie" Dundee must go undercover to find the killer. Were any of the inmates of the asylum insane enough to have committed the crime? Or, was it one of the staff, motivated by jealousy? And what was is the secret in the murdered man's past. Find the answer in... **One Drop of Blood**

AVAILABLE FROM RESURRECTED PRESS!

THE EDWARDIAN DETECTIVES
LITERARY SLEUTHS OF THE EDWARDIAN ERA

The exploits of the great Victorian Detectives, Poe's C. Auguste Dupin, Gaboriau's Lecoq, and most famously, Arthur Conan Doyle's Sherlock Holmes, are well known. But what of those fictional detectives that came after, those of the Edwardian Age? The period between the death of Queen Victoria and the First World War had been called the Golden Age of the detective short story, but how familiar is the modern reader with the sleuths of this era? And such an extraordinary group they were, including in their numbers an unassuming English priest, a blind man, a master of disguises, a lecturer in medical jurisprudence, a noble woman working for Scotland Yard, and a savant so brilliant he was known as "The Thinking Machine."

To introduce readers to these detectives, Resurrected Press has assembled a collection of stories featuring these and other remarkable sleuths in The Edwardian Detectives.

- The Case of Laker, Absconded by Arthur Morrison
- The Fenchurch Street Mystery by Baroness Orczy
- The Crime of the French Café by Nick Carter
- The Man with Nailed Shoes by R Austin Freeman
- The Blue Cross by G. K. Chesterton
- The Case of the Pocket Diary Found in the Snow by Augusta Groner
- The Ninescore Mystery by Baroness Orczy
- The Riddle of the Ninth Finger by Thomas W. Hanshew
- The Knight's Cross Signal Problem by Ernest Bramah

- The Problem of Cell 13 by Jacques Futrelle
- The Conundrum of the Golf Links by Percy James Brebner
- The Silkworms of Florence by Clifford Ashdown
- The Gateway of the Monster by William Hope Hodgson
- The Affair at the Semiramis Hotel by A. E. W. Mason
- The Affair of the Avalanche Bicycle & Tyre Co., LTD by Arthur Morrison

RESURRECTED PRESS CLASSIC MYSTERY CATALOGUE

Journeys into Mystery
Travel and Mystery in a More Elegant Time

The Edwardian Detectives
Literary Sleuths of the Edwardian Era

Gems of Mystery
Lost Jewels from a More Elegant Age

E. C. Bentley
Trent's Last Case: The Woman in Black

Ernest Bramah
Max Carrados Resurrected:
The Detective Stories of Max Carrados

Agatha Christie
The Secret Adversary
The Mysterious Affair at Styles

Octavus Roy Cohen
Midnight

Freeman Wills Croft
The Ponson Case
The Pit Prop Syndicate

J. S. Fletcher
The Herapath Property
The Rayner-Slade Amalgamation
The Chestermarke Instinct
The Paradise Mystery
Dead Men's Money

Fergus Hume
The Mystery of a Hansom Cab
The Green Mummy
The Silent House
The Secret Passage

Edgar Jepson
The Loudwater Mystery

A. E. W. Mason
At the Villa Rose

A. A. Milne
The Red House Mystery
Baroness Emma Orczy
The Old Man in the Corner

Edgar Allan Poe
The Detective Stories of Edgar Allan Poe

Arthur J. Rees
The Hampstead Mystery
The Shrieking Pit
The Hand In The Dark
The Moon Rock
The Mystery of the Downs

Mary Roberts Rinehart
Sight Unseen and The Confession

Dorothy L. Sayers
Whose Body?

Sir William Magnay
The Hunt Ball Mystery

Mabel and Paul Thorne
The Sheridan Road Mystery

Louis Tracy
The Strange Case of Mortimer Fenley
The Albert Gate Mystery
The Bartlett Mystery
The Postmaster's Daughter
The House of Peril
The Sandling Case: What Would You Have Done?
Charles Edmonds Walk
The Paternoster Ruby

John R. Watson
The Mystery of the Downs
The Hampstead Mystery

Edgar Wallace
The Daffodil Mystery
The Crimson Circle

Carolyn Wells
Vicky Van
The Man Who Fell Through the Earth
In the Onyx Lobby
Raspberry Jam
The Clue
The Room with the Tassels
The Vanishing of Betty Varian
The Mystery Girl
The White Alley
The Curved Blades
Anybody but Anne
The Bride of a Moment
Faulkner's Folly
The Diamond Pin
The Gold Bag
The Mystery of the Sycamore
The Come Backy

Raoul Whitfield
Death in a Bowl

And much more!
Visit ResurrectedPress.com
for our complete catalogue

About Resurrected Press

A division of Intrepid Ink, LLC, Resurrected Press is dedicated to bringing high quality, vintage books back into publication. See our entire catalogue and find out more at www.ResurrectedPress.com.

About Intrepid Ink, LLC

Intrepid Ink, LLC provides full publishing services to authors of fiction and non-fiction books, eBooks and websites. From editing to formatting, from publishing to marketing, Intrepid Ink gets your creative works into the hands of the people who want to read them. Find out more at www.IntrepidInk.com.

www.ingramcontent.com/pod-product-compliance
Lightning Source LLC
Chambersburg PA
CBHW070836250626
47159CB00003B/808